"I don't k...

Caroline straightened as she spoke, a woman trying to climb Mount Everest without oxygen. "I wonder what made Jake stick up for me."

"He's a good kid," Matt said. More than that, Jake knew about losing his own mother, and he loved Shelly too much to stand by while she made a big mistake.

Matt flexed his shoulders. He had to pretend he thought his son should marry Shelly and then convince Caroline they should help the marriage succeed. He had to lie to Caroline about his own doubts, because if he let her see he agreed with her, she'd use his doubts to cement her own opposition.

"Jake made me nervous the moment I met him," Caroline said, her tone reflective. She hadn't sensed Matt's agonizing inner struggle. "He and Shelly care about each other so deeply—but she's always tried to grow up too soon."

Though he didn't know Caroline, Matt would bet she'd just taken this conversation places she'd never meant to go. He steeled himself to move in now before she realized their situation imposed false intimacy.

"We can help them. Then they'll only have to deal with their feelings and the baby, not with survival."

Caroline went unnaturally still, and he waited for her to snap. He didn't have to wait long.

"What are you talking about? Marriage *isn't* the answer."

Dear Reader,

Imagine this. You've just emptied your nest. Okay, you thought you'd be happier about all that free time. After all, you undertook adulthood too early—loved a man before you were old enough to know love, had his daughter and learned he wasn't the man he seemed. After he left, you tried to prevent your daughter from repeating your mistakes. Now she's nineteen and living in a dorm at school. You start cooking classes, and you learn to let go. You're home free.

Then, because she's a Talbot like you, or maybe because you had her when you were barely older than she is, she makes the mistake you were trying to forestall. She's pregnant and she wants to marry her baby's father.

What now? Certainly, you won't listen to her prospective father-in-law, a test pilot with reckless tendencies that make your own outrageous family look conservative. But he loves his son, and he'll fight for your daughter—and he looks so good in a flight suit. Wait a minute—that's the kind of thinking you've tried to avoid your entire adult life....

Thus begins Caroline and Matt's story. While telling it, I learned a little more about Caroline's family, the Talbots, who appeared in July's *Unexpected Babies*. I'm sorry to finish these stories about THE TALBOT TWINS. While Caroline and Cate found their own true loves, I fell in love with a family that reminds me of my own.

If you'd like to share your thoughts on this story, please reach me at annaadams@superauthors.com.

Sincerely,

Anna Adams

Unexpected Marriage
Anna Adams

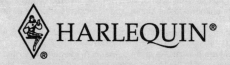

HARLEQUIN®

TORONTO • NEW YORK • LONDON
AMSTERDAM • PARIS • SYDNEY • HAMBURG
STOCKHOLM • ATHENS • TOKYO • MILAN • MADRID
PRAGUE • WARSAW • BUDAPEST • AUCKLAND

ISBN 0-373-71023-2

UNEXPECTED MARRIAGE

Visit us at www.eHarlequin.com

Printed in U.S.A.

To the women:
Birdie, Mamie, Margaret, Bertha, Mary, Dorothy and
Donna. How can I repay you for all you taught me?
And to my girls:
Jenny and Sarah, I love you.

CHAPTER ONE

"MOM, I'M PREGNANT."

On her hands and knees beneath her drafting table, clawing at the pencil she'd just dropped, Caroline Talbot Manning froze. Mid-June sunshine slipped between the plantation blinds to stripe the back of her hand as well as the pristine, sand-colored carpet. A second ago she'd had one thought: Grab that charcoal pencil before it marked the wool rug. Now her daughter's confession changed everything that mattered to her.

Shelly's voice echoed inside her head. "Mom, I'm pregnant. Mom, I'm pregnant. Mom, I'm…"

Caroline clamped her hand around the pencil, but she barely kept herself from snapping it in two. Gasping for air, she turned toward the crystal-clear windows she suddenly wanted to shatter. She needed air. She needed to scream. Her worst fear for Shelly had materialized on a sunny day that had promised nothing but routine.

How could Shelly—no, *why* would she stumble into the same mistake Caroline had made at almost the same age? How many times had they talked consequences, birth control—abstention?

"Are you sure?" Ridiculous question, *idiotic* question. She'd failed her daughter. She hadn't kept Shelly from repeating history.

"I'm positive, Mom. Come out and talk to me."

Caroline tried to back out from under the table, but her arms and legs refused to take orders. Twisting, she sat so hard the thud resounded up and down her spine.

"How positive?" She curled her fingers into the carpet, fighting intense anger. At twenty-one, unmarried, pregnant with Shelly, she'd learned the hard way to think before she acted.

"Mom, do you think I wouldn't make sure before I told you? I took four tests, and none of them came out negative."

Planting her hands on her knees, Caroline stared across the surly distance her daughter had put between them. Once, Shelly had trusted her—to help her up after she'd fallen off a playground swing, to cheer like crazy after she'd scored the winning goal in her middle school soccer game, to ply her with mugs of hot chocolate while she'd studied for high school finals.

Caroline had slaved to create those safe childhood pictures. She'd been five when her own parents had left her and her twin sister, Cate, with a maiden aunt and bachelor uncle. Both officers in the Naval Intelligence Service, her parents had accepted one isolated duty station after another. They'd sent home plenty of clothing and financial support, but not much else.

So many times in her life Caroline hadn't known what to do next. She took two deep breaths. What did a girl Shelly's age do when she found herself unexpectedly pregnant? Caroline had hidden in Uncle Ford's barn and howled like a baby until Cate had dragged her to their Aunt Imogen. After that, her family had supported her through the last rash choices she'd ever made—marriage too young, an irate divorce and later, a guy who didn't want children, but hadn't bothered to tell her until she'd thought she'd loved him.

Finally, she'd learned. She'd stopped believing in true love, realized commitment only came in fairy tales, but her family had shown her she could rely on them. Family was everything, and Shelly would be able to depend on those same reckless, but abiding Talbots.

Caroline swung into action, modeling her efforts on the care Aunt Imogen had given her. "Have you seen Dr. Davis?"

"Her test came out positive, too." Twisting her fingers, Shelly offered an unconvincing smile and looked hellishly alone.

Who was real? The scared young woman of nineteen or the defiant mother-to-be?

"Jake Kearan?" Caroline asked. She'd read the signs the day Shelly had slipped Jake inside the family circle at one of Aunt Imogen's barbecues. Both of them had been so touchingly conscious of each other.

Touching, unless you happened to be Shelly's mom.

"Why didn't he come with you?" she asked.

"Don't blame him. The two of us were involved in this." Shelly's steely tone surprised Caroline. "We know what we have to do." With a burst of temper that knotted her forehead, she turned as if she meant to flee.

Time to get out from under this table. Unfortunately, Caroline misjudged the distance between her head and the end of the table, and she bashed her skull on the laminated edge.

"Mom?" Shelly hesitated, concern slowing her down.

Caroline fell back onto her hands and knees and crawled into the spinning room. Determination had always been her strong suit. "I'm all right."

"Let me get you some water. You hit your head hard." She spun toward the hall again.

"I was trying to knock myself out," Caroline said low-voiced, as she watched her daughter walk away.

Pregnancy had dimmed the aura of joy that had always clung to Shelly. Caroline had blamed the undertone of melancholy, her disturbing weight loss on her busy new life in the dorm at Whitlock, the university all the Talbots attended, about an hour away.

Practicing her vow to give Shel space, she'd decided to wait until the end of spring term to grill her daughter about problems she might need help with. She'd expected a get-a-life-of-your-own-I-don't-need-a-mom response. Morning sickness hadn't crossed her mind.

Shelly sped back into the room with a glass of water that slopped a stream over its rim. In this perfect little house where Caroline had allowed no untidiness, the spill suddenly didn't matter.

"Here, drink this." Shelly pushed the glass into Caroline's hand.

As she drank, she studied her daughter, but Shelly plucked a picture from the drafting table. Her face softened as she looked at the family photo the minister had taken after he'd christened Cate's infant twin daughters.

Caroline knew the group by heart. She and Aunt Imogen and Uncle Ford had flanked Cate and her husband, Alan. Their son, Dan, sat in front of them, his infant sister, Mary, on his lap. Next to him, Shelly cradled Melinda. Shelly and Dan had just become the girls' godparents.

Shelly lifted her gaze, dark blue and achingly familiar. "You always say family counts most." She smoothed the back of her hand over the glass, as if she could absorb a little Talbot strength.

Biting back tears, Caroline snatched a pair of glasses from her desk and put them on. The lenses didn't hide a lot, but she was desperate. "When are you due?"

"Mid-December. I'm just over twelve weeks along." Shelly's smile thinned as she replaced the photo. "I've been trying to tell you, but I couldn't look you in the eyes. When I saw you under that table…''

"That end of me was easier to talk to?" For a guilty split second, Caroline wished she'd never had to know. "You still haven't answered me about Jake."

"I didn't want him here when you overreacted." Shelly had adopted that accusatory tone after she'd left for college.

"How can I overreact?" Adrenaline increased Caroline's heart rate. "You decided to become a mother at nineteen." What kind of life would she have? Caroline knew exactly.

"I don't need you to tell me how big a mistake I made."

Shelly's somber admission put the leash back on Caroline's emotions. *Think first.* Giving in to her impulses had always been a shortcut to catastrophe. "Let's talk in the kitchen." Anything for a few seconds to figure out a way to preserve Shelly's future.

When she'd become pregnant with Shelly, Caroline had already finished a design degree that had led to a job with Alan and Cate's construction company. She'd married Ryan Manning, Shelly's father, but he'd disappeared from their lives when Shelly was three. Caroline had sworn her daughter would never find herself deserted and penniless, the sole support of a child she adored.

Walking down the narrow hall, Caroline listened to the short, sharp breaths that betrayed Shelly's nervousness. Before last fall, Caroline would have hugged her and promised everything would be all right. Shelly no longer allowed comforting gestures.

In the kitchen, they climbed onto their usual stools at the counter. Shelly straightened the hem of her oversize white T-shirt. Jake's shirt, probably.

"Eventually, you'll have to tell me where Jake is and what he thinks of this. He doesn't seem the type to leave you high and dry," Caroline admitted. Unless the ones who looked like they cared most were always too good to be true.

"I told him I'd call after you got used to the idea. I didn't want you to say anything I'd regret."

Annoyed again, Caroline stood and snatched the kettle off the stove. She busied herself making tea.

"Mom, talk to me. I'm trying to be honest with you."

"I don't like your new honesty, Shel. It feels as if you're looking for someone to blame. You've seemed angry with me since you left home, I'm assuming since your relationship with Jake got serious."

Shelly blushed. "I knew you wouldn't approve."

"And you feel guilty around me because I was right. Do you know how many choices you had when you left last September? Everything was in your reach."

"I'll still have everything I want if Jake and I hang together."

"From now on, your life centers around your child."

Shelly ducked her head, letting her blond hair cover her face. "We're not like you and Dad. Jake and I will make our marriage work."

"Your marriage?" Had she rammed her head into another piece of furniture? "Don't get married and make this worse."

Shelly slid off her stool. "I knew you'd be like this." She laughed without humor. "You expect Jake to abandon me."

"How can you trust him after what your father did?"

"I don't care about Ryan Manning. He's a name—he's nothing, and I don't want to talk about him." Shelly clenched her hands into fists. "I love Jake, and he loves me. We're getting married, and we'll stay married."

Stunned, Caroline tried to bring sanity back to Shelly's world. "Why don't we talk about making your new life easiest on you?"

"You mean talk me into your idea of the right thing. My baby needs parents. That's what's right."

"Being pregnant is the worst reason to get married."

"For you it was." Accusation flamed in Shelly's eyes, and a hole opened beneath Caroline.

Did Shelly still blame her because Ryan had left them? She'd never defended herself against her daughter's childhood finger-pointing because she'd felt Shelly needed an outlet for her anger. Well, that wound went too deep to deal with now. Her priority was to keep Shelly from ever hearing such hurtful words from her own child.

"You don't have to marry Jake. You don't have to quit school. I can help you."

"I won't let you take over," Shelly shot back. "Jake is going to be my husband and this baby's father." With her hand, she outlined the slight bulge in her belly.

Eyeing her splayed fingers, Caroline felt sick. "It wasn't supposed to happen this way."

"You always wanted to plan my life, Mom." Tiredness infused Shelly's tone. "I'm a living checklist that was supposed to prove you succeeded despite the odds." She lifted her fist and uncurled her index finger. "I graduate college." She pointed the next finger. "I get a great job. I find Mr. Perfect, but I never have to depend on him, because I am the self-reliant product of Caroline Talbot Manning's oh-so-careful mothering."

Caroline licked painfully dry lips. "That's how you see me?" Sacrifices she'd made to keep Shelly safe suddenly seemed foolish—loneliness she'd embraced after Ryan left, after the only other man she'd let herself care for, a pilot she'd known as a girl, who'd come back into her life, had told her he didn't want children. Hope for her child collapsed in on her, a mountain of useless, dead weight.

Her pain must have touched Shelly, who softened her gaze and then her tone. "I'm a human being, not a cause."

"You want us to be honest with each other, Shel? You don't even have the same major you declared last September. How can you commit to a twenty-year-old boy for the rest of your life?"

"Jake's not a boy. We're both adults who want to keep our baby, and we don't need you or anyone else." Tears collected in Shelly's eyes as she plunged her hands into her thick curls. "You want to know the truth? I'm drowning. I'm ashamed I screwed up, but if you can't support Jake and me, we'll get married by ourselves."

"How can I help you throw your life away?" Caroline wrapped her arms around her own waist. "I've tried to keep you from doing what I did, but here you are, pregnant and unmarried." She fumbled for words. "I'm not asking you to leave Jake, but can't you both take care of your baby without getting married?"

"No—that's not even half a commitment. Jake and I want a family, and I won't let my child grow up without a dad." Fifteen years of abandonment trembled in Shelly's voice.

Caroline empathized. Her parents had claimed she and Cate wouldn't get a good education with them, but how could they have stayed away if they'd loved her? When Ryan had asked for a divorce, she'd expected they'd share custody, but Ryan had signed the papers and disappeared. He'd had no family. She hadn't known where to start looking, but she had searched because Shelly had wanted him back. She'd longed for her father's love.

The one thing Caroline couldn't give her. She choked back a sob—and gave in. For now. Surely Jake's father would help her make these two see sense. "Why don't you call Jake? We might as well talk tonight."

Shelly's sheepish smile exposed her uncertainty. "I invited them to dinner."

"Them?"

"Jake and Matt, his dad."

Both of them? "Tonight?" Caroline studied her cold stove. "What time did you tell them to come?"

"Six-thirty. Matt's flying. He's supposed to finish his debriefing around five-forty-five."

"You might have told me, Shel." She rushed to the pantry and yanked the door open. "Check the freezer."

"Who cares what we eat?" Shelly grabbed her arm. "Forget about making the perfect meal." Her hand tightened. "Most couples our age who get married with a baby on the way don't make it, but maybe they don't want to as much as Jake and I do. We both know how much a broken family hurts."

Caroline's heart cracked in sharp pieces. She'd tried to give Shelly everything she would have had if Ryan had been a father. She'd made a stable home, offered unwavering love. Now she realized nothing could make up for the loss of a father's love.

"We'll fix it," she said. "Please don't ask me to approve of marriage when you know it can't work."

"Jake and I have to make it work. Give me your support."

"I can't." Caroline let her go. "I'll give Jake and his father dinner, but I'm determined to make you all see marriage would be an even bigger mistake."

LT. COMMANDER MATT KEARAN adjusted the cold pack against his forehead to put less pressure on his stitches. Across the desk, Captain Ned Townsend, who ran flight ops at Leith Naval Air Test Center, slid his pen to the next line on his checklist.

"At what moment did you know the landing gear failed?"

"Moment?" Matt gave up on the cold pack. It was supposed to prevent swelling, but it was giving him a headache. "You want big hand and little hand positions?"

"Matt, I'm giving you a break. Either brief me informally, or we'll call in every system representative connected to the aircraft and let them question you before you go home. Where were you in the sequence of test steps?"

"I lowered the gear." Matt had a dinner date with his son, and he'd arranged to meet Jake here. He'd rather be waiting in the parking lot before Jake connected the mess on the runway with the flight Matt had had scheduled for today. "My instrumentation showed a successful deployment. When I touched down and kept falling, I figured my instruments were wrong.'' Matt pressed his fingertips to the gauze bandage that covered four fresh stitches above his left eyebrow. ''I was positive when the fuselage scraped the ground, and when the fire started, all doubt left my mind.''

Ned closed his green-bound notebook. ''Point taken. Do you want to try Jake on the phone again?''

''He must be on his way.'' Matt lightly bounced his fist off the edge of Ned's gray metal desk. ''I know you don't get it, but I don't want him to realize I crashed before he sees me.'' A member of the ground crew had pulled Matt out of the smoking cockpit, but his escape was a blank spot in his mind. The medics who'd attended him had diagnosed a slight concussion and congratulated him on the thickness of his skull. Information he'd rather no one shared with Jake.

''Matt? You with me? Should I call the docs back?''

''No.'' He tossed the cold pack in Ned's garbage can and yanked his flight jacket off the back of his chair. ''I'm going, but I'll cover all the details in my report.''

Ned's derisive expression mocked him. ''Jake's not a baby. What's the big deal about a slide down the runway and a bump on the head?''

''Happy to sacrifice my ounces of flesh, sir.'' They all pretended no one ever really got hurt. ''But Jake and I are meeting here to go to dinner." Matt paused at the door. "When do I fly again?"

"We have to determine what went wrong on the landing gear. I'll be in touch about that. Until then, I think the altimeters are ready for the other prototype."

"You know where to find me."

Ned waved him off, already turning to his next piece of paperwork. The yeoman, usually entrenched in Ned's outer office, had already left for the day. Matt opened the door to a blinding white hall and his son, rising from another gray metal chair.

Jake looked tense. "Are you all right? I saw the plane and the foam."

"The landing gear failed, and the plane's belly scraped up a small fire. Nothing to worry about. Didn't you talk to the yeoman?"

Jake nodded. "When you weren't waiting for me. He said you were okay." He looked Matt over, stopping at the gauze patch on his forehead. "Should I drive you to the ER?"

"After two hours in Sick Call? No, thanks. You didn't cancel dinner?"

Jake's frown deepened, as if he had something else on his mind. He slouched away, and his dirty white sneakers squeaked on the overpolished tiles.

Matt followed. "What's wrong, son?"

Already at the end of the hall, Jake looked back. "You may not want dinner after I tell you."

Matt pulled on his flight jacket and held the pale

green double doors open. He could guess what was up. His pre-med son had had more trouble with French than all the science and math Whitlock could throw at him. They'd talked about getting him some outside help. Matt's French, learned while he was stationed in the Mediterranean, didn't measure up.

"I knew we should have hired the French tutor before you started this term."

"It's not school."

His unhappiness stopped Matt dead. Still a little unsteady on his legs, he gripped the porch column. His son was in trouble, and, as usual, reluctant to say so. Nine years of visits, between the night Matt's ex-wife Lisa had left with five-year-old Jake and the day she'd died in a boating accident when he was fourteen, had eroded his trust. No matter how many times Matt came through for him, Jake expected the worst. And usually, he waited until he was neck deep in trouble before he asked for help.

"Better tell me, son."

With a furtive glance at the empty sidewalk and the other uniformed men pacing the parking lot, Jake shook his head.

His apprehension growing, Matt followed him off the wide porch, into lingering, afternoon sun and the scent of salt off the nearby ocean. Suddenly, Jake stopped and grabbed Matt's arm, reminding him of past painful goodbyes.

"Maybe here is better," Jake said. "Why not get it over with?"

"What?" When Jake stepped back at Matt's gruff tone, Matt reached for him, but his son executed a perfect military oblique out of his grasp. "Tell me. It can't be worse than what I'm imagining." Sex, drugs and rock and roll.

"It's about Shelly. And me."

Shelly? He hadn't even met Jake's girlfriend yet. "You two are serious?" Surely he wasn't about to say they were getting engaged. Shelly couldn't be more than nineteen—maybe twenty at the most. A breeze whispered through Jake's pale hair, and a shiver raced down Matt's spine. Proving he was still too young for a serious relationship, Jake clung to silence—as if the truth didn't have to come out. "What is it, Jake?" Matt marshaled his arguments against making such a serious attachment at their age. His own divorce had caused most of Jake's problems.

"She's pregnant."

Matt's mouth dropped open. "Pregnant?" His first foolish thought was, "How?"

Jake straightened stiffly, but his confidence looked shaky. "We're having a baby." He kept the blank panic in his eyes out of his voice.

Matt thought carefully, normally his strongest attribute, but the crash must have rattled him. Were Jake and Shelly talking marriage? He hoped to God not.

"Say something, Dad."

After Lisa's death, Jake had tested Matt with every

trick a teenager could dream up, but getting a young woman pregnant was no prank.

"What am I supposed to say?"

Jake walked away, and they'd never seemed farther apart.

"Wait." Matt chased him across the shell-paved parking lot, his head throbbing with each thudding footstep. "Jake, talk to me."

"I did. You lose. I need help, not judgment."

"Who said I judged you? Give me time to think."

"You were supposed to ask me how you could help us. Shelly says her mom is going to fall apart, but I don't know what Mrs. Manning will do, because Shelly's tried to keep me away from her family."

"Why?" Was she ashamed of him? For what? This got worse and worse.

"I'm not sure." Shoving his hands into his pockets, Jake met Matt's gaze. "I think she figured they all knew her well enough to guess we were having sex."

"My God."

Hardly the best response, but his son wasn't old enough to have sex, much less to get a girl pregnant. "What happens to med school?"

"That's why I'm asking you to help."

Jake paused as a khaki-clad Master Chief breezed out of the building. His feet crunched shells on the ground as he came closer. At the last minute, he slowed and muttered a brief "Excuse me" as he veered around them.

Jake nodded in the direction of his truck, parked beside Matt's vintage Jag. "Shel's telling her mom right now, and you and I are invited to dinner so we can all talk."

Matt kept pace with his son's loping stride. "Maybe you should have told us together."

Jake eyed him as if he'd lost his mind. "From what Shelly says, I'm not sure Mrs. Manning won't be armed."

"I'm not sure I'd blame her."

Jake stopped at his truck's tailgate. "I'm in trouble."

"I'm pretty clear on the colossal mistake you've made."

Shame hunched Jake's shoulders. "I know, Dad. I just don't know what the hell I'm supposed to do next. I never meant to mess up Shelly's life or mine. We were careful."

His misery finally got through to Matt. "What went wrong?"

"I don't know." Looking up, he dragged his palm furiously across his mouth. "But I'm responsible. I have to take care of Shel and the baby."

Matt backed off. "How is Shelly?" His concern was real as he tried to picture the young woman who carried his son's child, but Matt was also stalling for time to get used to the idea.

"She's sick," Jake said. "She's lost weight instead of gaining it, and she says her mom tries to sneak her cheesecake and stuff that makes her feel even worse."

"Sneak?"

"She's noticed Shelly's lost weight, but she won't just ask her why. I think they used to get along better, but Shelly started avoiding her after she left for school. She wanted to prove she didn't need any help." Jake glanced over Matt's shoulder, embarrassment wrinkling his features. "Then she didn't want Mrs. Manning to guess we'd…"

Matt grimaced. A little girl who needed to break away from her mom? "You don't think she—" He broke off, surprisingly uncomfortable talking about sex with his son. "She didn't become intimate with you to prove her independence?" Become intimate? How corny could he get?

Jake took a step backward. "Shelly wouldn't use me."

Matt realized his mistake instantly. However protective he felt toward Jake he had to avoid criticizing Shelly.

"Dad, I need you to help me convince Mrs. Manning I can take care of Shelly and the baby."

How the hell was he supposed to do that? He didn't believe it himself. "You haven't met the mother?" Best to avoid the issue of Jake's culpability while it still made him so angry.

"Once—at a barbecue Shelly's aunt invited me to. Mrs. Manning looked at me as if she thought I was going to steal the family car."

Matt felt for Shelly's mom. "She'd probably hand it over now. What about Shelly's father?"

"He left a long time ago, and after that, Shelly says her mom tried to make her believe she'd be better off if she never needed anyone else. She won't make this easy for us."

Matt put his hand on Jake's shoulder and tried not to mind when Jake shrugged it off. "I'm on your side—always, but what should Mrs. Manning make easy for you?"

"I told you I'm going to marry Shelly."

Jake always hid behind arrogance when he was uncertain of a decision, but Matt understood. The divorce had hurt him, and then Lisa had married a man who'd never managed to love him. By the time he'd come to live with Matt full-time after Lisa's death, Jake hadn't even trusted his own father to love him unconditionally.

Matt's conscience jabbed angrily at all the spots where he was most vulnerable to his son's pain. If he and Lisa had given Jake a "normal" family, would this mess have happened?

"You start med school year after next. How can you support a wife and child?" Matt headed for the Jag.

"I thought you'd understand, Dad."

"I won't let you down, but I can't pretend I think you should get married. You deserve the life you've planned, and so does Shelly."

"If you won't help, just forget it. I'll take care of Shelly on my own."

"You can't, and that's the point." Planting his

hands on Jake's shoulders, Matt propelled him toward the passenger seat. Surprisingly, Jake didn't resist. Matt thought hard about what to say next as he crossed behind the car.

Nothing came to him before he took the driver's seat. He wanted Jake to trust him, but a marriage couldn't be right. Not now—he wasn't even old enough to order a beer. Matt turned his key in the ignition.

"You can't tell us anything we haven't said to ourselves."

So Jake knew how much trouble he was in. Matt turned onto the road toward town. He'd figure it out. He avoided disaster for a living, though the throbbing in his head reminded him that he might be off his stride tonight. "Better give me directions to Shelly's house. Let's see if she's right about her mom."

CAROLINE WAS CRUMBLING feta cheese on a Greek salad as Shelly clattered into the kitchen in black platform sandals. Demure in a white skirt and lime blouse that emphasized her greenish pallor, Shelly looked more schoolgirl than expectant mother.

"What are you doing?" she asked.

Screaming inside. "Making dinner." Caroline had started cooking classes to celebrate all the extra time she'd expected to enjoy in her empty nest.

"I didn't invite them to a seven-course meal. Is that lamb?"

Shelly turned lamb into an accusation, and Caroline

decided to assume the aroma made her queasy. "I have some crackers if you're sick."

"No. I'm stronger than my stomach. I'm not giving in."

An attitude that came too late. "Why not take it easy on yourself? Eat the crackers."

Shelly swallowed with an effort. "No. Are you planning to put on clean clothes?"

Caroline studied the ink and food stains that vied for prominence on her linen shorts and cotton polo shirt. She opened a cupboard and fished out a box of saltines that she tossed to Shelly. "What's wrong between us?"

Shelly set the box on the counter. "You think you know what's best for me, but I'm responsible for myself."

Caroline stared at the crackers. Would pointing out the truth make any difference? No. "Okay." Best to get out of here before she exploded with all kinds of truth that would push Shelly even farther away. "Answer the door if Jake and his father come." She paused. "Where's his mother?"

"She died when he was fourteen."

Poor kid. Caroline stroked her hair out of her eyes. He probably thought he could manage without parents, too. "What does Jake's dad do?"

"He's a test pilot. He flies at LNATC."

That explained a lot. *Top Gun* images made Caroline want to bar her doors and board up the windows. She knew his type too well. Arrogant men who used trendy sunglasses and a cool leather jacket to paint a picture of character. Just what the doctor ordered to fill the gaps in Shelly's life. A reckless boy, brought up by a dangerous man.

"You'd prefer a dentist or a nice, solid mathematician, but I promise I'll never let Matt take the baby for a spin in his jet."

"Why do you assume I'm thinking the worst?" Shelly must remember Patrick, the pilot who'd returned to Caroline's life after Ryan's departure. Ryan had left her alone with a child, but Patrick had finally convinced her to put bars around her heart.

Shelly had been in kindergarten when he'd come back to town. He'd been Caroline's first love—a secret boyfriend, older and therefore too inappropriate for her sister or aunt to understand.

When Patrick had been stationed at LNATC again, they'd continued with the relationship that had ended when Ryan had come on the scene. Still the daredevil pilot she'd fallen for as a teen, Patrick's supposed maturity had made him more attractive. Until the day he'd told her he didn't care for children.

Somehow, he'd continued to believe they had a future, as if she'd choose a man over her child. It shouldn't have come as a surprise. She'd known about career Navy even then.

"I know the worst, Mom." Shelly dragged her out of her past regrets. "I saw it in your eyes. Why don't you try to find more satisfaction in your life and give me a break?"

"I was trying before today."

Shelly gasped, and Caroline felt sick, but she couldn't apologize. She hurried through the dining room and up the tiny cottage's staircase. Along with cooking lessons, she'd considered getting a dog. Now she'd have to learn to crochet those baby booties that seemed to dangle in front of Shel's starry eyes.

Usually, when she entered her room, she went straight to the gable window that framed the sea. This evening she stripped on her way to the small, adjoining bathroom. After a quick wash in warm spray, she snatched a lavender sheath dress from the closet.

Pulling it over her head, she stumbled to the window. Had Jake and his father arrived? No. She'd parked in the garage, and Shelly's car sat alone on the drive.

She had a few more minutes. Hurrying back to the bathroom, she stretched to zip her dress. As she wrestled her makeup bag out of a drawer beneath the sink, she studied the dark red hair that stuck out at odd, curly angles.

Tonight's meeting called for sober hair and plentiful makeup. Determined Shelly shouldn't have to face Jake's father alone, she painted as fast as she could and then clipped her hair into a plain ponytail at her nape. Heaven knew what a he-man pilot might say if he decided his son couldn't be at fault.

Caroline slid her feet into chunky-heeled lavender slides and then raced down the stairs as a car crunched into the drive. She peered through the glass

insert to the left of the front door. A Jaguar, beloved
from its gleaming insignia to its improbably black
tires, sat outside.

A tall man climbed out of the driver's seat and
shrugged a leather flight jacket off his broad shoulders. He dropped the jacket in the car and straightened
again to pull off his sunglasses. His surprisingly sensual mouth was set in a grim line. He made Patrick
look like an amateur.

If only she'd been wrong about Matt Kearan.

Turning, she flattened her back against the door.
Concentrate on Jake. Matt was just an extended part
of Shelly's problem.

The doorbell rang.

Caroline took three deep breaths.

"Mom," Shelly hissed from the kitchen door.

"How long have you been standing there?"

"Long enough to wonder why you're pretending
we're not home."

Caroline squeezed the doorknob in her palm. Her
heart was a block of ice. How could she open herself
to the idea of Matt and Jake Kearan as permanent
fixtures in Shelly's life? She'd been her child's only
protector.

If she didn't welcome Jake, she'd lose Shelly.

"Mom," her daughter said again and then hurried
down the hall. "I'll open it."

Caroline turned the doorknob. "I have to."

She met Jake's defiant gaze first. Still just a kid,

he'd made a bad mistake, but he was trying to pretend he hadn't.

"Hello." Any minute now someone would show up with an Oscar for her polite tone. Her maternal instincts demanded she blast Jake off the front porch.

Jake froze, but the man beside him smiled a silent greeting. Slightly taller than his six foot son, he sized her up with startling black eyes.

She respected his attempt to measure the enemy. Only she couldn't afford to think of Matt and Jake Kearan as the bad guys. For Shelly's sake, she had to see them as family.

"Mrs. Manning?" The older man offered his hand.

"This is my father." Jake's voice shook. "Dad, this is Shelly's mother."

"I'm Matt." His firm grip communicated the assurance of a man who routinely controlled millions of dollars' worth of hardware, software and firepower.

Caroline released her hand from Matt's and flexed her fingers as she widened the door. Her daughter, who'd needed her to be mother and father, required these men in her life. "Please, come inside."

CHAPTER TWO

SO THIS tightly wound redhead who'd clenched his hand with controlled fury—or possibly terror for her child—was Shelly's overprotective mom. Caroline Manning molded herself back to the wall in an effort to avoid touching Jake as he crossed the threshold. She'd asked them inside her home, but her flat blue gaze told Matt they weren't welcome in Shelly's life.

Jake stopped in front of her. "I never meant to hurt Shel," he said.

Caroline's mouth thinned. She cut Jake a sharp nod, but clearly the pain that clouded her gaze also kept her from speaking, and Matt stepped into the divide.

"Shelly must have told you about the baby," he said. "I wish they'd waited to tell us until we were all together."

She widened her gaze, surprising him as he realized neither she nor their miscreant offspring understood they were all in this together.

"Come in, Mr.—" She broke off, eyeing his civvies. "I suppose I should call you by your rank, but I can't tell what it is."

"I'm Matt."

She nodded—no smile. Waves of tension rolled off her, but he refused to be as afraid as Caroline. One of them had to stay calm. Allowing her to hold his gaze, he tried to share his strength with her—for Jake's sake.

He wasn't sure what to do—help Jake with this crazy marriage idea, or force his son to see he could be a better part-time father than Matt. He'd do what was best for Jake if he had to be ruthless on his son's behalf.

He ducked beneath the low door frame that grazed his regulation-cut hair. A scent of just-baked apple pie and a squeak in the hardwood floor offered homely welcome. His and Jake's house most often bore an unfortunate resemblance to the locker room at work.

Catching his eye, a young woman, blond and fragile, stepped out of the hall's shadows. "Jake." Powerful trust in her breathy voice punched Matt in the gut. She believed she and Jake could be together, despite obstacles stacked against them.

Matt's throat tightened. Shelly was no mixed-up young woman who'd played around, gotten pregnant and needed to be rescued. She loved his son. About a million years ago he'd felt the same about Lisa before reality had overwhelmed them, leading to their divorce and ultimately, Jake's determination to be his child's full-time father.

As Jake took Shelly's hand, Matt turned to Caroline. She hardly seemed to breathe until Shelly wrenched open another door and shoved Jake into the room beyond. Caroline exhaled a long breath and started after her daughter and Matt's son.

She stopped in the room's doorway. Lamplight silhouetted her body in the pale purple dress she wore. He tried not to notice gentle curves that suggested neither grandmothers nor apple pies. Suddenly, she took another deep breath and ran her hands firmly down her thighs, as if her own courage had flooded back.

"Shelly, offer Jake and his father a seat, and I'll bring drinks. Dinner should be ready in half an hour."

"Smells great." Jake's uneasy tone drew Matt closer.

He admired his son's touching effort to behave normally, but Jake had always risen to any challenge. He'd been a star athlete in high school. He'd won his choice of scholarships.

Would Jake achieve his childhood dream of becoming a physician? Matt had first noticed his aspirations when Jake had begun bandaging Lisa's perfect poodle. Frankly, the dog's looks improved in the makeshift bandages—and Jake's detailed reports of her injuries had fascinated his father.

"Matt, can I offer you a glass of wine?" Caroline's husky voice sounded faintly like Shelly's. "Or a beer?"

"A beer." Maybe he should have asked for a soda. Without the light shining through her dress, Caroline looked a little prim and pure. She might not approve of a man who swilled her beer at a time like this.

"Iced tea for you, Jake?"

"Yes, ma'am."

With a wry smile Caroline turned away. A young man who'd helped her daughter get "in trouble," couldn't have manners? She'd obviously assumed Jake was the one at fault. Just as he'd instinctively wanted to blame Shelly.

"I'm pleased to meet you." Shelly's shy welcome broke his focus on her mother, and he turned to her, taking both her hands.

"We should have met before." He should have known how serious Jake felt about her.

"We're all here tonight." She gestured to a big flowered chair, but she left her hand hanging in the air when she noticed his bandaged forehead. "What happened?"

If not for his dull headache, he'd have forgotten the stitches. "An accident. It's nothing."

"Dad's landing gear failed," Jake said. "Job hazard. Right, Dad?"

"Not usually," Matt said with a grin at Shelly. "How are you feeling?"

"Queasy." The tightness that had made her face seem so fragile while Caroline was in the room had eased. Why did her mother's concern threaten her? "Would you like to sit down?" she asked. As Matt sat, Jake pulled her to the sofa beside him. Her smile included Matt. "Looks like your confession went better than mine," she said.

Jake flashed Matt an anxious glance. "I'm not sure. Dad?"

"What you're asking is—" He didn't know how to say they wanted him and Caroline to help them throw their futures away. Jake hadn't listened to any of his arguments. Shelly'd already made up her mind. She wasn't interested in going over the drawbacks.

"You're doubtful," Shelly said, disappointment puckering her forehead. "My mom is, too. Actually, she said everything I ever wanted was open to me before this, and nothing is now." Looking at Jake with terrifying adolescent certainty, she looped her arm through his. "I believe in us. We want our baby. We want the futures we've planned, even if it takes us a little longer to get there."

Matt shifted in the roomy chair so that his pants rasped against the chintz. Where was Caroline with those drinks?

"Besides, Mr.—" Shelly paused.

"Matt," he said.

"Matt, I have a big family. They helped my mom when I was little. They'll help Jake and me."

She squeezed Jake's arm against her side, and Matt wanted to yank his son out of this small, comfortable home that had been built with loving hands. These two didn't care what he and Caroline thought. They wanted a stamp of approval.

"And you must have family, too," Shelly went on.

"Wonder why we've never talked about your family, Jake."

Jake's smile dimmed. He shifted his glance to Matt, who stretched his feet in front of him, accidentally scraping his heels on the spotless rug. Their family was no Norman Rockwell unit.

"My mom was an only child," Jake told Shelly. "My Dad's parents…"

Jake couldn't even call them grandparents, he'd seen so little of them. Matt's parents still lived in the farmhouse his family had owned since the first Kearan who'd landed on Ellis Island had traveled to Missouri with two horses and a plow. Matt had lost his father when he'd told him he wanted to be a pilot. Such a small thing—wanting to fly, rather than work the family farm, but his dad had never forgiven him, and his mother had gone along with her husband.

Did he want that kind of relationship with his son? Occasional phone calls? A hunger for love that embarrassed him with its connotation of weakness. He couldn't give up trying to make his parents love him, even when he'd finally given up trying to make them stay in touch with him. With every flight, with every award, he thought, "If they knew about this, they'd see why I needed to fly."

What if Jake turned away from him because he couldn't agree that marriage was best? What if Jake one day felt he no longer had any reason to share his successes?

"My parents live in Missouri," Matt said, his voice

unsteady enough to make him angry with himself. "We don't see them a lot."

"Well." Shelly sounded troubled, but, glancing at Jake, she didn't push for facts. "We'll have my family, and I think my mom will come around."

Jake wrapped a protective arm around her shoulders. "You and I are the parents. You may have to learn to put what you want first."

Shelly drew back. "You mean tell Mom she goes along with us, or I get out of her life? You know that's my last resort. She's given up a lot of freedom for me. I do love her."

Caroline came back into the room, a wide silver tray in her hands. Grateful to find an excuse for action, Matt rose to offer help. To the drinks, she'd added crackers dressed with tasty antipasto toppings, fresh-cut vegetables and a creamy dip. Regarding Matt with a lifted eyebrow, she let him tug the tray from her.

"You went to a lot of trouble." He set the food on the antique chest that served as a coffee table.

"To keep myself busy." She bit her lip, surprised at her own bluntness. "Sorry, Shel. I'm not complaining."

Shelly nodded. "We might as well get to the point. Jake and I want to be married soon. You know how small this town is, and I'm twelve weeks along. I'm getting huge—what if I'm carrying twins?"

Caroline's breath caught. "I have a twin sister," she said to Matt and then turned back to Shelly. "I wouldn't trade my relationship with Cate for anything, but you don't need twice the trouble. Besides, you'd know already.''

''I don't want to catch the guests whispering their bets on a baby pool.''

Distress darkened Caroline's gaze as she passed Matt a plate and napkin. ''You should be thinking about how this changes your lives. Neither of you is old enough to walk into a bar and order a drink, much less—''

''We made this baby.'' Jake challenged her. ''Now we have to be old enough to take care of our child. We don't need your permission to get married.''

His antagonism called for a referee. Matt set his plate on the chest. ''Wait a minute. Caroline has rights here, too. You want what's best for your child, and she wants to make sure Shelly doesn't make a mistake.''

''She's too late.'' Jake stopped as Shelly jerked her head in his direction. ''Not that I'm saying I don't want our baby, Shel.''

''I hope you aren't.'' She stood, moving out of their small, angry circle.

She looked so alone Matt allied himself with her. ''Why don't we calm down? Jake, you and Shelly are ahead of Caroline and me. We're still shocked our children are going to be parents. Let's not start an argument you don't want to fight. Don't make Shelly choose between you and her mom.''

Shelly flashed him a brief, tight smile before she

turned to Caroline again. "I'd have to choose Jake, Mom. My child needs a father."

Caroline slid her hands over her stomach as if Shelly had punched her. Moisture gleamed in her eyes, and in Shelly's, too.

"We should have given you and Matt more time before we all met." Shelly held out her hand to Jake, her face tight with dismay. "I can't stay here now."

"I'll take you away, but you know we can't wait much longer to make decisions if you don't want people to know you're pregnant."

"I'm leaving. Are you coming with me?"

"Don't go." Caroline swiped at the curls that clung to her forehead. "I want to be supportive, but I know what you're throwing away if you get married at nineteen. Let *me* help you with the baby."

Matt bit back a word Caroline and Shelly probably didn't hear too often. Caroline's attempt to cut Jake out of the picture went too far. Jake had endured enough estrangement in his life.

Taking Shelly's hand, Jake led her toward the hall, but he turned back with an apologetic smile that made him look younger than his years. "I can't help it, Dad."

Matt felt helpless, a sensation as unfamiliar as it was unwelcome. Caroline stood, wringing her hands. He'd never seen a human being actually wring her hands before, but Caroline twisted her fingers together with force that must have hurt.

"Go ahead, son." He'd try to smooth this argument over. Somehow, he could fly tons of metal out of the most dangerous situations a pilot ever had to face, but he'd never handled family drama with skill. "Talk until you feel better. We'll wait for you."

"We won't be back tonight," Shelly snapped.

"Shel, don't." Matt had never heard Jake's tone be so gentle before. "You want your mom on our side."

She lifted her face to his. An ache in Matt's chest made him put his hand on his heart. These two who had no idea what kind of commitment they were trying to force down his and Caroline's throats, but Shelly believed in Jake, and his tenderness damn near broke his father's heart.

Shelly finally shook her head and slipped into the hall. With a backward, desperate glance that ricocheted between Matt and Caroline, Jake followed.

Matt pivoted toward Caroline, frustrated with his own indecision, but clueless. How could he give in? But how could he risk his son's giving up on him the way his own parents had?

The front door opened and shut, and Caroline slumped over the closest chair, digging her fingers into the flowered upholstery. Matt felt for her, not recognizing the overprotective mother Jake had expected.

"I don't know what I'm doing. I don't want to ruin my daughter's life." Her pain providing a reflection of Matt's own, she straightened, a woman trying to climb Mt. Everest without oxygen. "And what made Jake take up for me?"

"He's a good kid." More than that, he knew about losing his own mother, and he loved Shelly too much to stand by while she chose a situation that continued to hurt him.

Matt flexed his shoulders. For the second time that day, he was going down and the wheels had come off. He had to pretend he thought his son should marry Shelly Manning and then convince Caroline they should help the marriage succeed. He had to lie to Caroline about his own doubts, because she'd been unable to see any merit in Jake and Shelly's plans. If he let her see he agreed with her, she'd use his doubts to cement her own opposition.

"Jake made me nervous the moment I met him," Caroline said, her tone reflective. She hadn't sensed Matt's agonizing inner struggle. "He and Shelly care about each other so deeply—but she always tried to grow up too soon. Not a single teacher ever complained about her." Caroline stretched. "Why couldn't she have hacked into the school computers or skipped class for the last half of her senior year? Why get pregnant to prove she wasn't a kid? She's not ready to be a mom."

Though he didn't know Caroline, Matt would still bet she'd just taken this conversation places she'd never meant to go. He steeled himself to move in now before she realized their situation imposed false intimacy.

"We can help them. If we make sure they can afford food and board, they'll only have to deal with their feelings and the baby, not with survival."

Caroline went unnaturally still. His muscles contracted as he waited for her control to snap.

"What are you talking about?" she asked in a wounded voice. "Marriage isn't the answer. Don't you know your own son? Is he ready to take care of a baby? The only babies Shelly sees are my sister's cute, cuddly twins. I never even let her baby-sit in high school."

"Why?" She intrigued him. This was the kind of behavior Jake had expected.

"Because so many crazy people live in the world, and some of them hire baby-sitters." She shook her head. "I'm overreacting, I know, but she's my child, and she comes first."

"I love Jake just as much. That's why I think we should help them."

She stared at him, her frustration, a living, raging thing, barely held in check. She all but ground her teeth as she reached for the tray. "I'd better not leave this stuff out."

He followed her, holding his own silence, hoping she'd cool off. In front of a closed door at the end of the hall, she balanced the tray on one upraised knee to free a hand. Matt leaned around her and opened the door.

"You don't have to stay." As she glanced over her

shoulder, her gaze told him she wished him out of her life. "If they come back, I'll have Jake call you."

"If they come back, you and I should be prepared to talk fast and say things they want to hear."

"Not about a wedding."

She set the tray on the long counter, and he resisted feeling at home among the clean, white fixtures that reminded him of the childhood kitchen he hardly ever saw.

"We don't know each other, Caroline, but I'm going to risk telling you about Jake. My former wife and I divorced when he was five. He lived with Lisa, and I saw him when I could, but I was never stationed near him, and Lisa didn't help him stay in touch with me. I never had him longer than a two-week period until Lisa died when he was fourteen." Matt paused, uncomfortable with the truth. "This is the hard part. Since Jake came to live with me, we keep distance between us. Maybe he's afraid of losing me. Maybe I try too hard to make him believe I won't let that happen again."

Color suffused Caroline's pale skin, jarring against her dark red hair. "None of this is my business."

Nevertheless. If his son married Shelly, Caroline would be an important part of Jake's future. "I'm explaining why I intend to support him if he wants to marry your daughter. How can I stand in his way, when I wasn't there for him? How can I *not* ask you to stay out of his way?"

"Jake told you I'm divorced?" At his nod, she

went on. "Did he tell you I got married because I was pregnant with Shelly? Did you enjoy your divorce so much you want your son to have one, too?"

Her sarcasm bit deep, but he stemmed his natural urge to respond in kind. It wouldn't help. "You and I are still young and still alone. Why not help them be happier than we are?"

She shoved the tray so hard he had to catch it to keep it from flying across the peach-and-cream tiled floor. The air snapped between them. Without speaking, she snatched the tray back and then turned to open the refrigerator door. She shoved the food inside.

She whirled to face him, her gaze shouting all the words she wasn't saying aloud. "I don't need a man to make me happy, and neither does Shelly."

"I'm suggesting we help them depend on each other—if we provide support, they'll stand a better chance. I want them to succeed where I've failed."

"How can I pretend I think Shelly should get married when marrying her father was the biggest mistake I ever made? He left her because he was angry with me, but she's the one who felt abandoned. Wouldn't she be better off if he were some faceless shadow she couldn't miss, because she couldn't remember him?"

Matt's control slipped as he understood her worst fear. "You're suggesting Jake shouldn't try to take care of his child?"

"Not if he can't stay for the long haul. If I hadn't married Shelly's father he might have left us before she really knew him. That piece of paper tied him to us until Shelly was so attached she can't get over him.''

''My son won't abandon his child.'' Against his will, he imagined how Caroline must have suffered. Knowing she'd reject any hint of comfort, he hid his concern, but fury toward the bastard who'd abandoned Shelly made his blood cold.

''Can you promise Jake won't make Shelly believe he loves her and then walk out and leave her caring for their child?''

If Shelly's wounds were still as raw as Caroline's, he admired her courage for wanting to try marriage. ''Did you tell her all this?''

Avoiding his gaze, Caroline took a box of plastic wrap from a drawer and set it on the counter. Then she pulled the tray back out of the refrigerator, her fingers trembling over its contents.

''I can't tell Shelly the truth about Ryan—her father. I never wanted her to feel responsible for my bad marriage. I don't want her to know how much I regret Ryan, but I'm sorry I haven't been enough for her. I overprotect her because I can't give her the one thing she wants. A father.''

Her frankness startled him. Courage ran in her family. Matt peeled a strip of wrap off the roll and then nudged her aside and began to cover the appetizers.

''You never told her the truth about him?''

''I hope I've taught her not to put up with a guy

as angry and untrustworthy as Ryan, but I never said he was the kind of man I hoped she'd avoid.''

Matt clenched the tray's handles in his hands. She wouldn't approve of him either. About six months ago, he'd stopped seeing a woman he'd almost thought he loved. When she'd forced him to choose marriage or moving on, he'd walked out of her life. Caroline wouldn't waste time with a man who didn't have the future on his mind.

Who was he to say he could help Jake? He'd never risked a serious relationship after Lisa. Maybe he didn't understand love between a man and a woman.

His throat seemed to close as he tried to speak. ''Maybe you should get to know Jake before you decide to stand in their way.''

''He may love her as much as a boy of twenty can, but I don't believe they know enough to commit to marriage and mean it. If they still want to marry when they're old enough to decide, and they're not under this kind of pressure, I'll support them.''

''Am I hearing you? You want Shelly to become a single mother until she's sure of Jake?''

''I don't care if everyone she knows is as shocked as you at the idea. I want her to know what she's doing when she gets married.''

He didn't believe in fairy tales any more than Caroline did, but for his son's sake, he'd lie to God. ''What if Jake and Shelly can be the exception if we're their safety net?''

She doubted him with her eyes. "When are you due for a transfer?"

Damn. She thought fast, but his responses felt dull. "I'll do everything I can to stay here or close by."

He hadn't exactly lied. With four months left on his commission, he'd have to transfer or retire from the Navy. Not even Jake knew about Icarus Aeronautical, the Maryland-based aircraft company that had already begun to court him. He loved the Navy, but he was tempted to interview because of rumors that had begun to filter through the test community. One of the largest providers of military aircraft, Icarus might be moving to Georgia, where they could continue to do business with their largest customer at a lower cost.

Caroline took back her tray. "What about your job? When will you take one too many risks and crash your plane?"

"I can't promise not to crash." But he'd been guilty in the past of working his personal life around his career. Caroline would consider him one of those men a woman should avoid. "My first job is to convince you we can help Jake and Shelly stay together."

"Not a chance."

SHELLY TURNED to Jake as he drove her car out of the flagstone entrance to her neighborhood. "I never thought you'd take up for my mom." She probably sounded like a baby, but how was she supposed to depend on him if he couldn't see they had to stick together?

He changed the unfamiliar gears, his arms tensing. "I'm on your side, but you don't want to turn your back on your mom."

"I've tried to hard enough." But she didn't mean it. She felt guilty and sad. She'd felt as if she were doing something wrong with Jake, and she wanted her mom to love her enough to help her.

"You wanted her to be on our side."

Shelly didn't want to talk about her mom anymore. She brushed the sweep of blond hair that blew back from Jake's face. Her air conditioning had long since broken, but she hadn't wanted to borrow money from her mom to fix it. In the heat, they had to drive with the windows down, and with his hair baring his forehead, Jake looked young even to her.

Their ages frightened her, so she tried not to think how old they were. "Why do we need Mom or Matt's help? I'll quit school and work. When you finish, I'll go back."

"You know how long it will take me to finish training." He glanced at her. "Put on your seat belt. You can't be reckless with the baby."

She straightened and pulled the strap over her shoulder. "Mom always expected this to happen. I don't want to owe her anything because she thinks she was right about me."

"Do you think she'll rub it in?"

She shook her head, her mom's hurt expression

sticking in her mind. "She has firm ideas about the way a good mother behaves."

"Will she hold her help over our heads?"

"Jake, this is our baby. We can manage." But she knew they couldn't.

He turned the car toward their favorite spot, the Leith pier. "We have to put the baby before anything we feel, Shel. I'm asking you to give Dad and your mom a chance, because I'm afraid we won't make it without them. How do you think I feel, knowing I can't provide for my own wife and child?"

"You know I hate it when you say that." Until tonight, when her mother had refused to consider marriage, Shelly's biggest worry had been that Jake wouldn't feel like the man of their family because they needed a hand. "That's why we should rethink our plan. The apartment we saw yesterday is small, but we could afford it if I worked forty hours."

Jake shook his head. "I'm not sure we should take that place. The building's kind of run-down. The neighborhood is—"

"We can't be choosy. Kids grow up in apartments all the time. Please don't ask me to live with Mom or your dad."

"I'm not, but why take the first place we looked at?"

His doubts scared her. She considered pretending not to notice, but they'd promised to be completely honest. "You're having second thoughts."

He turned into the pier's parking lot. As soon as

he stopped the car, he reached for her. Unlatching her seat belt, Shelly dove into his arms, the only place she felt safe.

"I'm sure about you and the baby," he said. "I'd just hate for you to suffer because I want to go to medical school. Maybe I should switch majors, just finish school and find a job as fast as I can."

She rubbed her forehead against his chin. "Don't pamper me because I'm scared. Mom's been where we are, and I thought once I came clean, she'd understand we want to raise our own child. I don't want you to give up med school because I'm one of the almost nonexistent percentage of women who get pregnant taking birth control pills."

"Shelly, we're both responsible."

"I know, but I don't think even my mom would want you to quit school. She believes in dreams." She straightened and looked into his eyes. "Let's go home, and I'll talk to her. I won't panic this time."

Jake crooked his index finger beneath her chin. His solid gaze made her heart beat faster. "We're getting married." He kissed the tip of her nose. "We don't back down, no matter what."

"I agree." She took his hand and flattened both their palms against her stomach. "Our child grows up with his—or her—mother *and* father. We love each other. We're both determined to be together. What could matter more?"

CAROLINE WAS wiping fingerprints off the fridge when the car rattled over the gravel in her driveway.

Matt brought a stack of her unused best china from the dining room.

"They're back." Wariness threaded his tone.

"I heard." Her extensive confessions made Matt difficult to face. Head-on, that was the way. "I'm sorry about what I said tonight. Everything I said." If only she could take half of it back. "I just wanted to make you understand why I don't want Shelly to get married the way I did."

He eased her plates onto the counter. "Consider me sworn to secrecy. I wouldn't do or say anything to hurt you or your daughter."

The warmth in his black eyes startled her. "You're still planning to help them, and you're trying to make me trust you, too." Matt awoke her strictly honest side. After she'd spouted the condensed version of her life story, she couldn't manage a tactful retreat.

"I just want to help Jake. And Shelly."

He'd had to add her daughter's name, but she forgave him his slight error. She couldn't begrudge Matt his priorities, when Shelly mattered most to her.

She braced her hands on her hips. "I'm not giving up."

"Maybe you could just listen to them." He held the door for her, and she edged close to the other side of the jamb. His maleness pervaded her kitchen as insidiously as he and Jake had invaded her life with Shelly.

She wasn't supposed to think of him that way. He

was Jake's father, and Jake had brought enough danger into her home. Walking ahead of Matt to the living room, she felt self-conscious. Surreptitiously, she sniffed the scent that wafted from Matt in her too-small hall. Man and soap and clean ocean air made her legs tremble. Because deep inside she was still the woman who'd fallen for both Ryan Manning and the pilot who hadn't loved her daughter.

Low voices came from the living room. Shelly and Jake turned as one from the stone fireplace. In a short span of time Shelly'd grown up some more.

"Mom, as I said, Jake and I want to have the ceremony before I'm showing any more. First thing we do is introduce Jake to the rest of the family."

This new tack—the wedding as a foregone conclusion—bemused Caroline, but she hadn't been Shelly's mom for nineteen years without learning a few tricks. "Jake's met everyone."

"Not as the man I'm going to marry. I hope they'll accept my child's father." Her mood changed rapid-fire, and tears pooled at the corners of her eyes.

Old guilt tore Caroline away from her determined stance. Was she fighting a losing battle? Could she be wrong? They always came back to reminders of Shelly's missing father.

Movement behind her back preceded the heat of Matt's body just behind her. He hovered as if he expected her to explode, and he'd appointed himself collector of the pieces.

Caroline stepped away from him. She didn't plan

to break yet. ''I'll call Aunt Imogen to arrange a get-together.''

She didn't want to lose her daughter, and a family gathering at Aunt Imogen's promised her another chance to make Shelly and Jake see sense.

CHAPTER THREE

"COMMANDER KEARAN?"

Matt looked up from his flight log. Captain Townsend's yeoman stood in the doorway, holding up a cell phone. "You have a call. Admiral Whitney Randolph."

Matt smiled at the yeoman's hushed tone. Whitney Randolph had started flying during World War II. Before he'd retired he'd flown every Naval aircraft he could get off the ground, and then he'd joined the astronaut program. Matt had been lucky enough to attend several classes he'd taught at the Naval Academy, and they'd become friends at a time when his own father had begun to pull away from him. Matt took the phone.

"Should I wait?" the younger man asked. "That's Captain Townsend's personal phone."

"I'll bring it to your desk." Matt covered the receiver. Whitney Randolph wouldn't want to share their plans with a kid who hero-worshipped him.

The younger man gave up under the pressure of Matt's steady eye contact. "Aye, sir."

Matt put the phone to his ear. "Admiral?"

"What's this I hear about Jake getting married?"

"How'd you hear?"

"Ned Townsend remembered I was stationed at the test center in the sixties. Thought I might know the family. Jake's marrying Imogen Talbot's niece?"

"Great-niece. How do you know Imogen Talbot?"

"She and my late wife volunteered together at the hospital. Evie and Imogen worked on a couple of committees. I remember when the young girls came to live with her after their parents were assigned to an isolated duty station with Naval Intelligence. One of them must be Jake's girl's mother."

"Caroline," Matt said. "Her last name is Manning now."

"Her married name. Those little girls grew up and made families of their own. I should have gotten in touch with Imogen before now."

From Whitney, it was a subtle suggestion. "Are you asking me to reintroduce you? Why don't you just call her?"

"Imogen and I belong to a different generation, Matt. I can't just march up to her door and call her to attention."

Whitney only worked at military humor when he was nervous, not a circumstance Matt had witnessed all that often. "She invited Jake and me to a barbecue next weekend. Why don't I ask Caroline if I can include a friend?"

"Is it a family thing?" Whitney sounded unnerved.

Before he could produce another bad armed forces joke, Matt rescued him. "Shelly wants to formally introduce Jake to the rest of the family. Come along. You'll provide cover for him.''

''Do I want to?''

''What's with you and Imogen?''

''None of your business, old friend.'' Whitney strengthened his voice. ''I'll come. I'm staying at the most grotesquely frilly bed-and-breakfast in town. Ned's wife set it up for me. I should have taken a room at the Navy Lodge. Anyway, why don't you pick me up on—what day is this barbecue?''

''Saturday.''

''Fine. Why don't you pick me up? What time?''

''I'll be there at ten forty-five.''

''Uniform?''

''What?'' Matt pictured the admiral in full regalia. ''What should I wear?''

''Do you own jeans?''

''Khakis.''

''Great.'' The knife-edged creases would be formal enough. ''I'll see you Saturday, unless you'd like to hoist a fortifying few before then?''

''I could fit you in after the 54th's squadron anniversary party Friday evening.''

''Call me when you're free and we'll meet at a pub I know.''

''You'll keep our conversation about Imogen in strictest confidence?''

Matt lifted his eyebrows. ''State secret, except I'll have to tell Caroline you know her aunt. See you Friday, Admiral.''

"See you then. I'm glad you're free."

Pushing the phone's off button, Matt spun his chair toward the window. On the other side of the runway, the ocean pounded ashore.

He looked forward to this barbecue with renewed interest. He'd like to see the woman who could reduce Admiral Randolph to begging invitations. If she was anything like her niece, Matt almost pitied his old friend. Matt had noticed something that seemed to have escaped Jake. Caroline had agreed to bring the family together. She hadn't agreed to the wedding. She could still churn up his son's happiness the way that ocean seemed to boil the sand.

On Saturday morning, Matt and Jake headed for Whitney's bed-and-breakfast. Jake had taken the Jag's less-than-roomy back seat, and he rolled down the window. In the rearview mirror, Matt watched his son lift his face to the salt-scented air. He was still so young, that kid.

"At least we don't have to go back to Caroline's house," Jake said with heartfelt relief. "That place smothers me—all those girly things and that teeny furniture."

"I'm betting that teeny furniture has been in her family for generations." Matt lifted one brow. He'd felt at home in Caroline's house. He'd put down any feelings of discomfort to the circumstances. "Shelly's used to the kind of home Caroline's made for her."

"She'll have to get used to my kind of house, won't she?"

Staring too long at his son, Matt had to brake the car as a boy steered his scooter off the sidewalk to cross the road in front of Leith's redbrick auditorium.

"Shelly's uncle is restoring that place." Jake pointed at a sign that read, "Palmer Construction." He continued, "Mr. Palmer won the contract after another company couldn't finish the job in time. Shelly works on it when she comes home for weekends."

"Shelly does?"

"Her Uncle Alan lost most of his business last summer. I've heard something about an embezzler, but I'm not sure what happened. The whole family pitches in now. They're all determined to do it on time and at budget. Caroline's decorating it for free on her off days."

Matt stared at the blue tarps and scaffolding that sheltered the building in metal arms. A family affair?

Guiltily, he thought of Icarus and their recruiter's persistent calls. Caroline's accusations burned in his conscience. He'd maneuvered his relationship with Jake around the demands of his Navy career.

Had he taught Jake that the rest of his family would have to work around his needs? What other bad ideas might he have created for his son?

"Do you like Shelly's family?" he asked.

"They're okay. I've met everyone in groups. She took me to golf at a course near the school where her cousin, Dan, works, but he came off all protective, like a big brother."

Matt laughed. "That much family is a different feeling for you after all these years with just the two of us." Whitney had moved in and out of their lives with barely more frequency than Matt's reluctant parents, but Jake had never been part of a family like the Talbots. Reckless by reputation, they were fiercely loving by nature, if Caroline was a prime example.

"They all come with Shelly."

"You'll have to find a style that suits you both." Had he been too subtle? He glanced at Jake, who seemed absorbed in the townhouses they were passing. "What I mean is, you can't just expect Shelly to follow you from medical school to the hospital you choose without considering what she wants. Her family is important to her. I wonder if my single-mindedness about the Navy caused problems at home with your mom."

"Don't glare at me, Dad."

Matt rubbed his forehead. "I didn't know I was."

"I think of Shelly. I'm just—I don't know—tense about today. I didn't have the guts to ask her who all knew about the baby. I like her Aunt Imogen, and I don't want to be the guy who knocked up the family's princess."

"Should you mention the knocking up part?"

"Isn't that what you'd think?"

"Maybe I'd think you were the responsible young man who's stepping up to the plate."

"God, Dad, you're getting old."

He sounded it, when he tried to relieve his son's

guilt. "Shut up, and help me look for the Sea Breeze. I think it's just around this corner."

He'd taken Whitney back to the B&B after they'd shared a beer the night before. Suddenly, Matt hoped Caroline had warned Imogen he'd invited Whitney. The breathless note in her voice when she'd repeated Whitney's name implied family secrets.

Since Whitney hadn't mentioned Imogen Talbot at the pub, Matt hadn't felt comfortable asking if he'd gotten in touch with her yet.

"I see the place." Jake indicated an ostentatious yellow-and-brown Victorian example of gingerbread. "Look at that monster. I'm poor this week, Dad, and I could use some money. How much will you bet me Caroline decorated it?"

Matt felt a startling urge to protect Caroline's good name. Jake meant more to him than anyone on earth, and he'd admitted today was upsetting him. Why shouldn't the kid blow off a little steam?

"I won't joke about the in-laws," Matt said.

"I probably shouldn't get in the habit."

As Matt parked at the curb, Whitney rose from a rocker on the B&B's front porch. The old warrior who'd been Matt's hero from the first day he'd climbed into a cockpit looked as nervous as Jake.

He smoothed his hands down the sharp crease in his khakis. As he opened the car door and then levered himself into the seat, a whiff of starch rolled off his blinding white shirt.

"So much for dressing down," Matt said.

Whitney grabbed the door handle. "I should change?"

"We don't have time. I was kidding." Matt stared at the other man and then started the car again while Whitney plucked at the folds of his pristinely pressed clothing.

They'd been friends for a long time, but friends with limits. They'd talked flying, but he'd never admitted his pain at losing Jake when Lisa had left him. Whitney had certainly never mentioned Imogen Talbot.

Those were the kinds of things families told each other. Matt glanced from his son to Whitney. He loved Jake more than he'd known he could love another human being, and Whitney was one of his oldest friends.

Deep down, Matt knew he hadn't been able to forge family ties with Jake that compared to the Talbot bonds. Why had he always been content to leave distance between himself and those who mattered most to him?

The answer came out of nowhere. He'd expected his mother and father to love him even though he'd disappointed them. They'd punished him for his betrayal—turning his back on the farm—by treating him as an acquaintance, and they'd never gone out of their way to love his son.

Oblivious to Matt's uncharacteristic musings, Whitney turned to eye the B&B, slowly falling behind them. "I can change clothes," he insisted, "but I'd have to iron."

"You iron, sir?" Jake said.

"I forgot to say good morning, young man." Twisting the other way in his seat, Whitney offered Jake his hand. "Good to see you again." He looked Jake over. "I meant I'd have to iron if I put on different clothes. Can't go around looking like a college man."

Jake grinned, taking no offense. He leaned over the seat. "Dad, you have to head toward the river." He gave directions to Imogen's house until Whitney cut in on the last turn.

"It's this sandy path—I still remember. Imogen's house has been the Talbot home for generations. Her brother, Ford, built his own house and barn on the family property. He did something with horses as I recall."

Whitney's mysterious relationship with the Talbots grew more interesting. Matt followed the dirt road until it curved and exposed the two houses.

"That one." It was a long, two-storied white home. "Do you remember the house, too, Admiral Randolph?"

"Like yesterday. This family made me their own. My wife and me. I've known Imogen and Ford for over thirty years. You're a lucky man, Jake."

Wondering how a man accepted such kindness, Matt kept his head down as he nosed his car into a cluster of vehicles in the pea-graveled parking area.

He looked up at the tall white farmhouse and tried to imagine Caroline as a carefree young girl playing on the wraparound porch, climbing the oak trees that squatted around the yard. Supported by the aunt and uncle who'd loved her enough to become her surrogate parents.

"It's hardly changed." Fondness deepened Whitney's tone.

Never knowing the kind of family life that had created Whitney's affectionate memories, Matt sure hadn't given Jake memories like Whitney's. Suddenly, he couldn't breathe in the car's close quarters.

He yanked open the door and stood. Why would Whitney, one of the smartest men he knew, and Evie, his extremely loyal wife, cut themselves off from the Talbots? The other man's anxious expression ensured Matt would never ask the question.

A screen door's complaint about being opened sent all the nearby birds scurrying from the trees. Matt felt Jake and Whitney turn toward the house as he did. In the doorway, Shelly clasped her hands in front of her as she grinned an exuberant welcome at Jake.

Behind her, an older woman came onto the porch. As tall as Shelly, and almost as slender, she wore her white hair in an elegant knot on top of her head. With wispy tendrils of hair around her fragile face, she still bore the beauty she shared with Caroline and her daughter.

"Whitney." Her Southern intonation floated across

the lawn. "I thought Caroline must have gotten the name wrong."

She had to be Imogen Talbot. She hurried down the wooden steps, her shoes tapping on the white boards. The breeze caught her dress, and Matt saw both Caroline and Shelly in her lithe stride as she hurried down the sidewalk.

"Whitney Randolph, I can't believe you've finally come back."

Only then did Matt realize his friend had stopped at the end of the walk. Matt shared a speculative glance with Jake.

"Imogen, I don't know what to say to you after so long."

"I wish you'd told me you were coming."

She held out her hands to him, but something shiny between her eyebrows caught Matt's gaze. Squinting, he inched a step closer, curious, but reluctant to interrupt Whitney's emotional reunion.

Tape? On her forehead? Matt turned to Jake, but his son had gone to greet the woman he wanted to marry. Striking Matt dumb, Jake took Shelly's hands and swung her away from the others, a man too deeply in love to notice if the sky fell on him.

Leaning into each other, the younger couple walked away, their connection as spiritual as it was physical. Jake was already tied to Shelly in all the ways that mattered.

"You must be Matt. I've heard only pleasant things about you from Jake and Shelly." Imogen's voice broke his concentration and Matt turned to her, trying hard not to look at the clear tape. "You've raised a fine young man," she said. "I'm Imogen Talbot."

"Thank you," he said, glancing back at Jake one more time. "And I'm glad to meet you. You seem to know my friend, Whitney."

"I can hardly remember when I met him."

Matt nodded, but, studying her wide, barely contained smile and the softness in her faded blue gaze, he doubted her. Suspecting he'd become a man who watched other people find happiness, Matt followed her gaze to Whitney, who couldn't look away from Imogen. She beckoned them toward the house.

"We've lost the young people. Come meet the rest of my family, Matt. Whitney, you're most welcome in my home again."

"Is Ford joining us?" Whitney asked.

"He is. He and I've argued about you all morning. When Caroline told us Matt was bringing a Whitney Randolph, Ford said it had to be you. I just couldn't believe you'd come back." She stopped, a blush tinting her cheeks. "How is Evie? She wasn't able to come?"

"She passed away, Imogen. Two years ago."

Immediately, moisture glazed Imogen's eyes. She reached for Whitney's arm, and Matt turned away, as much out of place with them as he would have been with Shelly and Jake.

"I'm sorry," she said. "So sorry."

"I've waited to get in touch with you."

Whitney's intense tone made Matt walk faster to give them privacy. As he came to the porch, the screen door opened again. Caroline came out, cradling an infant.

Seeing Matt, she stopped short. She looked down at the baby, and her obvious confusion made his heart skip a surprised beat. He stared at the baby, too. She wore pink, from her toes all the way to her squalling face. Matt, who took secret pride in his reputation for fearlessness among the test pilot community, searched for an alternate escape route.

"Hi." Caroline raised her voice over the baby's siren-like wails. "We're on our way upstairs for a diaper change, but I saw Shelly and Jake wandering off." Her guilty smile somehow charmed Matt. She could see her own failings. "I guess where they go is becoming none of my business, but I panicked."

"It's all right. You're not sure what comes next." He hadn't meant to tease her, and his words made her eyes widen.

"I'm sure," she said. "I've just failed at convincing the rest of you." She cupped her hand around the baby's head. "Come through the house with me, and I'll introduce you to someone more willing to include you in conversation." She flicked a glance over his shoulder and stopped. "Personally, I can't believe he's real."

Matt knew whom she meant. Already deep in their own talk, Imogen and Whitney had forgotten everyone else. Just like Shelly and Jake.

"You don't know Whitney?"

"He was transferred soon after my sister and I came to Leith." She pressed her lips to the baby's forehead. "Maybe they'll come back to us after they catch up with each other."

He didn't understand her half-sad gaze, but his curiosity about her felt inappropriate. Her slightly downturned mouth emphasized the fullness of her lips. Her troubled expression raised his protective instincts when he should have been concentrating all his concern on Jake.

"What's through the house?" he asked.

The distance in his voice, both unintentional and unavoidable, earned him a second look from Caroline, but she tilted the baby onto her shoulder, and the wailing finally faded to a mournful cry.

"We put the rest of the throng and the games outside. Volleyball, croquet, horseshoes and the traditional barbecue watch."

"Watch for what?"

"No one in my family can keep a fire going." She found her smile again, and her deep red lips tempted him more than before. "You'll be a hero if you can run a barbecue," she said.

"Thanks." He forced himself to smile as he tried to regain their old footing. "Before I take the family by storm, I'll go with you and the young lady. I'd better learn to change diapers again. Do you think the process has changed much since Jake was a baby?"

"You changed Jake's diapers?" she asked.

He opened the door for her and then followed her into a wide, cool foyer. "Maybe his mother needed more help in the diapering department than I did."

She started up a narrow staircase that split the dimly lit hall. "Sorry. I guess I was stereotyping. I saw this movie once—about pilots."

"Yeah? You shouldn't believe everything you see on a movie screen."

"Not much in common with the character, you're saying?"

"Right."

At the top of the stairs, she reached for the first door, but he opened it on a fully equipped nursery for two. Caroline carried the baby across the pale carpet to a dark pine dressing table.

"She lives here?" Matt gestured to the little girl whose diaper Caroline deftly removed.

"No. Remember I told you about my sister's twins? Cate—my sister—and her husband, Alan, are starting over with their business, and Aunt Imogen baby-sits for them sometimes. She set up the nursery to make Melinda and her sister, Mary, comfortable."

The aunt with the tape on her head took care of this baby and her sister? "May I ask you a personal question?"

"Sure." Caroline cleaned Melinda and maneuvered a diaper onto the wriggling, much more contented baby. "I may not answer."

"Did you notice your aunt has a piece of tape on her forehead?"

"She wears it to remind herself not to frown." Caroline lifted the baby to her shoulder again. "Frowning causes wrinkles."

Affection for her aunt filled her newest smile. "I guess that's true," he said. "I didn't notice any wrinkles."

"She has them," Caroline admitted, "but she's so beautiful no one ever notices. I'm surprised she didn't take it off for Whitney, but maybe she was trying to prove he didn't matter to her as much as we think."

Matt wanted to know about Whitney and Imogen, but his job was to find out more about Caroline. The more he knew, the better he'd know how to convince her to help his son. "Whitney tells me your parents were in Naval Intelligence."

"For over twenty years." She set her mouth and headed back to the hall, as if she'd rather not be alone with him and his questions. "They were still in when they died in a car accident."

"You don't like talking about them?" His sense of having let his own parents down made him reluctant to chat about them.

"They died before I understood them," she said, her voice firm. "They transferred to Turkey when my sister and I were five years old. They brought us here, and we never lived with them again. I love Aunt Imogen and Uncle Ford, but everyone Cate and I grew up with had a normal family." A deep breath lifted her shoulders. Melinda shoved a fist into her drippy mouth and jerked her head toward Caroline's face.

Matt smiled at the little girl. He liked looking at her aunt, too, at the emotions she couldn't hide from him, because her face showed everything. "I guess they loved the Navy as much as you do. They used to say 'the needs of the Navy come first.' You know how that works. When the time comes, you'll leave. You'll convince yourself you have no choice."

"You're talking about your mother and father, not about me."

"You can always prove I'm wrong." But she obviously didn't believe he would.

He knew how to pick his battles. "I can't prove anything until I know what my choices are." He wiggled his index finger under Melinda's nose, but the little girl only gnawed harder on her fist.

Caroline turned the baby away from him as if she needed to protect her entire family from contact with his. "I always sound angry with you, but none of this is your fault. I keep reminding myself."

"But I'm easier to blame than Shelly?" he guessed, uncomfortable with common ground when he should have been grateful. "I feel the same with Jake. I'm furious, but I'm afraid if I let him see how upset I am, he'll refuse any help from me."

She blushed, and he knew he was right—and that she felt as uneasy with him as he felt with her. With light makeup and her hair scooped into a loose curly ponytail, she looked young enough to be Melinda's mother, nowhere near old enough to be Shelly's mom.

"What should I have done to keep Shelly safe?"

Her pain and guilt reached inside him. As he'd tried to maneuver her toward a position that best benefited his son, he'd concealed his most painful secret—his absolute conviction he'd failed Jake from the day he'd let Lisa take him out of the home they'd shared.

"I don't have time for guilt." Massive lie, and it rasped against his throat. He didn't want Caroline to see how inept he could feel where his son was concerned. To help Shelly and Jake, he had to gain Caroline's trust.

When she didn't answer, he glanced toward her. She looked as if she were holding in laughter. Plenty of it.

"How do you say stuff like that with a straight face? 'I don't have time for guilt.' Admit you're scared stiff."

Her mind-reading caught him unprepared. "Do me a favor." He took cover behind a flip tone. "Don't tell Jake or Shelly I'm frightened."

She pressed her hand to Melinda's head, and her mouth worked as she tried even harder not to laugh, as if she didn't want to hurt his feelings. He stared. He hadn't seen her clearly until now.

She wasn't the victim of a bad marriage. She wasn't his son's enemy. Caroline was a beautiful woman who'd become a mother too early in life. Shelly's marriage spelled failure to her, and she was still brave enough to laugh.

His own breathing whispered inside his head. She hadn't thought less of him because he was afraid for

Jake. She'd only ridiculed his aversion to admitting it.

He'd hated dancing around the truth with women who'd wanted more commitment than he knew how to give. Caroline wanted honesty so much she didn't object to its bitter taste. He shook his head. Allowing himself to think of her as someone more than Shelly's mother would complicate Jake's life. He eased to the other side of the hall.

"Where's this grill you mentioned?" he asked. "Let's say I start the fire—will Jake's stock go up with your family?"

"Like a skyrocket."

He turned toward the stairs with alacrity. Better to take action than stand around mooning over the mother of the bride.

CAROLINE HALF EXPECTED a conflagration, a testament to testosterone. But Matt lit a perfect collection of briquettes and seasoned kindling.

Uncle Ford, infamous in the family for the way he denied his hearing loss, leaned on his cherry cane, close enough to hear every word Matt said. Caroline stood back, but Uncle Ford made an instant connection with Matt. He led the rousing cheers as the briquettes glowed around the edges, and once the oohs and aahs died down, Uncle Ford started interrogating Matt about the particulars of his job.

Caroline didn't want to hear it. Someone had turned on a Billie Holiday CD, and one couple swayed on the terrace to a soulful tune that made them forget everyone except each other and the infants they nestled between them.

Caroline smiled at her sister and brother-in-law, so newly back in love, so deeply unaware anyone else existed in their private world. As they moved together, they revealed Shelly, cradling her chin on her fists as she leaned on the brick wall that surrounded Aunt Imogen's terrace.

Her dreamy expression screamed a warning that dragged Caroline toward her. Shelly wouldn't be human if she weren't hoping she and Jake would find the same happiness Cate and Alan had fought for.

Shel was dreaming, and Caroline feared her daughter would wake up in a nightmare. Cate and Alan were adults. They'd already had a nearly grown son when they'd had to face the problems that had almost broken their marriage. Shelly didn't realize her only dependable asset was her family, which would support her no matter what she faced.

"Nice song." Caroline kept her voice low. Forget about confrontation. It never worked with Shelly. Better to ease into her point. Shelly and Jake weren't now and would never be Alan and Cate.

Shelly pivoted her chin on her hands. "I didn't notice the song. Aunt Cate and Uncle Alan look sweet, don't they?"

"A family, complete with mother, father and babies."

"And Jake and I don't stand a chance." Shelly

straightened. "Why do I keep hoping you'll help me the way I need you to?"

"I want to help."

"You want me to leave Jake, but I won't let my daughter grow up the way I did."

It hurt. Caroline had tried to make up for Ryan's absence, but Shelly had refused to attend father-daughter functions with Caroline as a stand-in.

"I'm sorry I couldn't be Ryan."

"It's not him." Taking Caroline's arm, Shelly turned her around. "Maybe it was at first, because I wanted to know why he could't love me—"

"Shel—"

"Let me finish. I don't want my child to feel unlovable, ever. Jake and my baby come first now."

"But why marriage? Why can't you take care of the baby without getting married? Wait until you're sure you want to be with each other."

"I told you I won't do that." Shelly backed away as if Caroline had threatened her. "Jake and I want a family like the ones we both envied when we were growing up."

Caroline wrapped her arms around herself. If wanting a fairy-tale family enough would bring it to her, Caroline would have managed to deliver it on a velvet pillow years ago. Playing house wasn't the answer.

"Shelly?" Jake spoke behind them. "I want you to meet Admiral Randolph. I've known him since I was born—and it turns out he knows your Aunt Imogen."

Caroline turned with Shelly. She'd learned of Whitney Randolph soon after she and Cate had come to live with her aunt. Town gossip had accused her aunt of having an affair with him before he and his wife moved away, but Aunt Imogen later told Cate and Caroline that while she couldn't help her feelings, she'd never acted on them.

Matt and Jake and Aunt Imogen surrounded the man who'd met her aunt in the driveway. He took Shelly's hand.

"Nice to meet you. Please call me Whitney. If you do, maybe Jake will follow your example."

"Thank you, Mr.—Whitney, I mean." Shelly turned to include her mother. "This is my mom, Caroline Manning."

"Mrs. Manning." Despite his polite tone, his gaze dissected her.

"Caroline." Uncomfortable with his scrutiny, she avoided his and Matt's gazes. Had Jake's father spoken to his friend about her?

"We know each other," Whitney said, holding on to her hand. "You don't remember me?"

"I remember you moved just after my sister and I came home." Those days remained painful and blurry to her.

"You were just a girl—you and Cate—Imogen was so proud of you, and happy to have you come to her."

Caroline turned to Aunt Imogen, who had eyes only for Whitney. Those days must have been horrible for her as well. Caroline realized she hadn't answered the man who clearly owned her aunt's heart, but Aunt Imogen rescued her.

"Where are you staying, Whitney? You know we have a guest house here on the property."

"I'm at the Sea Breeze."

"Oh, that place." Caroline's professional indignation got the better of her as she saw visions of overdone gingerbread. "I put in a bid for the Sea Breeze, but another company won the job and turned that lovely old place into a doll's house. Every time I pass it I want to tear everything out and start over."

Matt gave Jake a sharp look, and both men laughed.

"What?" Shelly asked.

"Never mind." Jake slid his arm around her waist and took her away.

"Let's let Matt explain to Caroline," Whitney said. "Show me the river, Imogen."

They meandered in pairs toward the woods where the river cut through the property. Even in mid-June a breeze off the water wafted Spanish moss from the tree limbs. Caroline felt alone in the face of affection that joined her daughter to Jake and her aunt to Whitney.

"Don't you have any other male family or friends, Matt? A couple of toddlers we can affiance to Melinda and Mary?"

He ignored her question. "Seeing that kind of happiness makes you feel alone if you don't have it yourself." Low and passionate, his voice raised a shiver that almost made her body dance.

What if he was right, and she was just plain scared? If Shelly and Jake truly loved each other and she stood in their way, would she lose her daughter? Was she trying to persuade Shelly to give up the man she loved and live alone like Aunt Imogen had?

"Maybe I should give up," she said.

Matt stiffened at her elbow. "Stop trying to persuade them they can't make it?" he asked. "Maybe they'll be all right." He tore his gaze away from the intimate image of Shelly and Jake leaning into each other as they turned the other way down the garden path Aunt Imogen and Whitney had chosen. "Look around you, Caroline."

She did, at her uncle tapping his cane to emphasize a point he was making with Alan, at Dan, hanging off the porch to shout a jeer that both Shelly and Jake laughed off.

"Your family amazes me," Matt said.

"What do you mean?"

"Whitney's a stranger, and so are Jake and I, but you all took us in. No one treats Jake as if he's slipped a ladder beneath Shelly's window to steal her away." He nodded toward Uncle Ford. "Your uncle acted as if I'd made fire for the first time, and then he started planning how I'd help him start the grill at our next barbecue."

"You expected a shotgun and a preacher?"

Matt shook his head, telling her she didn't get it.

"Jake and I don't have 'next times' when it comes to family. We've never had the kind of support you all take for granted. Look at you and your sister. You're as comfortable taking care of her babies as she is—and I don't think it's just because you're carbon copies of each other. As young as the twins are, they know they can depend on you the way they depend on Cate. No wonder Shelly thinks she and Jake can make it."

She stared at him, reluctant to hear what he was telling her, that he'd missed having her kind of family, too. "What about your support?" Eventually, the Navy would want to transfer him. Was he capable of putting his son and her daughter before his career?

"Maybe this is the last important thing we can do as their parents." Matt took her elbow. His warmth erased her inner chill, but another kind of shiver raced through her body. "We can do this together," he said.

She pulled away. He hadn't answered her question, and being "together" with his hand on her made her see him as a man, not as Jake's father. The father of the groom had no place in the mother of the bride's fantasies.

Even if the bride and groom never got married, Caroline and Matt would always share the child Jake and Shelly were having. Fantasy-type relationships, when they failed, sometimes forced people to choose sides. Shelly didn't need to add that to the pressures she faced.

Caroline had been as young as Shelly once. She'd

trusted Ryan. Shelly had suffered because Caroline had believed in the same promises Jake was making.

"She knows what happened to us because I got pregnant with her. Where does she find her faith in Jake?" Her voice startled her. The question undressed her own fears.

"They make each other believe. I've heard it can happen." But Matt stepped away, one long, lean-legged stride that was too casual not to be deliberate. "It just doesn't happen for everyone."

CHAPTER FOUR

ON THE FOLLOWING Thursday morning, as her political science professor droned on about election laws, Shelly's stomach revolted. Slapping her hand across her mouth, she fled.

She sensed her friends in the classroom staring at her. How many of them knew what was wrong? At times like this she needed Jake to tell her she wasn't alone.

In the rest room, she was so sick she felt faint. Finally, she dragged herself back into the hall, pressing a cold, wet paper towel to her upper lip. The colder the better. It eased her nausea. As she leaned against the wall, Jake pushed away from the classroom doorway he'd propped himself against.

Tall and sexy and just where she needed him to be. As if he'd sensed how much she needed him.

''You came.'' She caught his hands. ''I thought I'd die if I couldn't see you.''

Guilt flashed across his face, and she tightened her hands. Did she need him too much? Had he changed his mind? An alternate future bloomed in her mind, years of raising their child alone. In a flash, she understood her mom, irrational panic and all. She didn't want to be that kind of woman.

"Can we talk?" Jake turned toward the classroom door. "Where's your stuff?"

"In there. I ran out because I was sick, but I'd rather go back for my things after class." She braced herself for the worst. "Why don't you tell me what's wrong."

He peered down the hall. "Let's find an empty room."

It was that bad? Shaking her head, she sank down the brick wall to sit cross-legged on the cool tile floor. "I'm beat and I feel like crap. Why aren't you in class?"

He sat in front of her. "Something's been on my mind since last weekend at your aunt's house. I've put it off, because I didn't want to hurt your feelings, but I had to talk to you."

She clenched her fingers around the hem of her shorts. "You don't want to marry me?"

His horror-struck stare made her feel silly for worrying. "You thought I'd desert you?"

Did he consider marrying her a duty? "I don't want you to marry me because you think you have to," she said.

"Shel, you're the only one who ever brings that up. I know I don't have to. I love you. I want our baby, and I shouldn't have to tell you that every day."

Fighting mood swings that bewildered even her, she took a deep breath. "Then tell me what's bothered you since we were at my aunt's house.'' Her family hadn't interrogated him. What more had he wanted? ''Are you nervous around my aunts and uncles? You'll get used to them, and they already accept you.''

''I know,'' he said. ''But maybe I don't want to be one of the Talbots. I always thought the wife went with the husband.''

Nice. His mother had certainly gone with his stepfather, but Jake always said he'd felt as if she stopped loving him once she'd met Vince. He'd lost her two years before she'd died, because she'd decided her husband came first.

''Why don't we try blending our families? I thought that was the point of getting my mom and your dad on our side.''

He stroked her thigh all the way to her knee. ''I don't want to get married at your aunt's house. Your family is huge, and I'll only have Dad. We'll be lucky if his parents send us a wedding check.'' His pleading gaze softened her. ''How would you like to marry me someplace neutral?''

Her spine stiffened. ''Please try to understand,'' she said. ''I'm afraid. I tell my mom I'm positive about us, but I have doubts. We wouldn't be getting married if I weren't pregnant.''

''We would have gotten married later,'' he interrupted, because apparently he thought that made all the difference.

''My family has lived on that land for almost two

hundred years. I want to feel them with us. We need all those Talbots.''

''Even the ones who cheated and divorced and ran away?''

''No runaways.'' She cracked a smile that hurt her mouth. Not getting through to him scared her. When Jake didn't smile back, she rushed on. ''I know marriage isn't a Talbot thing, but we do family right. You and I can figure out our marriage on our own.''

''How can I make you see what I'm trying to say?'' He took her hand and twined their fingers together. ''I should be the one you depend on. I want to take care of you and all the children we ever have. I don't want your family looking over my shoulder, feeling they shouldn't hand you over to me because I'm not good enough.''

''Why would you think that?'' Tears came to her eyes so she buried her face in her hands. Her paper towel had dried and smelled disgusting. She felt sick again. ''No one thinks anything like that about you. They know you love me, and everyone except my mom has accepted us.''

''They accept me because you want them to.''

''Not true. They make up their own minds.'' She clenched the paper towel and met his gaze. ''I'm not asking you to do everything my way, Jake, but we'll remember our wedding the rest of our lives, and I don't want to remember it was in a place that doesn't make me feel anything.''

''I'm going to feel surrounded.'' He took her hand,

or tried to, but she was definitely about to be sick again. She pressed her palm to her mouth. "Are you all right?" he asked.

Shaking her head, she choked again. Jake pulled her to her feet, and Shelly searched his anxious gaze.

"Are you serious about holding the ceremony somewhere else?"

"Forget the wedding. You're sick all the time. Is something wrong with the baby, Shel?"

"No. Don't leave, okay? We have to settle this. Where do you want—"

She couldn't finish. Morning sickness rolled over her before she could ask where he wanted to get married.

"DAD, I NEED YOU to do me a big favor."

Matt tightened his hand around the phone. He stared through the slats of the blinds trying not to be so pleased his son needed him. "What do you need, Jake?"

"Shelly and I talked about the wedding, and I'd kind of like to see what it would be like to get married at the Officer's Club."

"The O Club?" When Shelly had that lovely old house?

"I just want to see what they'd offer us. Can you set it up? Or tell me how to?"

"I'll call the club manager and ask him what they do for weddings, but Jake, did something happen with you and Shelly?"

"What do you mean?" Jake's curt tone suggested Matt keep his questions to himself.

"I thought she'd want to get married at her family's house. Or maybe their church."

"We don't have time to reserve a church." Jake stopped, but Matt thought he heard something else in his son's voice, so he waited. You had to wait Jake out sometimes. "Maybe I don't want to be surrounded by Talbots," he finally said.

So that was it. "They'll be at your wedding no matter where you hold it."

"Okay, maybe I don't want to be surrounded by Talbots on their home ground."

Matt closed his eyes. He tried to see Jake's point, but he felt a measure of envy that his son would get to be part of Caroline's loving family.

"Why?" he asked. "They didn't seem to be trying to come between you and Shelly."

"I just want it to be our wedding, Dad, not a Talbot wedding. I can probably take care of this by myself, but I thought you'd have more pull."

Paying heed to the strain in Jake's voice, Matt gave in. "I'll call and set up an appointment with the manager and then I'll get back to you."

"Thanks, Dad." Jake's breath whispered over the phone. "We don't have to switch to the O Club, but if Shelly and I both like it…"

With any luck, Shelly's preferring the club to her family's home would be the only fallacy Jake tried to talk himself into. "I'll call you right back."

The club manager offered them a dinner from the wedding menu. Matt set up a time for the following evening and called Jake back.

"You're coming, too, aren't you?" Jake asked after Matt gave him the information.

Despite the diffidence in his voice, Jake wouldn't have asked if he hadn't wanted him. "I could if you'd like," Matt said. "How about Caroline?"

"I guess we should ask her. Do you want to call her, or should I?"

"Up to you, son."

"Why don't you call her, and I'll handle Shelly." Jake hung up before Matt could remark on the concept of his "handling" Shelly. That was talk Caroline would love to hear.

Matt glanced at his watch. In three minutes and forty-five seconds he'd be late for a meeting with Ned, but he'd make time for a quick call.

He'd already memorized her and Shelly's phone number, and he dialed it. He lifted his fist to his heart, which beat faster as he waited for the mother of the bride to answer. When Caroline spoke, her tone, textured in velvet and strength, rippled up and down his spine. He wasn't a man given to fantasies. Reality usually kept him occupied, but several inappropriate pictures that featured Caroline appeared in his mind.

She had to say a second hello before he found his own voice. "This is Matt," he said.

"What can I do for you?" The texture became sharpened steel.

"Jake's father," he said.

"I know. What do you need?"

She regarded him as the enemy—well, he had no qualms about using her to make his son's life easier. "I just spoke to Jake. He and Shelly have decided to look at the O Club for their wedding."

"The O Club?" Surprise made her forget to keep her distance. "I thought they'd want to get married at Aunt Imogen's."

He jumped on the fact she'd thought about a wedding anywhere. "Are you agreeing to help them go through with this?"

"The O Club is the worst idea yet. How is that personal to either of them? Do they want to rush through a wedding, or make it something to remember?"

"I can't say." He tended to agree with her, which made him feel as if he were being disloyal to his son. "But they want to look at the O Club, and the manager offered to make dinner based on their wedding menu. Jake asked us to join them."

Her deep breath raised the hairs on the back of his neck. He widened his eyes as the sensation rocked him. He didn't want to feel this kind of connection to the mother of his son's bride.

"I don't know what to do," she said, and perspiration glued Matt's hand to the phone. He wasn't sure he wanted to know any more about Caroline Manning, but his son needed her because her presence was important to Shelly.

"Come to dinner," he said. "If you hate the club, you'll have more ammo for your side. If you like it, maybe you'll start getting used to the idea."

"I can't stop trying to persuade Shelly not to marry Jake. I have nothing personal against him, but I don't think my daughter is old enough to know if she's in love with him or the idea of a father for her child."

"Give them a chance. See them together." What was he talking about? He didn't want his son tied to a marriage that could so easily go wrong either.

But Jake wanted it, and he'd so rarely given Jake everything he wanted. Maybe if he helped Jake build his own family, he'd break the cycle begun when he'd disappointed his own parents.

"Caroline, do you know where the flight line is?"

"No."

"Jake does. I'll ask him to drive you and Shelly out there, and then we'll go to the O Club together."

"I'll drive myself."

"Do you have a sticker for access to the base?"

"No."

"Then let Jake drive you. I have a meeting this morning and a flight this afternoon, and I don't have time to arrange a temporary pass on such short notice."

She paused again, but thank God she didn't breathe through the phone. "All right," she said. A paper rustled as if she'd moved on to her next item of business. "Anything else?"

"No." After they hung up he stared at the receiver.

How did he deal with Caroline? Her greeting, before she'd realized he was her caller, kept replaying in his head. He only wanted to persuade her she could trust him. Really. Trust was his only goal.

When he flew, he used checklists and mission plans to accomplish success. He had no such checklist to help him find the right relationship with Caroline.

He lifted his head. This thing with Jake and Shelly must be compromising his judgment. Just what kind of relationship could he expect to have with Caroline when he was trying to ease his son into marriage with her daughter?

ORANGE LIGHT HAD BEGUN to take the sky as Jake turned down the base's main road. Caroline clung to the door handle on her side of the truck. This ride had taught her everything she'd ever need to know about being a fifth wheel.

Her daughter had mastered the art of the proprietary handhold on Jake's thigh. Shelly treated him as if he were the grown man she loved, and Jake found time in the midst of his driving tasks to flash Shelly an occasional melting glance. After one of those quick peeks, he swerved into a pothole that tore Caroline's hand off the door handle and sent her toward the car's roof. She began to pray she'd vanish into thin air.

"Bad shocks, huh, Mom?" Shelly patted the dashboard. "We've decided to keep the shocks for now and buy a crib."

An instant headache wiggled into the center of Caroline's forehead. Shelly seemed to assume they'd agreed on a wedding as the next logical step.

"Did you hurt yourself, Mom?"

She forced a false smile. "I was trying to remember when I last went to the Officer's Club." As she spoke they drove straight past a sedate brick sign that proclaimed the equally dignified brick building behind it Leith Naval Air Test Center's Officer's Club. She'd said goodbye to Patrick there, and she couldn't consider it a good place to start a new life.

"I don't see Dad's car in the parking lot," Jake said. "He told me to drive out to the hangar if he didn't get here ahead of us."

"Cool. Men in flight suits." Shelly elbowed her mother. "You're in for a treat."

Caroline's headache boomed like thunder.

Jake drove through a stand of cypress and Spanish moss-draped oak. At the other side of the trees, rich dirt gradually gave way to tall, dry golden beach grass and sand. Down the beach, the hangar stood taller than Caroline had expected.

Jake had obviously been here before. He drove in and out of the cars that were still parked in front. After he stopped the truck, Shelly slid out on his side and Caroline met them at the hood. Jake pointed toward huge open doors in the center of the hangar.

"Come inside, and I'll find out if Dad's landed yet."

Inside, light slanted across most of the floor from

a twin set of doors on the opposite side of the wide building.

Several sailors in the flight suits Shelly had anticipated turned toward them as if scenting unfamiliar feminine flesh on the premises.

Jake reached for Shelly, his look of possessiveness startling Caroline. Reacting before she thought, she reached for her daughter's arm, meaning to free her from Jake's grip. Shelly simply frowned, a clear indication to back off.

Caroline fumed. Why would her daughter, a young woman brought up by the strongest females south of Washington, D.C., allow Jake to manhandle her? One of the other sailors broke away from the pack surrounding him. He crossed the few remaining steps, but when Caroline tore her gaze from Shelly and Jake, she found the young sailor was giving her the eye.

"How can I help you, ma'am?"

Caroline tried to stifle her laugh at the leer in his voice. Shelly frowned harder, as if she were trying to dissuade her mother from flirting with Matt's colleagues.

"We're looking for Commander Kearan," Jake said. "Is he back yet?"

The other man, hardly older than Jake, snapped to attention. "You must be the commander's son. Pleased to meet you. Commander Kearan left a message for you all to get comfortable in his office while you wait for him."

"Thanks," Jake said, and lifted his hands as if to usher Shelly and Caroline in front of him.

At the same time, noise from outside the hangar preceded shadows that fell across the sunlight on the cement floor.

Caroline turned, and Jake and Shelly looked back with her. Four men swung into the building, all in dark green flight suits and laced black boots. Carrying helmets, they all wore aviator's sunglasses. Matt, on the farthest left, stood out from the others. He carried himself with a hint of self-awareness the other men couldn't touch.

"Oh," Shelly said.

Caroline glanced at her, as did Jake.

"Remember that Patrick guy?" Shelly asked, not bothering to look away from the line of men. "Did he look like that?"

"Only on the outside," Caroline said, reminding herself not to be fooled by another excellent cover. Both Jake and Shelly gazed at her then, with twin expressions of curiosity.

"Glad you made it, Caroline." Reaching her side first, Matt took her arm. "Have you ever come out here before?"

She tried to match his casual tone while prickles of physical awareness ran up and down her arm. She nodded and began counting the seconds before she could decently pull away from his touch. "I've seen the hangar before."

"She dated a pilot for a while when I was a kid."

Shelly, a tad too helpful, seemed to enjoy exposing Caroline's mistakes. Caroline wouldn't have minded her daughter's relish, if only Shelly had learned to avoid the same traps. "You knew Patrick back when you were in high school, didn't you, Mom?"

Shifting slightly away from Matt, Caroline stifled her urge to follow the other flyboys who split up and walked around their small group. She'd never be able to forget she'd been a Talbot girl who'd courted danger and married a catastrophe. Even though she'd done enough penance. After Patrick, Caroline had tried to retire her spirit of adventure.

She turned to Matt, and the startled interest in his eyes surprised her, but she pretended not to notice. "Did you make reservations at the O Club?"

He hesitated, obviously looking for more information. Because of his son, Caroline told herself. Matt hadn't shared the surprising jolt of sensual pleasure that still tingled on her skin where he'd touched her.

"For seven o'clock," he said finally. "The chef is preparing their wedding salmon for us."

"Wedding salmon." Shelly's discontented gaze revealed a sudden aversion to salmon—or something.

Caroline glanced at Jake, whose lean face froze as he searched Shelly's expression. He glanced at his father and then away again, as if he found no answers there. Following Jake's lead, Caroline studied Matt for some clue to explain the undercurrents between their children. She should have been pleased at trouble between Jake and Shelly. Instead, she was anxious.

As if he hadn't noticed, Matt consulted his steel-banded watch. "Why don't you go on, Jake, so they'll know we haven't changed our minds."

Caroline turned with the others, but Matt pulled her back. "Wait and take my car. Half an hour in Jake's truck is like doing day labor on a jackhammer. You don't want to squeeze in with him and Shelly again."

Caroline rocked on her heels. He was offering the kids privacy. She didn't mind giving Shelly and Jake time to talk, but did she want to be alone with Matt?

With a sidelong glance at his fingers pinched around the stem of his sunglasses, his arm held tight against his narrow waist, his taut green-clad leg that ran for luxurious miles to his laced boot, she understood the difference between men like Patrick and a man like Matt.

Matt was just as eager to fly as Patrick, just as addicted to the rush, probably. But Matt had other facets to his life. He'd do anything for his son. He knew how to love.

Enough to stay and be the support his son and her daughter would need? Because if he transferred she wasn't sure she could be enough for them. Her family, as much as they'd loved her, hadn't been able to keep her marriage together. They'd just helped her pick up the pieces when it was over. Would she have to pick up pieces for Jake and Shelly by herself if she gave in to their crazy plan?

Did she have a choice about giving in? Jake and Shelly had already started toward the hangar doors. Suddenly, she couldn't let Shelly just walk out of here. It felt as if she were walking out of Caroline's life.

"I can't," she said.

"Can't what?"

He caught her forearm in his big hand again. He wrapped his fingers around her wrist with plenty of room to spare. He was strong and his touch made her feel safe, but her response horrified her.

"I can't let her go with him." But what she really meant was that she couldn't stay here with Matt. Jake's father had to be the last man on earth she should turn to for comfort. "I want her here with me. Always. I'll keep her safe." And she'd keep herself from harm, too.

"She's turning to my son. He'll keep her safe for you. He loves her."

"Please." She looked down at his hand on her. She wouldn't struggle to free herself from a man, not even figuratively.

Matt let her go. Maybe he knew how to read minds. "Wait for me," he said. "I just have to change clothes." He glanced at Jake and Shelly, near the door now. "We'll catch up."

Longing seemed to crush her chest as Caroline watched Shelly walk away with Jake. Caroline didn't know how to put her fears behind her.

"I don't want either of them to have the kind of

life I've led," she admitted. "I'm lonely. Not just because of Ryan, not just because of Patrick, who may have hurt me more. I'm lonely because I chose not to let in anyone else who could let us down."

Already on his way toward a set of metal stairs that led to offices along the hangar's upper level, Matt stopped, one boot scraping the floor. "Have I told you how much I like your honesty?" Softness in his wide gaze backed up his claim. "But you might be wrong about Jake."

"And you might be, too," she said. "Were they really so serious about each other before she got pregnant? I hardly knew Jake. You never met Shelly."

Matt came back to her. With his height, he could have intimidated her if she were that kind of woman. She wasn't, but Matt didn't back down, either.

"Give him a chance. I think he loves her."

His black gaze said something else. She saw doubt and fear and recklessness that made her shiver.

"I *know* they're too young to be married."

"You aren't talking about them, Caroline." His silky tone resonated with her quickening pulse. "You're thinking of what happened with you."

"I am," she said, disliking the truth, "but I've been through everything she'll face if it goes wrong."

He shook his head. "Why would you let Shelly's father and this Patrick character make you afraid to believe your daughter could love my son? Maybe you haven't known good men."

Her heart ricocheted into her throat. Matt roused

emotions she'd held under lock and key. His gentle tone suggested there were good men who could mean it when they loved, who could stick to a relationship.

She swallowed a groan. If he believed such men existed, did he think he was one of them? She didn't want to know. She looked away from him, aware of his quickened breathing, borne of concern for his son and her daughter.

His care made him too attractive, but she'd believed in words before. Actions spoke louder.

"What do you plan to do next, Matt?"

As if he were a machine, he blanked out the concern she found perilously appealing. "I'm going to drive you to the O Club."

"You know what I mean. I've asked you before when you were due to be transferred, and you've ignored the question. I'm no fool. Obviously, you're hiding the truth."

He gave up, and unease made his gaze almost vulnerable. "I think I'm going to interview with Icarus Aeronautical."

Immediately, the ocean seemed to roar in her ears. "You think?" She turned away, furious, now that he'd proven her point. He'd end up leaving Leith. Icarus was a huge, impersonal corporation based somewhere in Maryland.

"They want me, and I'd have more control if I went with them."

"Control over what?"

"Where I go and how often I can come back home."

"How could you pretend you'd be here to support Jake and Shelly?" Maybe she had no right to ask, but she'd been on the losing end of her parents' ambitions. She didn't intend to let Shelly suffer from the same career-comes-first attitude. Jake and Shelly wouldn't make it alone.

"I'll make sure Jake and Shelly know they can call me anytime."

"Until your job comes first."

"Stop holding grudges, Caroline. I'm not your parents. Jake isn't Ryan."

"We won't know that until you both have to prove it, will we?"

With a sharp nod, he spun away from her. "I guess you're right," he said. With a glance over his shoulder, he let her glimpse the anger he probably didn't dare speak. He might enjoy honesty, but he knew better than to say the words that leapt at her from his gaze.

One loping step took him up three stair treads. Rough, green cotton hugged every muscle in his lean body. "I'll be five minutes."

Caroline's courage faltered once his back was turned, but she couldn't look away from the fine shape of his posterior as he took the rest of the stairs and then hurried along the railed balcony that bordered the office spaces.

The sweet ache of desire could not have been more inappropriate.

CHAPTER FIVE

IN THE LOCKER ROOM, Matt avoided the other pilots. He stood in front of his locker until he stopped wanting to swear. What kind of woman assumed he'd abandon his son? He hadn't lied to her, and he'd admitted he was looking at the Icarus job. To Caroline, that meant he wanted out of the promise he'd made Jake.

So why did he feel guilty? He'd wrestled over the job. He didn't want to leave Jake, but he had to work. What did Caroline want from him?

Nothing. She wanted nothing, and that was best for Jake. Matt turned toward the showers. He'd admit it. He found Caroline Manning attractive. Not just those intense blue eyes and the dark red hair she shared with her twin, but the passion that simmered in her anger, and the love for Shelly that had driven her to accuse him of planning to do the one thing he feared most—failing Jake again.

Matt showered and put on khakis, a white shirt and a dark navy blazer. Something conventional enough to please the frightened woman who waited for him below.

What had she been like when she'd still trusted?

Trying not to imagine her the way Shelly was, vulnerable, willing to risk her heart on a happy future, he pulled a comb through his hair and then slammed his locker door. Nodding at a couple of friends as he left, he couldn't put Caroline out of his mind.

Through the balcony rail, he spied her. With her back to him, her shoulders looked unnaturally stiff. As soon as he stepped onto the metal staircase, she turned, and his heart tried to stop a little.

She'd used his absence to regain her bearing. Her burnished curls trembled against her shoulders as she lifted her chin. He'd hardly ever been more angry in his life than she'd made him, but now he saw himself gently tugging her head as he turned her mouth to his.

He wanted her the way she'd been for other men.

Matt rubbed his hand across his lips, appalled at his short, sharp fantasy. Caroline was about to become part of his family. She couldn't be more than Shelly's mother to him. And she clearly wasn't in the market for another pilot experience.

He attempted a placating smile. It felt like a grimace, and she met his gaze without emotion.

"Let's go," he said as he reached the bottom of the stairs. She let him move in front of her toward the open hangar doors. "My car is just outside," he added.

"I saw it." Did she disapprove, or did she find their unspoken truce difficult to maintain?

He'd show her who was in charge of his emotions. "You don't like my Jag?" Pretending he felt as unruffled as he sounded, he fished the keys out of his pockets and brushed at a film of dust over the car's trunk. Dust on his car? He was losing track of his priorities. "What do you have against antiques?"

"It's part of your image, isn't it? Did you buy it before you learned to fly, or was it a gift to yourself when you got your wings?"

Got his wings? She must watch a lot of movies. "Are you this touchy with everyone, or am I special?" So much for giving her an exhibition of control.

She opened her mouth and then closed it, uttering a squeak of dismay that made him want to look after her.

He pulled his sunglasses from the inside pocket of his blazer and put them on. Just in case his wandering gaze gave his thoughts away. "I didn't buy the car to build an image." He opened the passenger door for her. "Have a seat. If you can stand the softest leather that ever touched your skin, I'll deliver you to the O Club and you can make your own arrangements to get home."

"You're annoyed that I'm not impressed?"

"I don't know why you make assumptions about me. I'm not any man you've known in your past, and I have no designs on your future." He'd damn well quell any designs that popped into his mind.

She turned to him, putting her back to the door. "We don't matter to each other. We just agreed to help our children."

"Something happened when we were talking. You and I got personal with each other."

He opened the door wider. She ducked her head beneath the frame, and a whiff of some spicy flower floated back to him. She slid into the seat, but when she reached for the door handle, he gave in to an unfortunate streak of chauvinism. Catching the door before she could shut it, he eased it closed.

She'd make him pay for that.

Breathing harder than he had the day he'd lost his landing gear, he circled behind the car. As he put his key in the lock on the driver's side, the door popped open. He leaned down to peer through the window as Caroline slid back into her seat.

Scoring points off each other was a waste of time. He got in and started the engine.

"Thanks for opening the door," he said.

This time the sound she made was closer to a snort, but it ended with an unwilling smile that didn't quite make it to her shell-shocked eyes. Even when she might be wishing him dead, she had a nice mouth.

"I hope Jake and Shelly went inside without us." He turned toward the road. "I ran late getting back." She said nothing, and he concentrated on driving to keep from thinking about her nice mouth.

USING HER WATER GLASS as a shield, Shelly avoided showing Jake her utter dislike of the club. She searched the people who stood waiting at the dining room's wide entrance. All those men looked alike in their uniforms.

This was not where she wanted to get married. The place seemed like just another club. Surely her mom and Matt would understand and make Jake see sense.

Not that her mom had even agreed to help with the wedding. But why had she shown up today if she hadn't started to change her mind?

"You hate it, Shel?" Jake asked.

She tried to pretend for him. She wasn't sure why she couldn't just tell him the truth, except that getting married in a place neither of them knew seemed to mean so much to him. "It's nice." Her teeth hurt as she said the words.

"You do hate it." Jake sagged against the table, bracing his head in his hands. "They just redecorated." He looked at her. "The wallpaper's new."

That made all the difference. She took a deep breath. She didn't want to be like her mom, instantly opposed to any idea she hadn't thought of herself. "I like the wall sconces. They almost look like candles."

"They're cheesy." Jake's defeated tone turned her around for real.

Shelly reached for his hand. "I'm sorry. I just wanted to have the wedding in Aunt Imogen's backyard. Let me start over."

"No, if you hate it we shouldn't bother."

His quick surrender shamed her because she'd come prepared to turn down the club. "I'm sorry," she said again. She looked over the room, anxious to like something. Anything.

Jake waited. She skimmed over wallpaper painted to resemble brocade, the already tarnished light fixtures, the chair rail, newly painted, but already as scuffed as if the officers' brats had bounced their shoes off it. "I give up," Shelly finally said, tightening her hand on his. "But I love you, and I want you to be happy. Let's try the food. I'll keep an open mind if I have to borrow a can opener from the kitchen."

Jake's smile was weak, but she didn't blame him. She tended to forget she wasn't the only one in this fix when she felt constantly seasick and her mother kept reminding her she was too young and clueless to attempt marriage—much less motherhood.

What if her mood swings finally drove Jake to agree with her mom?

"Where do you think my mom and your dad went?" She hoped she sounded cheerful.

Jake didn't trust her new mood. He leaned away from her as if he expected the top of her head to open so the snakes inside her brain could come out and dance. "They're here," he said. "At the podium."

Turning, she smiled, but her mouth hurt and her stomach jumped at her mother's grim approach. Something had happened between her and Matt. Shelly knew the signs.

"Sorry we're late." Matt pulled out a chair for her mom and gripped it with the look of a man who'd resolved to stand there as long as it took her mother to sit.

"Thank you, Matt." Careful enunciation removed every hint of her mom's faint accent.

"You're welcome." Matt matched her formality.

"What's wrong?" Jake asked, raking his father with a suspicious gaze.

"Not a thing. Have you started without us?" Her mom lifted her water glass, apparently unaware that not one morsel of food had made its way to the table in front of her.

Which might have been part of the reason for the temper Shelly was hardly able to control. She might just consider a trip down to the beach to spear her own salmon if someone didn't show up soon with a meal.

"What do you think, Mom?" she asked.

"I think I see Aunt Imogen and Cate and Alan." Standing, her mom squinted at a table across the room. "Is that your Aunt Cate, Shel?"

"Unless you're looking into a mirror," Matt said, staring bemused between Aunt Cate and Shelly's mom.

His interest caused Shelly a twinge of alarm, but her mom tossed him a look that should have stopped his heart. When he laughed, widening his eyes as he gazed at her mother, Shelly bit her lip. Surely the sparks between them came from her hormonal imagination. The last thing she needed was to have her controlling mother hook up with Jake's dad.

"Go speak to your family," Matt said to her mom. "We'll wait."

"Do you want to come?"

At first Shelly didn't realize her mother was talking to her. When she figured it out, she shook her head. "Say hello for me." Two things—no, three—occurred to her. She couldn't cross that room with her mom right now without quizzing her about Matt. And Jake might realize he came first with her if she stayed put with him. Third, someone might bring something edible past their table now that it was fully occupied.

"Don't wait for me." Caroline dropped her napkin on the table.

"Thank God," Shelly muttered.

"Is that what's wrong with you?" Jake asked.

She almost hated him for the hope in his eyes.

CAROLINE SIGHED WITH RELIEF as she left Matt and their respective children. She knew her daughter well enough to sense Shelly was still fed up about something. The club, probably. Who'd want to get married in a place like this?

Plastering a smile on her face, she greeted her aunt, Uncle Ford, Cate, Alan and Whitney. "What are you all doing here without me?" she asked, trying not to stare at the man who'd come back into her aunt's life.

"Whitney invited us to dinner," Cate said. "We tried to call you. Did you turn off your cell phone?"

Caroline patted her pocket—it was empty. "I must have left it somewhere. On my desk, I hope." She smiled at the older man, whom her uncle appeared to approve of. "Thanks for the invitation."

Whitney nodded his dignified head. "I wish you had been able to join us. You're all welcome."

Caroline glanced toward her table. "They've prepared their wedding salmon for us to sample."

"Why?" Aunt Imogen's sharp tone drew interest from the diners around them. "They're not getting married here, are they?"

"Why do you all assume they're getting married?" A better time to ask the question might come up, but Caroline was starting to panic.

"I think I'll say hello to Matt." Whitney pulled his chair back. As Aunt Imogen slid into it, to be closer to Caroline, Uncle Ford stood as well.

"I have something I want to ask that boy," he said, and Cate slid into his seat.

Caroline and the women who meant most to her turned to Alan.

"I think I'd better find a reason to visit your table, too, Caroline."

She grinned, as well as she could with a lead weight pressing her into the floor. "Thanks. Maybe Matt and Whitney could give you a tour. The room we'd use looks over a park."

"I'll certainly ask for that," he said.

"Now what is it?" Aunt Imogen said. "Have you so annoyed that girl she wants to get married in a military club?"

"They hold weddings here all the time, Aunt Imogen."

Cate tapped the table for attention, and Caroline looked into her extremely comforting blue eyes. "You don't care about the place," Cate said. "If Shelly wanted to get married in the swamp and you were for it, you'd find a way. You need us to convince you she should get married."

"I think she's going to marry Jake whether I want her to or not. Why doesn't that bother you?"

"It does." Cate took Aunt Imogen's hand. "Look at us. Aunt Imogen nearly gave up on love. I took some strong convincing. You've vowed chastity—"

"Leave my chastity out of this. We're talking about Shel."

"And we don't have much time," Aunt Imogen said. "Matt took Whitney and Alan somewhere, but Jake and Shelly've started without you."

Actually, Jake was feeding Shelly something.

"Caroline, leave them alone," Aunt Imogen went on. "Let's make this brief. I didn't come here to have a girl talk we could have managed any time before this, and I won't ask why you've avoided talking to Cate and me about this. We did all right by you."

"But you let me get married."

"How could we have stopped you?" Cate asked.

The question lay there, ugly because it was too true, painful because it was the same question Caroline had begun to ask herself about Shelly.

"Balance the good you might do against the damage you'll surely cause," Aunt Imogen said.

"But I'm furious with her," Caroline said through gritted teeth. "Thank God I didn't let her see Patrick enough to get attached to him, but after him, I never let myself get attached to anyone either. I stayed alone for Shelly. I tried to teach her she could have the life she wanted if she just avoided my mistakes. Instead, I feel as if she made a checklist."

"Why are you so afraid?" Cate touched the tips of her fingers to Caroline's and strength flowed between them.

Caroline looked over her shoulder as Shelly caught Jake's hand, smiling at him with a softness Caroline hadn't seen since her daughter graduated from high school.

She smiled, but then Shelly pressed her lips to Jake's, and her touch was not a child's. Caroline turned away. Truth cracked like lightning over her head. She understood with a horrible sense of shame what frightened her most about her daughter and Jake's son.

"I've lost her," Caroline said, her face burning. "I thought I gave her up when she moved into the dorm. I know we haven't gotten along well since then, but I firmly believed she would come to me if she needed help. Now, her way is with Jake, and she's going to be his wife before she's my daughter. And there's nothing I can do about it."

"Is she going to be his wife?" Aunt Imogen asked.

Caroline heard her, but through a deafening roar. ''I'm so used to being mother, father and all the other important roles in her life, I don't know how to stop.'' Caroline used her fingers to blot the tears that had escaped her efforts to hold them back. ''But I have to, for her sake.''

''You want her to have a healthy relationship with her husband,'' Cate said, reading Caroline's thoughts as they came.

''Husband.'' Caroline fought her sense of panic this time. ''She's only nineteen. She was supposed to grow up first, figure out what she wanted. She was supposed to make her own choices, not accept a huge mistake.''

Aunt Imogen wrapped her arm around Caroline's shoulders. ''You're not giving her up. Once I felt just as you do now, and I still have you and Cate. Shelly's relationship with Jake has nothing to do with how she feels about you.''

''Unless you make her choose between you.'' Cate nodded toward the doorway, where Alan, Whitney, Ford and Matt stood, trying to look inconspicuous. ''Should we let them come back?''

''I guess,'' Cate said. ''Before they throw Matt and Whitney out of here. Can they be court-martialed for their dinner guests' bad manners?'' Caroline tried to put despair behind her—as if she weren't still persuading herself the most difficult decision she'd ever made was right. But horror at her own selfishness pushed her harder than all the good sense Cate and

Aunt Imogen could offer. She had to give in if her own feeling of loss was her most compelling reason for standing in Shelly's way. Matt was right. They could help Jake and Shelly over the hard parts. She hadn't accepted monetary help from her family. Maybe their financial straits had helped drive Ryan away.

Cate patted Caroline's hand, and Caroline smiled weakly at her sister. They'd always come to each other's rescue. Without having to be told, Cate knew when to avert Aunt Imogen's attention. "That Whitney's a sensitive guy."

Her aunt's blush made Caroline smile. "What do you mean?" Imogen asked.

"Alan and Uncle Ford know us, but they didn't leave us to talk. He gave us a moment."

Their aunt beckoned the man in question back to their table. As Matt came with him, Caroline noticed their own table was now empty.

"All done?" Uncle Ford's voice boomed as the men drew near.

"Satisfactorily," Aunt Imogen replied. "I don't think we'll have any more problems with Caroline. But where has Shelly gone? I want to tell her we can start making plans."

Matt closed his hand around the chair Caroline was sitting on. "You're willing to help them?"

She leaned away from the heat he exuded. "I'd rather do anything else," she admitted for the last time. She'd hold back her honest feelings from now on.

He smiled, and his eyes mesmerized her. Never in her life had she seen gratitude mixed with a warmer emotion so compelling she had to look away before she fell in and drowned.

"Where is Shelly?" Caroline had to think of her daughter, not of Matt.

"She and Jake went back to the kitchen to sample desserts." His husky voice urged her to meet his gaze again, but Caroline resisted.

"Are they serious about getting married here?" Uncle Ford asked. "Doesn't seem right for a family wedding."

"Jake's serious." Matt's disapproval drew everyone to him. "You aren't like any family we've ever known. You're deeply attached to each other, and he feels overwhelmed. I hope that doesn't hurt your feelings, but he's looking for neutral ground, and it is his wedding, too."

"We don't blame him for Shelly's pregnancy," Aunt Imogen said.

That wasn't strictly true. Caroline stared at her fingers linked so tightly in her lap her knuckles were white and pink.

This time Whitney came to the rescue. "You're not overwhelming, but he's in a delicate position."

Cate's hand on her wrist helped Caroline resist stating the fact he'd gotten her daughter into a delicate spot as well.

"Maybe we should let them see what the club has to offer," Cate said, "and get back to our own dinners. Matt, we were just wondering if the Navy would fire you for our rowdy behavior."

"I don't think I'd get court-martialed. Maybe I'd get a strong talking-to, but I'm a good pilot."

Caroline smiled, but Matt's husky voice shook her. She stood, but he must have thought she needed help returning to their table. When he dropped his hand on her waist, she gasped. The hem of her jacket had ridden up, and Matt's palm rested against her bare skin. Her own two feet had long ago learned to hold her up, but she wanted to lean into Matt's palm.

His strength threatened her because she wanted to let him help her and Shelly. Despite her family, she'd made herself independent after Ryan left. First, she'd curbed the part of herself that wanted to depend on others. Then, after Patrick, she'd killed the weakling who let herself become attracted to inappropriate men. Or so she'd believed until Matt came along.

No man could be more inappropriate than Jake's father. She forced herself to walk quickly enough to escape his warm fingers. If she was going to help her daughter marry Matt's son, she had to avoid getting addicted to Matt's hand against her skin.

"What are you going to tell Shelly?" he asked, his voice still too close for comfort.

Caroline twisted her head to avoid the phantom sensation of his breath on her neck. "I don't think

I'll have to tell her. I'll just start going along with her preparations.''

Matt caught her arm and turned her around. ''Don't you want to tell her?'' he asked. ''I'd tell Jake such good news.''

She had a picture of him laying good news like a gift before his son. ''That's not the way she and I are anymore. She'd think it was all part of a neurotic plan on my part.''

Matt looked startled. ''Must be the hormones.''

Caroline shook her head. ''I think our problems started when she met Jake. She knew he was the one, but I guess she didn't want to tell me.''

''It'll be okay, Caroline. We'll make it okay for them.''

The concept of a ''we'' that represented her and Matt was terrifying her. More news she'd better keep to herself.

LEANING AGAINST THE PIER RAILS, staring into the moody twist of the sea, Shelly tried to decide how to tell Jake they should rethink getting married.

''Shel.'' He pulled her into the curve of his arm. ''What's wrong? Tell me.''

''What if Mom was right?'' She lost her nerve the moment she looked into his loving eyes. ''What if we screw up everything by getting married?''

''We love each other, we're having a baby and that's all you and I have to know. Besides, I think she changed her mind.''

"She gave in, but she doesn't think we're right. She just can't stop us."

"What's the difference in the long run?"

"I don't want to owe her anything when I know she doesn't believe in us."

"I don't understand you, Shel. Do you want our parents to help us or not?"

"I want you to finish school and be a good doctor."

Jake rubbed his hand across his forehead, and his frustration frightened her. "You're not making sense. Your mom offered you her mother's earrings for the wedding. If she didn't want you to get married, she wouldn't offer you her jewelry."

"She's up to something." Shelly pulled his hand down. "I sound crazy, don't I?"

"A little," he said, relaxing. Then he leaned around her to kiss the side of her mouth, and his smile comforted her. It said he loved her, crazy or not. "Shel, I don't want you to put up with your mom because you think that's the only way I can go to school."

Leaning against him, she pulled his arms around her. "You know what happened between my mom and me? I didn't want her to know we were lovers. All my life, my mom warned me about boys like you." She tried to make it a joke, but she sounded bitter to herself. "She never trusted me to take care of myself, and she was right."

"Be honest. You're miserable because you can't

talk to your mom." His deep breath lifted her off his chest. "Why don't we forget about neutral ground, and call your aunt tomorrow? Ask her if we can get married at her house."

Shelly stiffened in his arms. "Do you think I've been trying to make you feel sorry for me?"

"No. You need your family, and I was trying to come between you and them, because I feel like the bad guy when I see how much they love you." Jake cupped her chin and tried to make her look at him. "Your mother included. I don't know why, but she's on our side now."

She pulled away. "I don't like the club, but I don't want to force you to marry me at Aunt Imogen's." She ran her palm over her belly. Hard to believe a baby was growing in there. "I just want this—you and our child."

"You're not forcing me. We need to concentrate on us and the baby. If you'll be happier on your home ground, I want to be there, too."

She tried to believe him, but her mom's sudden ability to compromise had put her completely off her stride. "I don't want you to think I'm inflexible, Jake. The desserts at the club were delicious. Did you like their room?"

"Don't pretend for me. The room was fine. The food was great. I wouldn't mind if we ordered that cherry chocolate cake thing, but I kept thinking I'm supposed to make you happy, and you won't be happy if we get married in a room that doesn't mean anything special to either of us."

"I'm supposed to make you happy, too." She hadn't learned anything from her mother if she hadn't learned to think about someone else even when she was positive her way was best.

"Then call your aunt tomorrow." He turned her around, and the moon over his head backlit his gorgeous, shadowed face.

"Don't give in just for me." She tried to mean it. She wanted their marriage to be equal.

He grinned as he leaned down to kiss her. "I'd never give in just to please you. I'm not as nice as your mom."

A WEEK LATER, Matt undertook his second tour of barbecue duty at Imogen Talbot's house. Ford and Alan flanked him again.

"Are you as good a pilot as the admiral over there?" Ford jutted a thumb toward Whitney.

Matt shook his head. "No one's as good as the admiral, but I am a pilot. Do you fly, Mr. Talbot?"

"Always wanted to. Call me Ford. How long have you known Whitney Randolph?"

"My whole career. He spoke at my graduation from OCS."

"Officer's Candidate School?" Alan said.

"Don't interrupt, Alan." Ford rapped his cane against the brick barbecue. A chink of mortar clattered onto the patio tile. All three men looked at each other. "I'm going to have to fix that." Ford kicked it to the side. "Now, Matt, this Whitney interests us. I remember when he and his wife lived in town, but they left rather abruptly. Rumor was, Imogen had something to do with his transfer."

Matt hid his surprise at this thread of gossip. Should Imogen Talbot's own brother spread the buzz? "Whitney has more integrity than just about any man I've ever met, and Caroline speaks highly of your sister."

"My sister is and was the soul of morality," Ford said stoutly. "So I'm not surprised she sent the man away if he was married. Maybe I'm being too subtle. What are Whitney's intentions now?"

His question, at the decibel level of a shouting plane captain on a carrier, drew surprisingly little attention. However, Alan put his hand on Ford's arm.

"Hold it down, Uncle Ford. Aunt Imogen thinks she can run her own life."

"Sorry," Ford said in an even more obvious whisper. "Did she hear me? She'll give me pure hell."

Matt laughed. Imogen Talbot, in an extravagantly flowered straw hat and a highly feminine floral dress, hardly looked as if she had hell on her mind. "I'm not sure she'd know how."

"She'd surprise you." Ford settled the grill screen over the flaming briquettes and smoky kindling. "I don't know how you keep a fire going the way you do."

"SERE school," Matt said. "Survival, Evasion,

Resistance and Escape. They dumped us in the desert, and we had to find our own food. I don't like raw—''

Alan and Ford eyed him expectantly, but they were a touch too civilized to contemplate the kind of eats he'd found on land that had been used for the same kind of training for decades. Besides, they were about to cook their own dinner.

''I can take it,'' Ford said, ''but you'd better go easy with Alan.'' He launched a jab at Caroline's brother-in-law and caught him on the muscular forearm. Alan grinned, returning Ford's affection. Watching them, Matt felt more alone than ever. Would Jake have time for him after this unruly gang took over his life?

Finally, Ford made his way to a seat built into the brick wall that flanked the barbecue. ''I've been trying to ask you this since the club the other night, Matt. What are my chances of getting a flight out of you?''

''In a Navy aircraft? Not a single chance.'' Matt grinned to soften his response. ''I can't afford the rent.''

''How about a private plane? You can fly those, can't you?''

''Sure, and I'd be glad to take you up.''

''Wait.'' Alan sipped his beer as he cast a careful glance toward Cate and Caroline, hovering over the twins. ''You'd better see if they mind.''

''Say what?'' Ford hissed in his irritation. ''I don't ask permission to have fun. Imogen didn't check with me before she took up riding my horses with her fella there.''

Alan moved around the barbecue. "Get a grip. Aunt Imogen rides that slow old nag of Dr. Barton's. She, Cate and Caroline aren't about to let you start flying.''

"Alan, stay out of my leisure activities.''

"I don't want to get on Caroline's bad side,'' Matt cut in. "If she doesn't want me to take you flying, I can't.''

"I thought you were a soldier.'' Ford showered him with a helping of disdain.

"A sailor.'' Matt resisted an urge to brag about the courage in his branch of the service. "And Caroline holds part of my son's happiness in her hands. I can't risk making her more annoyed with my family.''

"I never thought a fighting man let women push him around,'' Ford observed.

"Not all women. Just Caroline, because she and Shel are about to become part of my family, too.''

Alan narrowed his gaze. "How well do you and Shelly get along?''

"My son's marrying her. She can rely on me.'' Without thinking, he turned to look for her. She and Jake were wandering along the riverbank again. She loved his son. He'd learn to love her.

"Since you're all determined to treat me like an old fogey, I'll ask Caroline for permission to fly with you.''

Matt laughed. He liked being included in Ford's insult. "If Caroline says okay, I'll take you."

"I think I'd better come along." Alan looked reluctant.

"Do you fly?" Matt asked.

"No—but I'd feel better." Alan's grin mocked himself. "I've been around those women too long. I don't even like to fly."

"Safer than driving," Matt said.

"And I don't need a nanny, Alan. Besides," he said, his gaze on Matt intent, "we'll make a list of questions I should ask him. We need to know the Kearans a little better, and I won't have those womenfolk getting in the way on a plane."

Matt smiled, but Alan's amused nod suggested the older man wasn't joking.

"What are you all doing to Matt?" Caroline sounded appropriately suspicious.

Matt turned to her, but Ford answered first. "I'm badgering him to take me flying. He wants your permission first."

Caroline blushed, and Matt's fingers tingled as he imagined the heat coming off her skin. Why was she embarrassed?

"Why ask me?"

"Because he thinks you'll be mad at him and make Jake's life a misery if he takes me."

Her blush faded, but she looked annoyed. "I'm not your mother, Uncle Ford."

"I guess that's a yes." Triumphant, Uncle Ford

pried himself off his brick perch and took Alan's arm. "We'd better go spell your wife with those babies. You want to get the carriage? We'll run them down to the barns to look at their foal."

"Okay, but Uncle Ford, this time we keep our distance. The girls will hurt that little horse if they keep pulling on her tail."

Matt caught Caroline's scowl as the other men left to collect Alan's twins. "They have a horse?"

"Uncle Ford bought it to grow up with them. We'll be lucky if they don't break their little necks."

"He's careful with his family. He says he's planning to interrogate me."

She lifted both eyebrows. "I don't envy you."

"Funny—I'm glad you're all so careful of each other. When I'm not here, I'll know Jake's in good hands." He almost admitted how much he enjoyed spending time with the Talbots, but he stopped himself. No reason to flaunt the pathetic family-envy he'd developed since he'd met her and her clan.

"What do you want to do about your parents? Jake gave Shelly their address, and we sent an invitation, but they haven't called."

Why bother to explain? She'd never understand. "They'll probably send a check. They didn't come to Jake's graduation. He's likely to get a card that says, 'call if you need anything,' and then he won't hear from them again."

"Why?"

"They didn't want me to join the Navy. We have

a farm—or they do. I didn't want to work it, and I think they thought they could punish me into coming back if they didn't write or call. Over the years, they've drifted away, and I guess I have, too."

"You don't see them?"

"Not often. I don't want to talk about it, Caroline." He didn't like her pity.

"Maybe if I called and asked them to come?"

"I don't want you to."

"Then you should call them soon." She stared at her nails, possibly realizing he wouldn't let her push him overtly. "We have to hurry with the wedding, or Shelly's right. Someone will notice she's pregnant."

"I'd like to see anyone say a word to her or Jake about the baby."

"I don't care about after the ceremony, but I don't want anyone to say anything during the wedding. She should have the opportunity to remember it fondly. Ryan and I eloped, and the justice of the peace who married us took his favorite kind of payment—a case of Jack Daniels."

"When kids as young as Shelly and Jake get married someone always wonders if they're having a baby," Matt said. "Someone's bound to say something, but I'll take care of them. Don't worry."

"I'd rather you didn't turn the place upside down on Jake's behalf, but I'm glad you care so much."

"He's my son."

Caroline nodded at his simple statement. She understood.

CHAPTER SIX

CAROLINE SAW the days spin by. In the next two weeks, she discovered how difficult it was to persuade all her relatives to agree on the simple family wedding Shelly wanted.

As the mid-July day drew closer, Shelly and Jake retired into their own world. Caroline went doggedly forward, trying to put her doubts out of her mind.

On the night before the wedding, Alan and Matt hung paper lanterns in the yard. Dan and Shelly and Jake found time and friends to strew ribbon and garland around the moss-laden oaks. Cate, a genius at floral arrangements, worked a deal with the florist who owned the beach shop two doors down from her and Alan's office. She finagled the bouquet as well as table settings for lunch. Then she directed the kids as they ''prettied up'' the decorations in the trees.

Caroline studied the crowd of Shelly's friends. Their enthusiasm comforted her with the knowledge her daughter would be able to depend on a wide range of support. At the least, she'd have a never-ending supply of baby-sitters.

The morning of the wedding dawned on one of Leith, Georgia's best days. Sunshine and a light breeze that tasted only slightly of salt. A promising lack of humidity.

Wandering in an uneasy stupor around Aunt Imogen's house, Caroline caught glimpses of Shelly, in Cate's altered wedding dress. Maybe she was imagining the worst because of her fear for her daughter, but Shelly had already moved on.

When her bridesmaids arrived—in their prom dresses from the previous year—they all disappeared upstairs, and Caroline drifted out to the backyard, where Cate and Aunt Imogen and the twins were admiring their work.

Caroline attempted a smile. "Promise me she'll be happy and safe."

"Second thoughts?" Cate asked.

"She's gone already." Strands of Mary's silky reddish-blond curls lifted with the air. Cate smoothed her baby's hair, and Caroline remembered holding Shelly just the same way, as if she could feel her daughter's warmth in her arms again. "She's excited about her new life, her new apartment, her baby, but I wonder if she'll have enough to eat, if she and Jake will start to hate each other in direct proportion to their money problems."

"They may hate sporadically," Aunt Imogen said, "but you have to finish what you've started. Let her go, Caroline. Uncle Ford and I jumped into your lives whenever we thought you needed us. And maybe we made you too dependent on us when you should have turned to your husbands. I wonder if our strong family makes us less open to the people who marry into our happy little group.''

''I wouldn't have been able to support Shelly alone after Ryan left, and Cate wouldn't have found her way back to Alan without us to lean on last year. You talk as if we're bad for each other, Aunt Imogen.''

''Not bad for each other,'' Cate said thoughtfully. She and their aunt shared a look of understanding that made Caroline feel left out. ''But I came to you all when I should have gone to my husband. You don't want Shelly to use our family to hide from making a commitment to Jake.''

''She's committed.'' Caroline understood what her sister was saying, but she refused to believe her commitment to her family had anything to do with her own failed relationships.

''I wonder if Cate's right,'' Aunt Imogen said. ''Don't shake your head at me, Caroline. Why was my true love a man who was absolutely unavailable to me? Are we Talbot women afraid to commit except to our family?''

''That's nonsense. We don't *choose* the wrong men.''

''I'm holding back now because I don't know why I care so much for Whitney. What kind of trust is that?''

''What are you saying? I trusted Ryan. For that matter, I trusted Patrick, but neither of them wanted family. For family, I had to turn to you. What if Jake decides he's too young to take on the responsibility of a child? Are you saying I should send my daughter back to him?"

"No one can predict what a twenty-year-old boy will do, but don't assume he'll abandon his child." Aunt Imogen already defended Jake as if he'd become one of the Talbots' own.

"Look at Matt," Cate said. "He raised Jake, and family obviously matters to him. You can trust them both to stick around for Shelly."

"You forget he's in the same business as Mom and Dad."

"Matt's not cut from that cloth." Aunt Imogen grew impatient. "Don't judge him or Jake on the basis of your parents' attitudes or your past. You're also committing for life today."

"Not to Matt." Caroline stared at her sister and aunt. For the first time in her life, they'd let her down. She'd come to them, hoping to find comfort, and instead they wanted her to question her most sacred value—her family.

Cate tried to ease the tension. "Calm down, you two." She kissed her aunt's cheek, absently rubbing Melinda's head at the same time. "We should get dressed so Shelly won't have to apologize when all the women in her family show up late for her wedding."

"You go ahead." Caroline was almost glad to send them without her. The breeze, still surprisingly cool, tossed her hair against her face. She held on to the back of the closest chair and breathed.

Caroline and Aunt Imogen had to be wrong. Otherwise, she'd wasted too much time.

She turned toward the porch, quickening her steps as if she could outdistance the loneliness that chased her like the ribbons that dripped from the trees, angling, rolling, reaching for her.

Upstairs, in her old bedroom, she showered and put on makeup. Then she leaned over to dry her hair without grooming it into the smooth bob Cate preferred. At last, she slipped her lavender silk dress over her head.

She turned to the mirror with a twinge of guilt. The dress had probably cost more than all the decorations outside, but her reluctance to be mother of the bride had seemed to call for something extravagant.

She smoothed the silk over her breasts and then her hips and thighs. From the mirror, her eyes glittered back at her, more blue than she'd ever seen them.

Gutless panic. Giving in to so much doubt fed her image of herself. First Ryan, and then Patrick had turned her into a woman who refused to need a man. She'd refused because she'd considered her failures weakness.

But everyone needed love, and she was no exception. Her attraction to Matt came from the longings she'd put behind her. They weren't based in fact. As the concerned father of the groom, he just happened to be playing a role that appealed to her.

She tried to shuck off her needling doubts. She pictured the wedding plan in her head. Today's cere-

mony was the last checkmark on her list. She just had
to keep her mouth shut and not snatch her daughter
to safety that held no charm for Shelly.

A soft rap on the door had Caroline turning from
the mirror. Cate came in.

"I thought you might like some help with your
hair." Cate looked uncertain.

Caroline considered. If she sent her sister away,
she'd be running from the uncertainty Cate had pro-
voked with her questions. "All right, but I don't want
anything formal."

Cate plumped the back of the dressing table chair.
"Put yourself in my hands, sister dear."

Caroline sat in front of her and shook her hair over
her shoulders. "I don't think I've seen you in months
without Mary or Melly."

Cate made a sour face. "Don't call her Melly. Alan
does that to annoy me."

Caroline studied Cate in the mirror, trying to see
how else her sister might have changed. "A twist?"
Cate asked, twisting Caroline's hair into a rope.

"Go ahead and try it." Caroline never bothered.

"I'm sorry if I hurt you before."

"I'm not hurt, but I don't like feeling as if I've
made a mistake when I was only trying to take care
of Shelly."

Cate unpinned the twist. "I don't like this. Let's
try a braid." She parted the top of Caroline's hair.
"See if you can find another hairpin. I lost the one I
had."

Caroline opened a glass jar and fished out a couple of pins. "Do you think my life is a mistake, Cate?"

"Do you? That's what matters."

"I made some mistakes, and then I tried to fix them so my daughter wouldn't have to suffer. What else could I do?"

"Nothing. I would have done the same, but isn't it a shame you've been alone this long? And wouldn't it be worse if you really believed Shelly would be better off alone than taking a chance with Jake when she's carrying his child?"

"I can't change the way I feel." But she didn't have to make Shelly afraid. From today, Caroline had to protect Shelly from her own doubts. She didn't want Shelly to live without love just so she could be safe.

"You can talk to me when you're afraid," Cate said. "But give Shelly a break."

"You still read my mind."

"Shh." Cate pulled Caroline close. "Don't cry. You won't be able to hide it. Now, come help me dress. You'll probably end up holding Mary or Melinda, but they'll keep your mind off Shelly."

Cate was right. As soon as they opened the door to the nursery, the girls woke up in foul moods. Cate nursed them and passed them to Caroline while she changed. By the time they'd dressed the twins, the guests had begun to arrive.

Their noisy greetings filtered upstairs as Caroline eased into Aunt Imogen's room where Shelly stood alone in the dress Cate had worn for her wedding over twenty years ago. Shelly turned to greet her mother with a woman's smile.

"You're lovely," Caroline said, a little awed. "It's trite I know, but you are."

The dress hugged Shelly's newly voluptuous body. They'd had to let it out to accommodate her growing child. She pulled at the veil that trembled on the crown of her head.

"If we don't find some superglue, I'm going to lose this," she said.

"Let me see." Caroline straightened the veil and then pressed her lips to her daughter's forehead. "I'm sorry if I've overstepped, but I just want you to be happy."

"Jake makes me happy. And we're counting on you and Matt, so I know we'll have an easier life than most kids in our situation." Shelly hugged her as tight as she used to. "Trust us, Mom."

"I'm trying."

Shelly held her close again, bringing back memories of the affectionate child she'd been until she'd met the man she loved. "You're doing a whole lot better than I expected." As if she remembered her newfound maturity, she pulled back, and Caroline sensed her mentally separating herself. "Go downstairs now so we can start."

"All right." She left the room. She had to let go so Shelly could make her own life. Caroline found the minister and told him Shelly was ready. He disappeared toward the trees where Matt and Jake were waiting.

A trio composed of Shelly's friends from her high school orchestra played softly near the porch. One of Jake's friends ushered Caroline to her mother-of-the-bride chair. Thankfully, she was seated next to Aunt Imogen, who took her hand and held on.

The minister brought Jake and Matt out of the trees. In a gray morning coat and crisp, white shirt, Matt looked as confident as he had in that lovely flight suit Caroline had tried to forget. For a brief, intense second, his black eyes locked with hers. His mouth, the full lower lip tight with tension almost curved in a smile, and she remembered what Cate had said about how hard he tried with Jake.

Caroline looked down at her hands. Every instinct screamed for caution. She'd be crazy to try to share her feelings for Shelly with this man, but no one else could understand the combination of fear and joy that twisted her inside out today.

Shelly, so sure and so happy, almost made her believe. Jake, as nervous as his father, but as proud as Shelly, came to attention when the strains of the bridal march heralded Shelly's entrance.

Caroline stood, and somehow Matt drew her gaze again. This time she tried to smile, but something had changed since those brief moments when they'd joined gazes before. His solemn appreciation had nothing to do with the children between them.

His gaze traced the lines of her pale purple silk.

She almost felt his touch, awakening her body from a long and lonely slumber. Matt looked startled, as if he didn't entirely welcome the emotions so clear in his eyes. He dropped his hands to his sides, but his fingers moved, and Caroline's pulse sped up as he flexed them into fists.

Again, she broke the connection between them. She'd probably looked at him the same way that day in the hangar. She had a thing for flight suits. He liked purple silk. No big deal.

She turned her attention from him to Shelly, who came down the aisle on her Uncle Alan's arm. Rather, he held her back as she tried to fly to Jake.

Caroline's tears tasted of pride and hope. When she wanted to look at Matt, to share her unexpected joy, she held back.

Her undeniable awareness of him had more to do with the uncertain future Jake and Shelly were embracing with all their hearts. She was hungry for love like the passion that exploded all over her aunt's homely backyard. But her hunger wasn't Matt's responsibility.

ONE OF Caroline's clients catered the wedding lunch. Matt had to admire Caroline's business sense. He'd picked her up the afternoon she'd browbeaten the caterer into providing a meal in return for an upgrade on countertops and cupboard organizers.

Once they finished their delicious, bartered meal and the traditional toasts, the trio started playing dance music. Matt found himself counting the seconds until he could take Caroline in his arms.

As he held her, she looked away. She didn't speak, and he couldn't come up with words, but their dance ended far too swiftly.

He tried to understand the inexplicable urge to take her in his arms again, to run his fingers down the purple silk that clung to every delectable curve of her body. Hardly appropriate behavior for the father of the groom.

His son and new daughter-in-law flitted everywhere at once. They barely stopped long enough for him to speak to them. The afternoon flew by, marred only by the departure of Matt's stoic parents. He watched them say goodbye to Jake. They'd surprised him by coming. They didn't surprise him with their short waves as they left. No wonder he'd never known how to give Jake a family like the Talbots.

Even Whitney seemed under the wedding spell. He cut in early on Matt's dance with Imogen, and Matt had to stop himself from asking the admiral when they planned to make their own announcement. He was ashamed of his sadness at the thought of losing his old friend to stronger ties.

"Hey, Matt, good news." Ford appeared at his side, dapper in a dark suit, the epitome of every rumor the townspeople of Leith spread about him. "Caroline was surprised you made me ask her again for permission to fly with you."

Matt already knew the older man well enough to be suspicious of his bluff manner. "You asked her again, the way you promised? Because it wasn't fair asking her in front of everyone.''

''Didn't I just say I asked her?''

''Yeah, but you called me a granny for making you. She said I could take you?''

''Yes.''

Ford seemed to be laughing at him.

''Now I'll have to ask her, because I can't tell if you're amused because I don't want to cross her, or you're happy because she didn't object.''

Ford abandoned even his halfhearted effort not to laugh. His guffaw drew stares Matt ignored.

''You ask her yourself, flyboy. I hope she doesn't lose all respect for you when you abase yourself in front of her. Don't think I didn't notice you ogling her during the wedding.''

Matt stepped between Caroline's uncle and the wedding guests. ''Ford, you always say just the wrong thing.''

''She's my niece. I'm not entirely joking when I tell you to be careful with her.''

''I'll make you a deal. You don't warn me to stay away from Caroline, and I'll give you a safe flight.''

''You won't shove me out in midair you mean?''

''Copy on staying in the plane.''

''Is that pilot talk?''

There was something about this man. Matt understood how he'd charmed the rest of Leith's inhabitants. ''Let's go raid the kitchen, Ford. I think I could take you better on a full stomach.''

''Picked at your lunch, did you? My girls do that

to men. Charm is a Talbot curse. Look at your boy. He succumbed.''

Matt caught a glimpse of tux and white wedding dress, whirling on the makeshift dance floor in the center of the tables. Caroline and Cate had insisted on proper wedding attire, maintaining that Jake and Shelly would remember what they wore today. With visions of utility bills dancing, unpaid, in his head, Matt had given in. If need be, he'd find a way to persuade Jake to take a loan on those bills, but Caroline and her sister and aunt had put on a beautiful wedding.

''I guess you're right, Ford. Those Talbot women are formidable.''

He and Ford rummaged through the lunch leftovers. They finished their second meal about the time Shelly and Jake fell through the porch door.

''Dad,'' Jake said, ''what are you doing in here? Hello, Uncle Ford. I can call you that now, right?''

''I told you to call me that weeks ago, son.'' Ford stood. ''You two getting ready to leave?''

''We're going to change clothes now.'' Shelly hugged her uncle. ''Thanks for all your help.''

''Don't be too stiff-necked to ask for assistance in the future if you young people need anything. You know I'm flush, Shelly, and I'll always help you.''

''I know, Uncle Ford, but we should try to manage on our own.''

His nod was short and sharp. ''Fine, as long as your baby doesn't want for basics.''

"My neck can't get that stiff," Shelly said, while Jake looked uncomfortable.

"You'd better hurry if you want to get out of here before someone decorates your car." Matt stood to give Jake a gentle push.

Jake's smile offered silent thanks for getting him out of the room. He was too young to realize Ford had paid him the compliment of talking to him like family. His and Shelly's laughter floated behind them as they headed upstairs, but Ford jabbed Matt's arm.

"About the car, Dan and Jake's buddies ran past the windows about fifteen minutes ago. Do you think the boy will mind if they slightly vandalize his truck?"

"Nah." Matt picked up their dirty dishes. "He'll welcome the traditional ambush." He looked at the older man. Ford might try to come across as a gruff old guy, but his concern for his family spoke volumes. Matt felt more at ease with him than he had with the rest of Caroline's family. "I'm worried about Shelly and Jake, but they don't seem to know what kinds of problems they'll face."

An easy smile creased Ford's normally stubborn face. "Caroline and Ryan were the same, but they had a problem Shelly and Jake don't share."

"What do you mean?" Mention Caroline, and he was all ears. He couldn't help himself.

"Ryan no more wanted marriage than I do. Jake may not be ready for marriage, but he wants it as bad as any adult I've ever seen."

"Caroline's sister and brother-in-law have been married a long time. It can work."

"They've had some rough times, but like Jake, they want it to work. Your boy and Shelly are both good children. I just hope they'll be mature enough to last out the rough parts."

"They have to." Matt ran water in the sink and began to wash the dishes. "I wonder if Caroline feels as sad as I do right now."

"Sad?" Ford said.

"Alone might be a better way to put it. I'm not sure I've done the right thing." He glanced at Ford, surprised at his own willingness to confide. "Something about your family makes me talk too much."

Ford's laughter boomed around the kitchen, but Matt suspected the volume of his amusement had nothing to do with his hearing impairment. Matt bet he'd laughed like that all his life.

"I trust you, too, Matt Kearan, or I'd have found a way to keep your son and my niece apart."

Matt eyed him carefully. "You trusted Ryan Manning?"

"Never, but I was twenty years younger. Nowhere near as smart as I am now." Ford limped across the room and took the sponge out of Matt's hand. "Why don't you find Caroline and offer her a ride home? I'm sure she does understand how you feel right now. We felt the same when she and Cate married."

Taking Caroline home was the last thing he should do. He wanted to be with someone who understood him, and his loneliness made him restless.

He dried his hands. "I'll find her."

He eased through the clinging plants on the porch and stepped outdoors just as everyone headed toward the other side of the house.

He followed and arrived in time to wave at his son, who was standing on the running board on the driver's side of his ribbon-and-can-festooned truck. Shelly rolled down her window and shouted words Matt couldn't decipher.

He forgot to look for Caroline as Jake slid behind the steering wheel. His heart constricted. More afraid than he'd ever been in his entire career, no matter what had fallen off his plane or what enemy had looked back at him from his radar, Matt pressed the heel of his palm to his breastbone.

They'd be okay. In a week they'd return from their mystery honeymoon, and life would go on like normal.

Besides, this was no way for a man to behave. Hyperventilating in a very nice elderly lady's yard. He straightened the ridiculous coat his son's mother-in-law had forced him to wear and raked both hands through his hair.

Why shouldn't he offer Caroline that ride?

Cate and Alan, each laden with a pink, ruffled bundle of confusing softness, looked up as he yanked the screen door open. The rest of the family and an assortment of their friends, minus the woman he sought, slowly faded to silence.

"Caroline already left." Cate Palmer had read her

sister's mind several times since he'd known them, but this was the first time she'd read his.

"She's gone?" What'd she do? Park her own jet behind her uncle's barn?

"She went home, I guess." Cate swayed gently with her baby to music only she heard. "We usually make her help clean after a party, but she seemed to want to be alone."

"Thanks," he said. A titter ran through the mob. Add humiliation to his unaccustomed lack of an idea as to what he should do next. "And thanks for giving my son a great day."

"You're welcome, but I don't think the father of the groom has cleanup duties either." Ford rescued him. "Why don't you hit the road and get some rest, too? You and Caroline have been through as much as the children."

"We should stop thinking of them as children," Alan said.

"Finally someone notices we stop being children when we turn eighteen," Dan said.

His father tried to quell him, but a quirk in Dan's eye faded as he met Matt's gaze.

"Sorry, sir." But then Dan laughed.

Matt beat it before his son's new in-laws realized he had no place here without Caroline or Shelly.

CHAPTER SEVEN

BOTH HAPPY for Shelly and appallingly lonesome for her at the same time, Caroline closed the door and leaned into it, as if she could press her body through the wood and get back outside again. The silence screamed at her. Nothing would ever be the same. Her empty nest had become an empty home. Shelly didn't live here anymore.

Trying not to cry, Caroline kicked off her shoes and padded to the kitchen. Shelly had worn happiness like part of her wedding outfit all day. Caroline had never looked or felt like that—maybe Shelly's kind of happiness only came with true love. Maybe Shelly and Jake loved each other enough to make their ill-timed marriage work.

Praying her daughter was wiser than she'd ever been, Caroline started a pot of coffee and turned on the radio. She tuned in a jazz station. A sad, Sarah Vaughan song lifted her spirits.

Naturally she was restless. Since Shelly had told her about the baby, she'd had something to do almost every second of every day. She'd have to get used to a crisis-free life on her own.

She searched the fridge for something worth eating.

They'd spent so much time at Aunt Imogen's lately the pickings in her own pantry had grown slim.

Rummaging in the vegetable bins, she pulled out a stalk of celery and went to the sink to wash it. One bite was too much. It tasted stale and bitter.

She tossed it at the wastebasket, but it missed and bounced beneath the table. She was on her hands and knees fishing it back out when the doorbell rang. Caroline slid out from under the table and skated down the hall in her stockinged feet. She hoped it was Cate, who must have realized how much she needed her, but she'd welcome a call from the taxman about now.

Instead of the IRS, Matt stood on her doorstep. He'd shed his jacket, but he looked even better with his white shirt open at the collar, loosely tucked into his black trousers.

Caroline opened her mouth to ask him in, but his heavy-lidded gaze struck her speechless. He seemed to reach into her soul without any effort, and she felt naked in front of him.

They'd never been together without Jake and Shelly before. His being here felt forbidden, and she'd always been a sucker for the forbidden.

"I didn't want to be alone," he said.

"I don't, either." She was in trouble. She'd been smart so long. She'd been *careful.* She'd protected herself from physical need when it hadn't been anywhere near as plain as the longing in Matt's eyes.

"Come in." Her voice failed her. She sounded as if she'd been crying, when she was only crying out for a connection to this man who'd fought her so that her daughter could be happy. "I can offer you wilted celery."

"I've had more attractive offers at your table."

"When I got home the cupboard was bare." She stood back, at a disadvantage without her shoes.

"Do I hear Louis Prima?" Matt asked.

"Do you like Louis?" Did he have to talk? She started toward the kitchen, and he followed, moving around her to open the door so she could enter ahead of him.

"I'm surprised you know him," Matt said. "I never heard of him until I was stationed in Iceland in the late seventies. Armed Forces Radio couldn't afford top forty, so they revived the seventy-eights."

"I discovered him at Uncle Ford's."

"Uncle Ford." Matt stood still, and his stillness backed her toward the wall. "Did he really ask you again if I could take him flying?"

"Why do you keep making him ask me?" He seemed so much taller than she'd noticed before. Where had she put her shoes?

"I pictured you losing your mind at the idea of him risking his life in a plane. Shelly wouldn't want me to worry you. Jake would give me hell for worrying Shelly."

Caroline faltered. "I hadn't thought about him risking his life. Would he be?"

Matt laughed. "No, but I tried to see the situation through your eyes."

Caroline blinked. She'd been wrong about him. She wanted him, but he didn't feel the same about her. She was just Shelly's mom. He'd placated her so she wouldn't keep her daughter from marrying his son. "Why are you here?"

"I miss Jake." Coming closer, he curved the tip of his finger beneath the purple ribbon that held her dress on her shoulders. "I thought if you and I saw part of this night through together, we wouldn't remember what we've helped our children risk."

Damn him. "Risk?"

"You were right. You were always right about them." He lifted the ribbon slightly. It tugged at the material that sheathed her breasts. Her nipples tightened, and she felt betrayed by her body and by him.

"You didn't believe any of the lines you fed me for the past month?"

"All of it intellectually, but I can't seem to make my heart agree with my head. I had dreams for Jake." Looking down, he caught his breath, and Caroline pushed his hand away from her.

"Stop touching me. You lied."

"You're beautiful. I can't stop thinking about you, about how you'd look if I touched you." He moved his cupped hand toward her breast, but he didn't touch her with any part of himself other than his naked need. She ached for him to close the few inches between his palm and her taut nipple. He widened his eyes, reading the signs her body offered. "I had to choose between doing what my son needed and giving in to what I thought was best. If I'd admitted I agreed with you, you wouldn't have gone along with them.''

''How often do you imagine I've gone along with what someone else thought I should do for Shelly?'' She arched toward him. She couldn't help herself.

He finally looked up again, lifting his head first and then his gaze. ''My son wanted to marry your daughter. No matter what you say, Jake had a responsibility to marry Shelly. I consider the fact he loves her a bonus.''

''He shouldn't have married her because of the baby. What can Jake and Shelly know about real life at their ages?''

''How did a couple of shallow guys kill your faith in marriage?''

''Maybe I believe in marriage, but Shelly and Jake are too young.''

''Let's try not to lie to each other.''

''What about you? I don't see any sign of the second Mrs. Commander Kearan.''

The corners of his eyes crinkled at the mockery in her tone. ''Jake and a wife and the Navy and I don't seem to mix,'' he said. ''But I won't give up the concept. If you could do it right, it might not be a bad thing.''

Caroline tried to look as if the nebulous image of a second Mrs. Kearan didn't hurt her.

''You know you would have lied to me for Shelly's sake.'' He closed both his hands around her shoulders, his eyes a little wild, just frightening enough to be irresistible to Caroline. "Tell me we're both good parents and we've started our children on a future they won't regret."

She caught his wrists, her hands sliding his already rolled sleeves up the corded muscles of his forearms. His plea gave her power. "I don't intend to let them regret anything."

Matt laughed softly, his breath stirring her senses. "You're in charge, Caroline Talbot Manning?"

He moved his thumbs, massaging the flesh just beneath her collarbones. It wasn't enough. As she slid her arms around him, his shirt rustled, starch and linen protesting her every move. Uncertainty flashed in Matt's gaze, but then he locked his arms around her waist.

"What comes next?" he asked, his voice pitched so low he might have been talking to himself.

She simply didn't pull away. She linked her hands at the nape of his neck. His close-cut hair scraped her palms as he covered her mouth with his. Sweeping hunger turned her into another woman who knew she wanted Matt and knew how to tell him the things she'd like him to do.

She kissed him, teasing him, taunting him. She opened his mouth, but when he tried to take over, she held back, retreating until she was just out of his reach.

"Caroline," he protested, and his pain made her realize she resented him for making her need him.

Cradling her face, he kissed her forehead and then each eyelid. Slowly, he traced his mouth along her cheekbone, tasting her as if she'd been created for him to explore.

His desire was a low rumble that transferred from him to her, a meeting of breath and possession and passion that made her abandon every truth she'd ever known.

He lifted his head to stare into her eyes as he smoothed his fingertip across a tear she hadn't known she'd cried. He put the pad of his finger to his lips and licked her salty tear off his skin.

Want assailed her. She tightened her arms around him, craved his strength, the power in his muscles as he strained against her body.

He caught her mouth again, and she trembled, trying to get closer to him. As she opened her lips, he pushed her against the wall. Bracing his hands on either side of her, he kissed her again and again, easily as starved as she.

When she twisted her head away, overwhelmed, a little frightened, he gently scraped his teeth against the column of her throat and dragged her hands to his chest. She unbuttoned his shirt and flexed her fingers on the planes of his flat, taut belly.

His pulse seemed to race all over his body. His skin was fever hot, but she longed to warm herself against him. Quickly addicted, she stroked, learning the distance between his rib cage and his navel, the sweep of silken hair that arrowed to his waistband. He straightened, a big, dangerous cat absorbing heat from his god-given place in the sun.

His lashes were like tangled black lace against his tanned skin. Gentled by her touch, he brushed his lips against hers, nudging her mouth open. Mindlessly, Caroline smoothed her index fingers over his tight nipples. Matt drew a ragged breath and dragged her hips against him.

At first, the jut of his hardness brought her relief, but they were moving too fast. He was offering her pleasure here against the wall, in the shelter of his arms, in the most sensual tangle of clothing and lust and not-so-gentle consideration for her need.

It was too much.

"No," she said while she was still able to breathe.

As she twisted out of his grasp, he turned his own back against the wall, his face defenseless and drawn. His gaze drilled all the way to the depths of Caroline's sense of herself.

"And you think I was keeping secrets," he said.

"I'm sorry." Who knew what she meant? She was sorry she'd stopped them, sorry she'd started. Sorry they were Jake and Shelly's parents and couldn't be involved with each other without adding extra pressure to a marriage that had too many strikes against it.

"Don't say that, Caroline."

She averted her face from his. Looking into his ravenous gaze, she wanted him too much.

"Staying would be a mistake." He began to button his shirt.

Who knew buttoning could be even more seductive than taking his shirt off? Lethargic with need, she summoned the strength to nod. "Maybe you should go."

"Don't make too much of a kiss between adults, Caroline."

"That's all it was," she said, as if he'd forced her to finish the trite thought.

"Yeah." His glance fell to her mouth, to the broken ribbon she hadn't noticed on her right shoulder. "Right."

The last of her strength seemed to melt through the floor beneath her feet. She couldn't have moved if the house burst into flames.

Matt tore his gaze from her lips and stalked toward the front door, his stride stiff.

She closed her eyes. Loneliness was a horrible, pervasive poison, but look what the hell she'd almost done.

She opened her eyes, desperate for a last glimpse of his long, straight back, the narrow width of his hips, the arrogant tilt of his head. She pressed her hand to the wall.

Regret hurt more than loneliness.

THE NEXT EVENING, after Matt returned from a meeting with Captain Townsend, he peeled a small green square of paper off his locker. Caroline had left him a message. She'd asked the yeoman to leave her number and requested that Commander Kearan return her call.

At least she hadn't retired to her cottage and boarded up the windows. He crumpled the note. She knew he'd memorized her phone number weeks ago. She'd long since stopped leaving it when she'd needed to talk to him. Today's message must signal her return to being the woman she claimed she was—the one with the plan he'd blown to bits.

What had come over him? The purple dress that had seemed to serve her body on a silk platter? Their shared sense of loss? What would Jake have said if he'd walked in on them?

He had to make sure Jake never discovered he'd slobbered over Shelly's mother like a teenager with a terminal case of heartsickness. And to think, for the past two months he'd tried not to rage at Jake for behaving irresponsibly.

Matt checked his watch. It was after five. Tomorrow morning he had to fly to Maryland for his first meeting with Icarus Aeronautical, and he'd promised Ned he'd turn in his reports before he left.

Since the hangar was almost empty, Matt changed into civvies and put off calling Caroline. The woman with a plan had probably decided how to deal with what they'd almost done last night, and he expected her strategy to annoy him.

He filled out his reports and then carried them down to Ned's office. The door was already closed.

The hangar echoed, pipes clanking as the building settled. Only sailors on watch were hanging around. Matt dropped the file in Ned's mail slot.

Going back to his own office, he tried to plan his conversation with Caroline. He'd been curious about her, attracted and concerned for her, but he hadn't planned to make love to her against the wall in her kitchen. And he would have if she hadn't stopped him.

He dropped into his chair and spun to face his desk. He didn't know what to say. He dialed her number and then ignored the way his pulse quickened as he waited for her to pick up the phone. She answered on the fourth ring, her tone absent, as if he'd interrupted her at something important.

"It's Matt," he said.

"Oh." Metal clattered at her end of the phone. She'd dropped something. "I'm glad you called," she said.

"I'm sorry about last night." He wasn't. He kept thinking about what they hadn't done, how much of her he hadn't touched.

"No, you were right. It's no big deal." Determination infused her voice. "We need to make sure we can talk to each other without a kiss making us uncomfortable."

A kiss. She'd either gone without real passion or her latest plan involved lying to herself big time.

"I'm fine," he lied, as annoyed as he'd expected to be. "How about you?"

"Couldn't be better. I'm considering turning Shelly's room into a sewing room."

"What?" His voice squeaked the way Jake's used to.

"I had to drag my sewing machine down today, and now it's cluttering my work area. I need it fairly often, but I don't have room to leave it up."

"So you're going to put it in Shelly's room?" He didn't believe her for a second.

"Sure. What could convince her more that I believe in her marriage? Shelly's moving on. I'm going to follow her example."

Exactly what did she want to move away from? He also had an idea about that. "Caroline, we only kissed each other. I hate to think what you'd be doing today if you hadn't stopped us last night."

"I'd still be designing my sewing room." Iron reverberated from her voice. "You give yourself too much credit."

Too much credit? The woman had practically turned herself into a nun to hide a passionate streak a mile wide. "You know last night changes things." He regretted his sputtering accusation the moment it left his mouth, but her flip attitude pissed him off.

"Nothing changes between us, Matt."

He ached to prove her wrong. "I wish I were with you right now."

"I wanted you last night. Not tonight, not ever again."

"You've made a hell of a plan, Caroline."

"Maybe." Doubt made her sound more like the woman who'd nearly reduced him to a shivering boy. "But I'm right. I feel sick when I think what might have happened if someone had walked in on us. My aunt and uncle show up all the time without warning."

His frustration subsided instantly. "You're right."

"Why don't we have dinner and try to behave normally?"

Her suggestion staggered him. She had led a sheltered life if she thought he could sit with her, talk to her, remember what they'd been like together for those few moments and not try to feel that good again. "I can't." He resisted the temptation. "I have to fly to Maryland tomorrow."

"Icarus?"

A note of anxiety in her voice made him smile, when he should have felt bad about upsetting her. "The initial job interview. It doesn't mean they'll offer or that I'll take it."

He'd finally agreed to do the interview because the company's recruiter had confirmed rumors about Icarus' moving to Georgia. The recruiter had refused to say where the company planned to stake its new headquarters, but Leith made sense, because of the naval air base. When one of the vice presidents, an old friend, called to second the recruiter's request for an interview, Matt had agreed to talk to them.

"Are you flying yourself?" Caroline asked.

"No, I'm going commercial." Icarus had treated him to a first-class ticket. They were serious.

"When are you coming back?"

He couldn't resist an answer that was bound to aggravate her. "I knew you cared."

"About Shelly and Jake. They'll be back in six days, and I wonder if you'll know everything by then."

She didn't take jokes well after a night of almost-passion. Whether she was able to admit it or not, she'd been as involved as he. "I'm flying back day after tomorrow, but I won't know anything for a while."

"I'll probably see you after the kids come home then. Have a good meeting."

He hoped she didn't mean it. No matter what he had to do, he wished Caroline wanted him to stay here. "I'll see you, Caro—" The phone clicked in his ear.

He smiled as he replaced the receiver. He'd tasted her astounding passion. He no longer believed in her attempt to look tough.

And pigs would fly before she'd turn Shelly's room into a workroom.

THE NEXT MORNING found Matt sitting on an airplane in Leith for an hour while they waited for weather to clear at BWI. Based in the somewhat isolated town of Patuxent River, Maryland, Icarus wasn't easy to reach.

After he finally landed, Matt spotted a limo driver holding a sign printed with his name. They drove to Waldorf, Maryland, and then turned south toward Pax River. Matt had trained at Pax and then done another tour there in the late eighties. The town had grown since his tour, but it still lay at the back of beyond.

Icarus occupied a large complex south of the base. Henry Camp, Matt's friend, met him in the building's rotunda. Henry had been one of Matt's instructors when he'd trained at Pax. A little more gray hardly diminished his dark blond hair. A few more lines made him look more mature, but no less powerful.

"Morning, Matt," he said. "Sorry your flight was delayed."

"You control that too, Henry?"

The other man grinned. "If I did, you'd have flown on time. Come on in. I want you to meet the board."

"The board?" He'd expected a low-key interview with Henry and a couple of his subordinates.

"We have plans for you, Matt. Big plans. Which jobs have you enjoyed most in your career?"

"Test flight." The Navy differed from the other services in that test pilots left their test assignments to fly with squadrons who flew the planes they'd been testing.

"You're going to like working here."

Temptation. Caroline passed through his mind, and she silently accused him of biding his time until he could leave Leith. "It'd have to be a phenomenal of-

fer, Henry. My son got married a few days ago, and
he's having a baby.''

With a low whistle, Henry shook his head. "Jake
got a girl in trouble? I'll bet you'd like to ship him
off to boot camp about now.''

"About four months ago would have been more
beneficial.''

SHELLY SET A GLASS beside one of the plates Aunt
Imogen had given them. The table that had come with
the apartment rocked beneath the glass's minuscule
weight.

"Jake," she called. He stumbled out of their bedroom, covered in dust and sweat. The elderly air conditioner had died before light this morning—their first
Saturday morning in their new apartment. By noon,
she was barely able to keep him from pushing the
unit out of the window. He'd finally announced he
could repair the cord if she'd leave him alone.

"I thought you were going to fix that table leg,"
she said, "and I don't want you to kill yourself on
the air conditioner.''

"I'm going to buy a fan and feed that box to the
landlord. Then I'm going to chop the legs off that
table. Do we have a sharp knife? Because we can't
afford a chainsaw.''

To Shelly's dismay, tears burned her eyes. "You're
not happy.''

"I'm burning up, Shel, but I'm not sorry we got
married.'' He opened the refrigerator that fit beneath

their sink and pulled out a pint of her favorite ice cream.

"Jake," she said, smiling through babyish tears. "Thank you for the treat, but that stuff costs a fort—"

He slammed it to his forehead. "Since we can't have air conditioning, I think we can use some ice cream. Do you think your mom will eat it after it's been on my face?"

She took the container from him and pressed it against the back of his neck. "A doctor should know where it'll do the most good. And I don't think we need to mention its superior use as a cooling agent."

"Something's burning."

She shoved the ice cream into the pit of his stomach and whirled toward the stove. Her casserole came out a little crisp around the edges, but her mom would eat it and keep quiet. "How does your dad feel about carbon?"

"He's fed me enough. I think he'll thank us as long as we don't make him cook. When are they supposed to get here?"

She glanced at the stove clock that had begun to tick long before digital was a word. "In about thirty minutes. Maybe if I shut the door my casserole will stay warm."

"Dry out, you mean. Come take a shower with me, Shel."

"Not a chance. You want to give my mom a stroke? Go get cleaned up, and I'll figure out how to make this table stop doing a boat imitation."

"Leave the table alone. You can't get those legs even." He started toward the bathroom, but he turned back. "Did you make up a list of things for the baby?"

"I left it on top of the television."

"I'm not sure we should let Caroline and Dad buy all that stuff."

She grimaced. "Giving us something we can't afford will make her happy."

He headed for the bath. "Seen any houses you like?"

He sounded as if he was joking, but how could she tell for sure? Jake hated the apartment. He sniped at her every time she went out by herself in the neighborhood, as if everyone in the building shoved air conditioners out the windows onto unsuspecting pedestrians.

As the shower pipes roared at the water rushing through them, Shelly took a napkin out of the holder on the table. She folded it into a small, tight square, which she then wedged under the table's short leg. She prodded the table. It hardly moved.

Close enough.

She made some lemonade and pried the ice tray out of a narrow cave in the tundra of their freezer. She'd heard of freezers you had to defrost, but she'd thought they'd all died with the dinosaurs. Somehow, this one had survived.

Maybe her mom could tell her how to defrost it. She'd call her after she went home tonight. After she'd eaten a perfect meal at her married daughter's new home.

Smoke curled out of the oven door. Shelly grabbed a dish towel and yanked the door open. Naturally, she'd forgotten to turn down the heat.

The shower pipes rattled to a halt. The bathroom door opened as Shelly stared, deflated, at the hunk of burned black cheese on a noodle and beef concoction.

"Shel?"

"What?" she snapped.

"What if we let Dad and Caroline buy us an air conditioner?"

"She doesn't need to get that happy. Jake?"

"What?"

"I'm throwing dinner out of the window."

He shut the door without answering. Coward. And she'd bet those hot dogs he'd eaten for breakfast were the last ones they had.

CHAPTER EIGHT

THANK GOD she drove a Jeep that was too old to steal. Caroline locked the door anyway and forced herself to look at Shelly's building. Rust that dripped from each metal window frame made her want to cry. Faded paint made her want to call Alan and beg him to donate a makeover. Only her intimate knowledge of her sister and brother-in-law's finances stopped her.

She looked at the nearby apartment buildings and the undergrown trees that lined the sidewalk, the cars—mostly older models—and people, who seemed to regard her with suspicion. From this square of sidewalk, only a faint hint of salt in the air reminded her the ocean existed.

Caroline dodged the traffic in the two-lane street and entered the somewhat dank, uncarpeted lobby of Shelly's building. Strange symbols decorated the taupe elevator doors. Hoping they weren't gang signs, Caroline barely held back a whimper. The building door opened behind her, and a pair of shoes stuck to the floor with each step that brought their owner inside. She managed not to turn defensively toward the newcomer.

"Caroline?"

"Matt." He was the only person on earth who could understand how she felt. She hadn't been wealthy. Uncle Ford, the family's financial genius, had helped her buy a tiny house on a piece of land at a time when land prices in Leith had been depressed. She and her family had done all the work on the house. She wasn't a snob, but she hated the idea of Shelly living in an area that felt unsafe. "Now I know why they wouldn't let us visit the apartment before they got married."

"It's not that bad. I lived in worse while I was in college. Did you push the elevator button?"

"I did, but maybe I'd better stay down here until I'm sure I can manage not to cry."

"Please don't cry." His imploring tone reminded her he'd compromised his own ego to help his son. "You'll make Jake feel inadequate, and I don't think Shelly wants to see you crying, either."

"I'm glad I didn't clear out her room."

He pulled her close, and she let herself sink against him. "I've just won a bet with myself on that whole room deal," he said with a return of conceit that charmed her. "Here's the elevator."

The metal doors clattered open. Caroline flattened her hand against the folded doors, holding them.

"What happened with the job interview?" She'd meant to be more subtle, but she had no time. She prayed he'd think she cared so much because of

Shelly and Jake. She'd die if he realized he mattered to her now, too.

"Nothing, Caroline." He tightened his arm around her. "I talked to them. They made me a good offer, but I'm trying to stay here. That's all I can tell you."

She stared into his eyes. He shrugged ever so slightly, and she nodded.

"It matters to me, too," he said.

She didn't ask him to clarify what mattered. Or whom.

Matt held Caroline's hand as they went inside the elevator. By the time they stopped on Shelly's floor, she released herself from his grip and stood on her own two feet again. An odor of burnt cheese greeted them as the doors reopened.

Matt sniffed, scrunching his nose. "Somebody burned dinner."

"You don't think…"

He smoothed her hair away from her eyes. "Prepare yourself in case."

Caroline squared her shoulders. "You have to stop touching me like that."

"What do you mean?"

"As if you had a right to fix my hair or comfort me about Shelly and Jake's latest disaster. It makes us look too intimate, and I don't want them to find out about what happened."

"Then don't talk about it right now." Looking surprisingly out of sorts, he drummed on the apartment door.

Shelly opened it, waving a towel toward the kitchen Caroline could see from the door. "Come in," she said. "Jake's not here right now."

The cheese smell got stronger, but none of the more offensive odors they'd experienced in the building's common areas came into the apartment with them. Caroline picked her way over the threadbare brown carpet, trying to look as if she wasn't. "I like your couch."

It was actually a plaid loveseat, adorned with one of Aunt Imogen's crocheted doilies. A real couch wouldn't fit in the small room.

"Mom, you don't have to think of something nice to say."

"Man, it's hot in here." In a transparent effort to head off trouble, Matt tugged at the collar of his dark green polo shirt. "Do you mind if I open those windows?" He pointed at the two behind the loveseat.

Shelly's lip quivered. "They're painted shut. We couldn't force them open."

"Do you have a screwdriver?"

"I don't know."

Caroline rubbed at the moisture on her upper lip. "I think I could pry them open with a butter knife."

"Jake couldn't," Shelly said.

"Let me at them."

"I'll look for Jake's tool box," Matt said with a reproving look Caroline took to heart. "Do you know where Jake's tools are, Shel?"

"In the bedroom with the dead air conditioner. I'll get you a knife, Mom."

While Matt searched, Caroline slid the plain white curtains out of the way and jabbed a knife into the paint between the window and the sill. With the strength of a mom whose daughter lived at a terrifying address, she broke the seal. She opened the first window before Matt came back, screwdriver in hand.

He took one look at her hot face and laughed at her. Imagining the picture she must make with sweat curling her hair and heat painting her face a bright red that clashed with those curls, Caroline laughed back.

Shelly burst into tears.

Bewildered, Caroline turned to her. Had Shelly, like Matt, hidden all her fears about this marriage? And now was willing to cry about it? "What's happened?"

"I don't think my life is funny," Shelly wailed. "I have to live here, and Jake hates it."

"Jake's worried about you," Matt said.

"He's talked to you."

Caroline stared as he backed up, his hands out, palms up, trying to look innocent. "Jake said nothing." He turned to Caroline for help.

She eyed him blankly, as if she were responding on a delay. Unsure what had put Shelly in such a despondent frame of mind, she couldn't possibly come to his aid. She focused on her daughter.

"Shelly, what do you want us to do? Are you having second thoughts?"

Shelly and Matt turned on her at the same time. Matt's impatience thinned his mouth, but Shelly exploded.

"Second thoughts? Jake went out to get something to eat because I burned dinner, and I'm afraid he won't come back. He's going to end up hating me because this place is all we can afford." She collapsed on Caroline's shoulder. "Two months ago, Dan was teaching him to play golf, and now we can't even afford putt putt!"

Caroline patted her back and shared a tentative glance with Matt. "You don't have to live here," she said, thinking with her mom's mind. "Come home, and bring Jake with you."

"He wouldn't come, and I don't want to, either."

"You're both responsible for the baby," Matt said. "He's not allowed to hate you because you had to find a place to live."

"Not allowed! I don't care what he's allowed to do—I care how he feels. He's supposed to be studying anatomy and vascular systems and I don't know what else. Instead he's been banging away at the air conditioner all morning, and he doesn't have a clue how to fix it."

"Shelly, I looked at the air conditioner." Matt laid his hand on her shoulder. "The cord's broken. I can replace it for you."

"Can you?" She lifted her head.

Mascara trickled down her face and streaked Caroline's shoulder, but hope shone in Shelly's gaze. Never in her wildest dreams had Caroline pictured an air conditioner being so important to her daughter.

"I've replaced a million cords." Matt turned with his screwdriver to the other window and quickly pried it open. "When Jake was a toddler, we lived in an apartment and he couldn't spend a lot of time outdoors. He ran his tricycle over every lamp cord in the place, so I had to learn how to fix them."

Just then, the apartment door opened. As one, they leaned toward it in time to see Jake appear with a bag of sub sandwiches. He frowned at Shelly's blotchy, mascara-smeared face.

"What happened to you?"

She ignored his question. "Your dad can fix the air conditioner."

"Can you?" He looked between them, at the white curtains wafting into the room. "You opened the windows, Dad."

"Just one of them," Matt said. "Your muscle-bound mother-in-law managed the other."

His teasing helped Caroline control her own distress. She took the sandwich bag from Jake. "I'll put these on plates. Shel, you've ruined your makeup."

"You look great." Jake carefully pecked his bride on an unbesmirched patch of cheek and dragged his father toward the back of the apartment. "Show me what to do with the air conditioner. I was trying to figure out how to tell Shelly we had to sleep on the roof tonight.''

Shel stared after him, her lip starting to tremble again. ''He doesn't even care that I'm miserable.''

''Sweetie, it must be true love if he can't see you look like a raccoon. I'm terribly fond of you, but I plan to send you a cleaning bill for my blouse. Go clean up, and I'll get the food on the table.''

''Wait, I have a favor to ask you.''

The last words Caroline ever expected to hear stopped her in her tracks. ''What did you say? I think the heat just made me hallucinate.''

''Funny, Mom.'' Shelly took a sheet of paper from the top of the television. ''We need some things for the baby, but we're too busy with school to shop, and we're broke. We thought you and Matt might like to give them to us.''

Caroline took the list and scanned the scrawled words. Crib, changing table, car seat and so on. ''It's just like Christmas,'' she said.

''You mean we asked for too much?''

''No.'' Clasping the paper to her chest, Caroline hastened to correct her daughter's misapprehension. ''I can't speak for Matt, but this is the best gift you've ever given me. I'm dying to do something to make your life easier.''

Shelly narrowed her eyes, as if she suspected sarcasm that couldn't have been further from Caroline's feelings. ''Shut up, Mom, or I'll take it back.''

Caroline made as if to zip her lips.

TWO WEEKENDS LATER Caroline leaned her elbow on a maple crib that looked exactly like the hundred or so they'd looked at in every infant "superstore" from Florida to central Georgia. This one, Matt had heard of in the locker room while he was changing after a flight.

Caroline sagged in despair as Matt grimaced at the crib. She recognized the look, and she sighed to make her own suffering known. Unimpressed, Matt crossed his arms and glared at the footboard.

A pregnant woman who regarded the crib with a more receptive expression almost tripped over him, but the gorgeous hunk of glaring man took her mind off the baby bed. Recognizing signals each of Matt's conquests had thrown at his oblivious head, Caroline grimaced, disgusted with him and his admiring audience.

Another thing she'd discovered in her search for baby goods. Nothing proved a more powerful aphrodisiac to a woman—any woman—often the more pregnant the better—than a man shopping for a crib. Still afraid he was planning to leave and far too involved with him herself, Caroline discovered she could feel jealous when other women gave him the eye.

Despairing, Caroline paid no more attention to the sparks of interest the mother-to-be emitted. Weren't any of these moms married to interested men of their own? "I can't wait for you to tell me what's wrong with this one, Matt."

The other woman grinned at Caroline. "Your first?" she said. She eyed Caroline's unrounded stomach askance. "Don't worry. By the time the baby comes, you'll have the whole room ready, and then you'll never have time to make it as pretty again."

Matt smiled politely, and the woman beamed back at him, continuing on her way. Caroline remembered when his smile had melted her, too. But that was before she'd shopped with him.

He didn't uncross his arms, and he didn't smile at her. "I can't believe you don't see the problem—what if the kid's a boy?"

"What if he is?" She straightened and marched around the crib where painted bunnies rioted across the maple footboard. "What, Matt? I don't get it— boys like bunnies—and I can't believe you're not ashamed to be such a sexist."

"Caroline, that bunny—" he prodded the one that offended him "—is wearing pink."

She jabbed a smaller rabbit. "That one's wearing purple. Manly purple."

"I don't like it."

"You can't be serious."

"Maybe it's not the pink overalls. I just don't like this bed. Can't we look at the darker woods?"

"We can look at hammocks in the sporting goods store, but you and I will never agree on one item on this list or any other list ever created in the annals of list making."

"You're overreacting," he diagnosed smugly.

"Why don't we wait until Shelly has an ultra-sound? If Dr. Davis tells her she's having a boy, we'll buy a bed of nails, and if it's a girl we'll buy silk-worms to spin her a tiny nest of silk."

A reluctant smile curved his lips and Caroline had to admit she recognized his charms. But she didn't want to.

He brushed his fingertips across her cheekbone. "I like your sarcasm."

"Don't." But she caught his hand instead of push-ing it away. "We agreed not to be—"

"Nice to each other," he finished.

Caroline frowned. They hadn't said they wouldn't be nice. Just not intimate. He turned to the crib.

"Maybe it's okay."

Annoyed with herself for mooning over him, she pressed her hand to the small of his back and pushed him toward the front of the store. "I should jump on the opportunity to actually buy something Jake and Shelly asked for, but let's wait until we agree." She veered away from him as another couple took up the middle of the aisle.

After they passed, he came back to her, his gaze taking in the crowds. He always remembered what they'd seen in each store. His powers of observation were so acute Caroline wouldn't have been surprised if he listed what the other shoppers had worn.

"A lot of people have babies," he noted.

She laughed. "To think, you have commanding officers who probably feel the fate of the free world rests in your hands.''

"I can detect the obvious," he said. "I'm sorry I don't share your taste in baby stuff."

"Me, too, but we'll find something."

"Not today though." He held up his watch as if she knew when and where he was due for an appointment. "I have to pick up Ford in about forty-five minutes. Today's our first flight."

"Your *first* flight?" She opened the door and held it for him. Pointedly, he placed his hand on the glass above her head, and she let him take the door. It would be silly to fight about who held the door for whom. "First implies you plan more. Uncle Ford hasn't talked you into teaching him to fly?"

"No, but I assume he'll want to go again."

"Who wouldn't?" she said.

"If we go now, I can drop you off before I pick up Ford."

An idea struck Caroline. "I must be out of my mind. I know where we'll find baby furniture."

Groaning, Matt dug his keys from his pocket. "Not another store. I told you I don't have time."

"Aunt Imogen's attic. Shelly's things are up there. Cate found enough stuff for the twins."

"Will anything be left with twins in the family?"

"Cate and I are twins. Our cribs are there. A lot of Talbots have had babies."

"I won't even voice my opinion of such foolhardy behavior in a family like yours." His teasing tone touched her as he turned her toward his Jag in the crowded parking lot. She knew he liked her family.

"I'll drive you out now. You pick out what you like while Ford and I are flying, and then I'll look at what you've chosen."

"And give me your approval or hold it back as you see fit?"

"I don't care what you say—I'm not being sexist this time. Why argue our way through your aunt's attic when you can choose what you want, and then I can choose a subset of that?"

Engineer types. She sighed as they came to his car. He'd been right about those soft leather seats. She always let him drive on the fruitless expeditions she'd miss if they ever managed to fill Shelly and Jake's list. "It's a deal. I'd like to spend some time with Aunt Imogen anyway."

"FORD, YOU CAN ADJUST the volume on those headphones." Matt lifted his voice over the roar of the Cessna 152's engines in case Ford couldn't hear him. He'd mentioned the volume control because Ford kept trying to answer him when he was actually transmitting to the tower.

Ford nodded and fiddled with the knobs. "Thanks, son. I'm sure I'll like flying better if I can hear what you say to me."

Startled, Matt turned toward him. "You're not having a good time?"

"I'm a little seasick. Is it always this bumpy?"

He tried not to be disappointed. Ford was not the first guy who failed to understand flying was the best thing that would ever happen to him. "It'll smooth out once we're over the ocean." He made his turn and headed for the beach not far north of Caroline's house. He pointed, to take the older man's mind off his stomach. "Look down there. Caroline's. Do you see it?"

Ford nodded. "That takeoff. Did you think it was smooth?"

This time Matt managed not to look at Ford since his question seemed to imply dissatisfaction. A herd of rogue elephants practiced more tact than the Talbot family. "Fairly smooth in such a strong crosswind. I'm sorry if I shook you up." Apparently, they didn't know he was the pilot everyone expected to follow in Admiral Whitney Randolph's footsteps. He'd have to slip them a couple of clippings from *Stars and Stripes.*

"I'm okay." Ford sat up as soon as they crossed from land to ocean. "Well, that's already better."

Matt forgave him his lack of reverence for the soul-stirring experience of flight. "We'll keep the land in sight, but you'll like the ride better from here."

"I do."

"Have you ever lived anywhere but Leith, Ford?"

"No, I even went to college at Whitlock, like Dan and Shelly. Look at the church spire, Matt. It's a lovely town from this vantage. You can't see all those strip malls." He twisted to peer behind him at the fat green treetops and neat roofs. "But we were talking about me. I couldn't ever go too far away for long because I come from a family that sticks together. We depend on each other."

"I've noticed." Matt wanted at least part of them to depend on him, but his latest phone conversation with Harry Camp nagged at his conscience. Icarus management had decided to make the move to Leith.

The whole operation would come south, and he could be in charge of all testing programs. The part of being in charge he liked. But it was all two years away.

He surveyed the intense blue sky with joy. "Do you like it yet, Ford?"

"I'll reserve my judgment until I see how you land, but I definitely see more merit from here than I did over the town."

"Do you want to take the stick?"

"Hell, no!"

Matt laughed, and Ford punched him in the arm. Just a bug bite of a punch. "I'll tell Caroline you flew for a little while," Matt said.

Ford grinned. "She'll froth at the mouth. Make sure you tell her in front of Imogen."

"Two birds with one stone?"

"Lovely birds," Ford said, "but they're awfully meddlesome. Imogen and Caroline and Cate need to learn I can take care of myself. Hey—there's the Tybee Island lighthouse."

"We'll turn back around Hilton Head."

"So soon?"

His disappointment pleased Matt. Ford's opinion mattered to him. "I knew you'd get flying. You do, don't you?"

"Like I said, I'll let you know after we land. We feel as if we're moving much slower than we are."

"We'll schedule a longer flight next time." In his ear, another pilot announced he was close by. Matt searched for the other plane and then spotted him off his right wing. "I wasn't sure you wouldn't get sick all over me."

Ford scoffed, but he tapped Matt's arm. "I might have if we'd stayed over land much longer."

"We'll make that turn back over land at the last possible second."

"I do like flying with you. You've always got your eye on the contingencies."

"That's my job." Why had his own father preferred tractors to airplanes? This newborn connection with Ford made him happy, but he wished he'd found a way to meet his own father on common ground. He was determined not to lose Jake, never to leave his son drifting, looking for a family who'd love him.

They turned back at Hilton Head. As he wanted to begin his approach at Leith, he pressed the microphone switch on the yoke. "Leith Tower, Cessna 552kilo 10 miles north, inbound for landing."

"22kilo, Leith tower, runway 32, winds light, report downwind."

Ford tapped his shoulder, and Matt glanced at the

other man. "Is military flight this good?" Ford asked, a hint of envy in his gaze.

"Even better." It was true. Nothing compared to the moment he lost sight of where his body ended and the body of the aircraft he was piloting began. Especially in test flight, when he was one of the few human beings who'd ever flown such a machine.

Civilians didn't understand that kind of high. Caroline, for one, wouldn't understand the risks.

At the airport, he brought the Cessna in smooth as silk. They landed so softly Ford didn't seem to notice they were on the ground. Noting his tense expression, Matt nudged him.

"We're down."

"We are?"

"Sure. Now we just roll down to the gas tanks, and I'll refill it."

"Wait, do you mind if I try your headphones?"

Matt lifted an eyebrow. "Why?"

"Humor an old man."

"Okay, when we stop."

When they parked at the tanks, Ford reached for Matt's headphones and handed his to Matt. "Put these on, and then say something to me," Ford said.

Matt slipped the headphones on. "What do you want me to say?"

"What?"

The question reverberated in Matt's head and he yanked off the headphones. Ford adjusted the volume on the other set and nodded at Matt.

"You could see an audiologist for this kind of test," Matt suggested.

Wonder widened Ford Talbot's eyes. "Good lord, I think I'd better. I thought those women were crazy." He looked sheepish. "Alan may have occasionally implied I didn't hear well, but that boy's too polite."

"Well, he wasn't born a Talbot, but he'll probably learn your brand of brutal frankness eventually."

CHAPTER NINE

CAROLINE TUGGED Shelly's old changing table to the space she and Aunt Imogen had cleared in the center of the attic. She placed the table beside the high chair Uncle Ford had broken his teeth on. The two pieces fit together, but would Shelly want them for her baby, or would she consider them old junk her mom had culled from the family attic?

"I like those," Aunt Imogen said, "but you still have to decide on one of these cribs."

Caroline held up her hand, seized by a strong urge to sneeze. The air up here was so dry her nose burned, and the floorboards flexed beneath their feet.

Wiping her nose, Caroline stood in front of the crib Aunt Imogen had painted white for Dan nineteen years ago. Even in the attic's slightly orange light, the white paint still gleamed. "Matt would consider this 'girly.' How about that big monstrosity?"

Made of oak, it was as large as a toddler's bed, and it looked like a modified throne. "Too heavy," Aunt Imogen said. "Your mom bought it from a couple in London who were modernizing their townhouse. She was walking down the street and found it sitting on the side of the road as if it were rubbish." Aunt Imogen tapped her chin. "I don't see it fitting in Shelly's apartment."

"You're right." Caroline slid an old blanket beneath the crib's legs and hauled it back to its corner. Then she put Dan's back. "I think we have to buy something."

"Maybe not. I've been thinking. Shelly's baby is due around Christmas, and she'll probably use my grandmother's cradle for the first few weeks. By the time she needs a crib, Mary and Melinda may not need the ones I bought for them."

Caroline eyed her aunt with admiration. "Perfect!" But then she remembered. "Aunt Imogen, you painted those flowers along the rails."

"Babies like flowers."

"But Matt doesn't."

"Matt?" Aunt Imogen's interest rattled Caroline, who wanted no one seeing her inappropriate attraction to Jake's father. "Have you all asked Jake and Shelly what they want?"

"Shel said she'd like whatever we gave them. She swears they're too busy to shop, and when I suggested she look at catalogs she rolled her eyes as if they were a couple of pinballs." Caroline shrugged. "She's taking a full course load this summer."

"She just wants those classes out of her way," Aunt Imogen said with a shake of her head. "Dan's the same. He started classes last summer a few weeks after he finished high school. I don't understand why they're so eager to grow up when you and Cate gave them such happy childhoods.''

''Shel has no choice.'' Caroline took her continued misgivings back into the shadowy depths of the attic. Shelly was only doing what she had to, for her own child.

Mere steps behind her, Aunt Imogen's voice startled Caroline. ''Why don't you take that vanity to your place? You've always liked it, and it reminds me of the stained glass windows at church.''

A piece her grandparents had commissioned, the vanity's mirror was set in three gothic-pointed panes. Caroline had loved it when she was little, but it hadn't fit in the room she and Cate had shared, and they'd resisted separate rooms.

She rubbed the brass drawer pulls. ''I should come up here more often. I forget about all these things.''

''You can always take whatever you want. It's all in the family.''

Caroline hugged her aunt. ''Do you think Shelly is as attached as we are to family pieces?''

''You want comfort from the association, but Shelly may not need that. You gave her a strong family.''

Caroline looked into the past, at all the times Shelly had done without her father. ''Lately, I don't know how well I did with her, but I guess she assumed I wouldn't vanish like Ryan did.''

''Ryan's the only reason you've avoided other commitments?''

"He's one of the reasons I tried. You remember—"

"Patrick, the one who didn't want Shelly. You could have chosen among several persistent suitors, and I remember how many of those men wanted to know Shelly. Are you afraid you can't make a healthy relationship with a man?"

Caroline looked at her. "You're throwing stones, Aunt Imogen," she suggested gently.

"But I don't live in a glass house. I love Whitney, and I never wanted anyone to take his place."

Startled, Caroline felt a sudden longing for Cate. They should be together when their aunt finally announced her intentions toward the love of her life. "You *love* Whitney Randolph?"

"Yes, ma'am, I do. Notice I've given up tape."

Imogen's forehead was bare. "I hadn't noticed." Admitting it, she felt guilty. Her family was her strength. They formed a wall against the rest of the world. She should have noticed her aunt had stopped wearing her shield.

"How much do you love Whitney? I feel guilty for asking this when I seem to be hearing before Cate." But she couldn't help herself. "Are you talking marriage?"

A frown puckered her aunt's bare forehead. "What if we were?"

Caroline tugged her close. "I'd say better late than never, and I'd envy you for your courage to try with Whitney."

"He hasn't asked, but if he does, I'll say yes so fast his head will spin like one of his jet engines."

"How did all this happen behind my back? Does Cate know already?"

Aunt Imogen shook her head. "I wasn't sure how you'd both take it. You think you've become the mother figures around here in the past few years. You're used to having me all to yourselves, and, Caroline, change doesn't seem to be your strong suit lately."

"Shelly's changes," Caroline agreed, "but she's so young, and I'm afraid she's making the kinds of choices I did. You know what you're doing, and you deserve this happiness. You did the right thing with Whitney all those years ago, but now you're both free."

"Give yourself a little credit, too. You may not agree with Shelly's decisions, but you're helping her as much as I ever helped you. Better, maybe. You're helping her stay with the man she loves."

Caroline flushed, pleased to accept her aunt's approval. "Did Matt put you up to this?" Teasing, she hugged Aunt Imogen. "Hey," she said, "does he know about you and Whitney?"

"I don't know what Whitney's said to Matt." Suspicion entered Aunt Imogen's gaze. "What do you and Matt talk about? Do you think he'd report to you if Whitney talked to him about our plans?"

"Report to me?"

"That's military talk." Aunt Imogen grinned. "Do I speak it well?"

Laughing, Caroline put gentle arms around her aunt's fragile-seeming shoulders. "You're inspired. Tell me about your plans now." Suddenly, a change that would be hard to swallow occurred to her. "Will you have to leave us?" What would this home be like without Aunt Imogen in it? What would her life be like? she wondered selfishly.

"If Whitney needs me to go with him, I will. We've been apart so long, I'm jealous of the time he has to spend away from me, but I'll always be around here, Caroline, in bits and pieces, in that wallpaper I messed up in the kitchen, in the hats you'll have to wear while you walk my horse."

Caroline recognized how unhappy she'd be if Matt had to leave for his job. There'd be no question of her going with him, but that thought had no place in her mind. "Oh, yeah, Polly," she said vaguely, alarmed that she could think of Matt at a time like this. She pictured wearing one of Aunt Imogen's big flowered hats to walk Polly. Would she be the next eccentric Talbot?

After Aunt Imogen had retired Polly from plowing, she'd made the horse a hat to match her own, and unmarried Imogen Talbot, who wore tape on her forehead, had suddenly added dressing like her horse to her reputation, but she and Polly had never been troubled by the sun on their daily walks-for-exercise. Now, Polly expected all her walkers to show up prop-

erly attired, and Caroline could see herself doing pe-
culiar things to hide from the truth. She'd begun to
care for a man who wasn't available to her, but she
didn't want anyone to feel sorry for her.

"Will you be all right, Caroline? Cate has Alan
and the babies, but I worry about you now that
Shelly's left home."

"I'm not alone." She'd have to remind herself of
that before she started getting tattoos to prove she was
tough. "I have Cate and Alan and Dan and the twins
and Shelly's baby and Jake. But I don't need any of
them to keep me from having a nervous breakdown
if you finally marry the love of your life."

"I worry about you the way you worry about
Shelly."

Caroline squared her shoulders. "You don't have
to." She turned back to the other cribs and firmly
changed the subject. "We have to make a decision.
The old cribs or the new ones? I think the spindles
on these are too far apart. We'd have to replace them
all and drill holes for new ones."

"I've got it," Aunt Imogen said. "We'll take pictures of everything, and then Shelly and Jake can decide."

"Thank God you're so creative." Caroline hugged
her again. "Does Whitney know how lucky he is?"

"I think he's guessed."

"I hope I'll be as brave as you someday."

"You already are. You just don't know yourself
very well, and you're afraid."

More flights of fancy from Aunt Imogen, but she was in love. Her admiral loved her back. She had a right. "Do you have film in your camera? We'll take pictures of these and the ones you put in the nursery downstairs, and then I'll go back to the baby stores. I can't decide which crib they should use."

Aunt Imogen looked strangely pleased. "You're growing up, Caroline."

"I don't know what the hell you mean by that." But she suspected it might have something to do with not wanting to control Shelly's choice of baby furniture. "You want to go get that camera? I'll set up some of these lamps for better lighting."

FOR THE NEXT MONTH, Caroline and Matt delivered photos to Shelly and Jake. They maintained their platonic relationship, though Matt hoped she didn't notice how often he made excuses to stand too close to her, or how often he called with goofy excuses to talk, giving in to a compulsion to hear her voice.

Shelly and Jake decided they didn't want the ornamental family furniture, and Shelly couldn't chance waiting for Mary and Melinda to grow out of theirs. They set up the changing table and the high chair Caroline and Imogen had chosen, and Matt found a rocker in an antique shop in Pax River when he went up for a second interview.

When he found Caroline stroking the delicate lines of that hand-carved rocker with a mixture of warmth and regret he flattered himself her attachment had nothing to do with baby furniture. Until he knew where he'd live next, he couldn't explore the need he felt for her though they hadn't touched each other except in comfort since their children's wedding day.

At last, Jake and Shelly decided on the crib with the bunnies. Jake agreed with Caroline and Shelly that Matt shouldn't give the bunny in pink overalls any more grief. They set up the crib the day Shelly had her first ultrasound.

"We should have waited for today's results," Matt teased from underneath the crib, where he was tightening screws. "Shelly may find she's having a boy."

"Don't start your pink-is-for-girls lecture again." Caroline stuffed packing paper into the crib box. "Finish up there, or we'll get to the hospital late."

He tried not to notice the way her calf muscles flexed as she straightened with the box. "I don't know that we should be with them for this test."

"They asked us to come," she said, startled.

"They probably wanted us to feel included after we set up all this stuff." He rolled his head on the floor to look at the room they'd begun to transform into a nursery. "What do you say we paint it? And maybe you could put up a few babyish things?" Letting his hand drift over the tan carpet, he decided to clean that, too. "I can't imagine what kinds of things a baby likes these days, but you must have designed other nurseries, and I'll pay the expenses."

Excitement gleamed in her eyes. "We'll go halves. I read an article on using black and white patterns to make a room interesting for an infant. Apparently, they like the contrast.''

Matt slid out from under the crib. ''You're easy to please.''

''Low maintenance,'' she agreed. ''Are you ready?''

''Let me put Jake's tools away.''

Nodding, she held the box a little higher. ''I'll take this to the incinerator.''

They drove to the hospital in separate cars and met at the information desk, where a receptionist gave them directions to the correct room on the maternity ward. Caroline didn't speak inside the elevator, and Matt did nothing to ease the strain that rose between them. The closer they got to the maternity ward, the more Matt thought they should stay out of Jake and Shelly's ultrasound.

He didn't want to fight with Caroline about it. He enjoyed their new relationship. Friends, with the promise of something more.

She insisted she didn't want anything more, but Matt saw hints of a deeper bond, his own intense interest in conversations that would once have seemed banal—about infant care and safety features on car seats.

Caroline seemed unconscious of the way her gaze darkened on him when she thought he wasn't aware of her, the blush that covered her cheeks as she turned away from the desire he didn't bother to hide at such moments.

The tight leash Caroline cinched around her emotions challenged him. Even being with her like this, sharing silence, he felt eased, as if her physical presence took the edge off his hunger.

If only he could convince himself she'd forgive him if he decided to take the Maryland job—if only he could believe Jake and Shelly would accept the kind of relationship he wanted to investigate with Caroline. But even Jake would think it was weird to have his dad lusting after his wife's mom.

And then there was Caroline's past. Those two men she'd allowed herself to care for. They'd broken her ability to trust even a man who'd try his damnedest never to hurt her.

"Here we are," she said as the elevator opened on a pale blue hall, but as she glanced his way, uncertainty lowered her voice and put a question in her gaze. "Matt, is something wrong? Does the ultrasound make the baby more real to you?"

"This baby can't get more real." He took her arm. "But I wonder if we should try to pull back from Shelly and Jake's lives a little."

"They don't include us when they don't want us."

Was she really so blind? "They know you want to see the test."

She stopped, but a wariness in her gaze told him he had hurt her after all. She reached for the curls that teased her smooth throat. "You think I'm interfering?"

"No. As you said, they asked us to come, but I

think I'll wait outside for you." He stopped at the waiting room, and Caroline hesitated.

"What should I tell them?"

"That I can't wait to hear their news." Striding inside the otherwise empty room, he reached blindly for one of the magazines scattered over a Formica-and-chrome table. He looked back at Caroline as he dropped into one of the vinyl chairs.

She hovered on the doorstep, but finally, she twisted her mouth into a hard-fought expression of self-assurance and spun away. Matt opened the magazine, but the pages might just as well have been blank.

His mind wasn't with his son or Shelly. He wanted to be with Caroline, to reassure her he didn't think her concern for Shelly was wrong or even necessarily obtrusive. He'd just gone as far as he could with Jake. The ultrasound felt too personal.

Nevertheless, he couldn't stop staring at the scuffed waiting room door. He willed someone to come. Jake or Caroline—or maybe even all three of the people who'd become the center of his attention.

Matt imagined Jake and Shelly, laughing at their own secrets, curving their hands over the mound of the baby she could no longer hide. Dread prickled his spine. Caroline was right. He wasn't ready to see his son as a father yet. And inside that other room, Caroline and Jake and Shelly were seeing the first pictures of the newest Kearan.

Suddenly, a door opened down the hall. He recognized the feminine footsteps that sped up as they came closer. He stood before Caroline appeared in the doorway.

"You were right." Surprise dulled her eyes. "They didn't need anyone else." She took the chair beside his. "I shouldn't have gone, but I'm glad I did."

"Why?" Again, she interested him more than any other woman on earth—and he'd talked to other women about subjects other than babies on the way. More sexual subjects, more intellectual subjects, but never more personal subjects.

"What I said to you, about the baby seeming more real." She shifted to smooth her short skirt over lovely knees. Reminding himself she didn't want him to want her, he trained his gaze on her face. "That didn't happen, but I finally saw Jake and Shelly as they are now. They'd make it together if we weren't with them. I wish you'd seen the way he looks at her."

Matt knew what she meant. "I've noticed."

"She lets herself need Jake. He's going to be a good father." Caroline's slight, embarrassed smile touched Matt with its vulnerability. "And I believe he's going to be a fine husband to Shelly."

Matt relaxed against his chair. "If you saw all that, maybe I should have gone. Why were you so determined?"

"I thought you were afraid to see the baby," she said. "You've admitted you hide your doubts from Jake. I've noticed you two keep distance between you—like privacy between roommates. He tells you what he needs, you arrange it for him, and then you step back.''

Unsettled at her too-correct diagnosis, he hoped he hid the rest—that he was afraid he hadn't been a good enough father to Jake, and now he'd never get the chance to be a dad again. ''What would scare me?''

''That you won't have a chance to be involved with Jake the way you want to be. I know Shelly won't ever feel the same about me. She's a mom now, and she's not my baby anymore. The good thing is, now that I see that, I think I'm ready to do what you said— start backing out of her life.''

She amazed him. Where was the woman who'd looked terrified when he and Jake showed up on her doorstep? How had she changed so much when he felt as if he were standing still? ''How do you intend to put this plan into action?''

''I'd like to decorate the nursery, but let's make it a family project. Uncle Ford is heroic with a paint-brush.''

Time with the Talbots? He thought he might just be able to stand it. He'd like to know if Ford had taken action on getting hearing aids. ''We'd have to work in shifts. There's no way everyone will fit in that room.'' He glanced toward the door. ''Now I wish I'd seen the ultrasound. Seems as if you had a spiritual awakening.'' He grinned, only half joking. ''Did they say if it's a boy or a girl?''

''I ran before they had a chance.''

"I'm astounded at you. You are a good mom, you know."

She shot him a stricken glance. He lifted both eyebrows, but he couldn't tell Caroline how he really felt—that her courage made him care for her, too. He probably looked as if he'd lost his mind, waggling his brows at her, but words deserted him. Even if he stayed in Leith, they still had to deal with Jake and Shelly. And what if they started a relationship that went wrong? Which parent would Jake side with? Matt didn't want to be responsible for making more confusion between Shelly and Caroline.

Saying, "I'd like you to be my girlfriend" would be both juvenile and reckless. And Caroline wanted no reckless men in her life.

A WEEK LATER, Caroline knocked on Shelly's apartment door at the appointed time—an hour before the rest of the painting party was due to arrive.

Her misgivings mounted by the moment. Matt had asked Jake and Shelly if they could come early because he wanted to talk to them. Caroline arrived with a fairly bad attitude because she figured she already knew what he wanted to say. He must have heard something about his transfer.

Shelly opened the door. "Mom." She looked as wary as Caroline felt. "Be nice now, okay? Everything will be fine, no matter what."

"Matt must be here already?"

"He got here a few minutes ago." Shelly led her

mother to the small kitchen. Matt rose from his chair behind the table.

"Caroline," he said.

"Hi." She'd practiced looking indifferent. She didn't want anyone, especially Shelly, to know how much Matt's decision mattered to her. She turned to Jake. "How's school?"

"Fine. Better once I finish my anatomy finals." He glanced at his father. "Why pretend we don't know what's coming? What did you have to say, Dad?"

Matt waited while Caroline sat across from him, and Shelly took the seat at his right. Then he sat again. "Have you heard of Icarus Aeronautical?"

"Sure," Jake said.

Shelly nodded, and Caroline held her breath. Don't say anything, she told herself. It's his decision. Whatever happens, Shelly and Jake will be all right because they had her and Cate and Alan and Aunt Imogen and Uncle Ford. What did she really expect a Navy man to do?

"Icarus has offered me a spot as director of test flight. Right now, Henry Camp has the position—you remember Uncle Henry, Jake?"

"Sort of," Jake said. "You're taking his spot?"

"He's being promoted. I'd set up their test flight plans for all new aircraft, and they want me to fly. You know, if I stay with the Navy, Jake, I wouldn't be testing in my next assignment."

"But can you stay here, Dad?"

Thank God Jake had asked, and Caroline didn't

have to. She laid her hand on top of his, and felt warmer when he twisted his fingers around hers. She must have grown attached to him without noticing, but she felt his pain at his father's imminent departure.

"If I take this job, I'll come back here," Matt promised. "Icarus is relocating their plant within the next two years." He stopped. "You all can't tell anyone that until the company announces it in the press."

They nodded, Caroline with clenched teeth. Matt narrowed his eyes at her, no doubt feeling the anger she could barely contain. She cared about him, too. She hadn't meant to, didn't want to need him, but she wanted him to wrap his arms around her, hold her as he had in her kitchen that day. She wanted him to tell her he wouldn't leave Jake and Shelly. Most of all, he wouldn't leave her.

"Where is Icarus Aeronautical?" Shelly asked.

"In Maryland, a town called Patuxent River. I'll have access to the company jet, so I won't miss the baby, Shelly. Henry knows I want to see my family as often as I can, so Jake, I'll come back, every free weekend I can take the plane."

Caroline held on. Of course he wouldn't make any more promises to her. He'd already broken the one that mattered most. She held herself perfectly still. She had no right to expect him to care if she didn't want him to leave.

But when he finally looked at her, his intense gaze nearly broke through her guard. She mustered a smile that hurt all the way to her stomach. He curved his mouth uncertainly in return.

"When do you have to give Uncle Henry an answer, Dad?"

"In a couple of weeks. I wanted to know how you and Shelly felt."

Jake looked impossibly young, and Caroline shivered, realizing anew how this young man held her daughter's happiness in his hands. He obviously loved Shelly, but how could a man his age bear up under the responsibilities he'd shouldered?

"Jake," Matt said. "How do you feel about this job?"

"You don't have a choice. You have to take the one job you've always wanted."

Shelly reached across the table for Jake's hand. "But how do you *feel,* Jake? Don't you want your dad with you when you become a father?" She glanced at Matt. "We've talked about this."

"Dad, I think you should take the job."

"But you think I shouldn't, Shelly?"

"Can you stay here? Or would you have to leave Leith even if you stayed in the Navy?"

"I'd have to leave," he said. "I might talk my way into another six months, because of the stage we're at in testing the plane, but then I'd be stationed somewhere else with a squadron."

Shelly closed her eyes, and Caroline felt proud of her strength. "Then you should take the job." As she glanced her mother's way, Caroline bit the inside of her cheek in an effort to remain stoic. "It sounds as if you'll be able to make more time here with this job than you would if you let yourself be transferred in the Navy. And you'll be back in two years, right?"

"Right," Matt said.

"But, Dad, are you ready to retire from the Navy?"

"I won't pretend I'm not excited about the job with Icarus." Matt slid his fingers beneath the woven placemat in front of him. "I'll miss the people I've worked with, and I owe the Navy a lot for my training, for helping me grow up when I was a child, myself. But my family needs me, and this is the best way I can see to be here for you." He touched his son's forearm. "You and Shelly are important to me."

"I know, Dad." Looking embarrassed, Jake gently shifted out of Matt and Caroline's reach.

"And you, Caroline?" Matt's direction change startled her. "What do you think of my plan?"

Even though she'd known he was interviewing, her disappointment cut deep. She felt as if he'd lied to her, back when he'd said he'd be around for Jake and Shelly. He'd wanted her to go along with the wedding, and nothing else had mattered. "You'll enjoy the job, and you'll be here when you can for Jake and Shelly." Not for her. She hoped their children didn't hear her anger, but she no longer cared what Matt thought.

"Is coming back good enough for you, Caroline?" His tone asked more. She almost read his mind. He wanted to know if he mattered to her, and she marveled at his unexpected cruel streak.

"Your job is none of my business." She stood. "I'll pour paint in the buckets before the others show up." She meant to walk away. Matt's choices really weren't her concern. He owed her nothing. "I wish you'd been able to fulfill your promises to Jake and Shelly." *And to me. Damn you, and to me.*

He glanced at Jake and Shelly, who were staring at each other, newly aware of the undercurrents that flowed between their parents. "I'll help you with the buckets," Matt said.

"I'd rather do it myself, but I left some brushes in my car. Maybe you could go downstairs for those." She took her keys from her purse and tossed them at him. "And the drop cloths, too."

His expression hard, he nodded. He left the apartment without looking back, and emptiness seemed to fill the place. Caroline went to the baby's room. She wouldn't give in to the unexpected depth of pain that numbed her. Matt had decided to move away. There was no more to be said.

In the baby's room, she spread newspapers in the center of the floor. Then she opened the paint cans and poured paint into small buckets. One for each of her family members—Jake, Shelly, Matt, Aunt Imogen and Uncle Ford. Cate and Alan were working this afternoon.

Caroline turned in a circle. They'd paint this room

inside an hour. Two, if they talked a lot. As her family tended to do. A knock on the door made her jump.

"Mom? I'd like to come in."

"Door's open." Caroline turned in time to see Shelly enter.

"What's wrong between you and Matt?"

"Nothing. I just wish he'd made a different choice."

Shelly stared at her. "I get the feeling Jake and I aren't the only problem you have with his moving."

"Why else would I care?" Caroline set the buckets around the room, careful to make sure she didn't drip on the carpet.

"We have no right to ask him not to take this job, Mom. What else could he do? Come when I have a flat tire? Coach Jake for his exams? Jake and I do those things for each other now, and if we can't, we'll always have you."

Caroline nodded. "You do," she said. It ought to be enough. She had her family. When had she needed more?

The apartment doorbell rang, and Caroline touched Shelly's hand. "Let's go. If we don't corral them right away, they'll scatter and chatter and we won't get any work out of them."

"I'm glad you all came." Shelly hugged Caroline and quickly let her go. "This place will feel like home now."

Caroline glowed a little. Between them, they put everyone to work. Except Uncle Ford, who was late.

Caroline was taking tea to the others when the bell rang again. Uncle Ford at last.

"I'll get it," Caroline called, balancing the tray of glasses so she could open the door.

Uncle Ford marched over the threshold. "Whisper to me, Caroline. I'm a new man."

"Huh?"

"Whisper, I said."

"Whisper what?"

"Anything, woman. Can't you see I'm trying to tell you I've had my hearing adjusted?"

"How do you adjust your hearing?" she whispered.

He popped a small device out of his ear. "This little gadget is a marvel. Put it in your ear."

Visions of germs danced in her head. "Don't go offering that to people."

"Take off your white gloves, girl, and join the real world."

"Lay off today, Uncle Ford." Bending carefully, she kissed his dry cheek. As he grinned, she edged behind him to shut the door.

"What made you take the plunge?"

"I listened through Matt's headphones when he took me flying. The difference convinced me I had a problem."

Matt again. What did he have that the rest of them lacked? They'd each suggested a hearing test at one time or another in the past twenty years.

What did it matter if Matt had achieved the miracle? Uncle Ford could hear again. "What do you notice most?" she asked. "That you couldn't hear before?"

"Birdsong—and night sounds. Every night in the trees outside my bedroom window—it's a frat party."

Caroline laughed. "A frat party?"

"Rowdy night animals, carrying on in a most unrespectable manner, and before you ask, yes, I do envy them."

She nudged him with her elbow, risking the glasses as tea slopped gently toward the rims. "Come back to the nursery. Everyone's in there."

"Couldn't you commandeer a paint team you've hired before? I'm not sure I've raised you well, because I'd have taken advantage of business resources rather than family."

Caroline grinned at her impossible uncle behind his back. He and Aunt Imogen were still raising her. Her smile faded as Matt came out of the nursery.

"Hey," Uncle Ford said. "Talk to me in a low voice." He glanced back at Caroline. "Can't ask a man to whisper to me."

"You did it." Matt gripped Uncle Ford's shoulders. "Let me see."

The older man popped the device out of his ear again, and Matt inspected it, much more suitably interested than Caroline had been. Which riled her.

"So when can we fly again?" Uncle Ford asked.

"When?" Matt's reflexive glance Caroline's way made Uncle Ford laugh.

"We need her permission?"

"I'm afraid so."

"Uncle Ford, aren't you too…"

"Can't say it, can you? Because you don't really want me to feel old."

"You aren't too old for most things," she said, "but what if you had a heart attack?"

"The ticker's fine. Only my ears were defective. Why don't you fly with Matt? If you think he's safe, you tell Imogen and Caroline, and I can fly without a guilty conscience."

"I'll take you," Matt said.

"That's crazy." And besides, she was scared.

"He's safe, Caroline. Go."

"If you don't, I'll have to disappoint Ford."

"Say that in a whisper, son. I love to hear whispers. I'll bet you never thought to see me hearing like everyone else."

Matt laughed, and Caroline marveled at the connections he'd made with her family. The man was everywhere.

He planted his fist against the older man's shoulder. "Aren't you going to show the others?"

"Come with me. See how amazed they are."

"In a minute." Matt's gaze brushed Caroline's face, and he took the tray out of her hands. "I want to talk…for a minute."

Uncle Ford assessed his niece with surprise. "Okay," he said, but doubt drenched his agreement. "Okay with you, Caroline?"

She smiled to thank him for noticing her discomfort. "We'll be in soon, Uncle Ford."

He was still looking back when he turned into the nursery. His curiosity boded ill for Caroline. He wouldn't be able to keep his suspicions to himself, which meant the entire family would find a way to interrogate her about Matt.

"I know you're angry about the job."

"I feel as betrayed as Shelly and Jake should."

"I didn't betray you." Matt stood too close. His scent pervaded the tiny hall, musk and spice and everything oh-so-nice.

Caroline refused to back away. "I didn't want you to go. Maybe I had no right to ask, but I hoped you'd know."

"Because of that night at your house?"

"Yes," she snapped. "Maybe it was just one night with a woman to you. Maybe you hold women like that all the time, and maybe those women make you want to forget every lesson you've ever learned about life, but that's not the way I've lived. I've tried to pretend nothing's happened since that night, and I guess I convinced myself you were just waiting to find out about the job before you said you felt the same."

"The same what? I do care about you. I want you." He lowered his voice as she flinched, looking toward the baby's room. "But I have to work, and our children won't want us to be lovers, Caroline."

"I know." Her heart was pumping. Perspiration

damped her palms. She went for broke. "You're Jake's father, and you owe him and Shelly, not me, but I let myself care, and once again, I picked the wrong man."

Taking her arm, he pulled her farther into the small sitting room, glancing over his shoulder in a way that emphasized the furtive nature of their fledgling relationship. Caroline tried to take an emotional step backward. Their children couldn't afford for them to make a mistake.

"Maybe I'm the right man," he said. "I don't know, but I'm trying to find out. How far are you willing to go to meet me?"

"To the edge of hurting my daughter," she shot back. "And no further."

He let her go so fast, she fell away from him. "Then that leaves us nowhere. We have to realize if we take our feelings for each other any further, Jake and Shelly could be upset. If we screw up, we could hurt them."

She twisted her hands together. No answer came to her. "I don't want you to be right." She had trouble breathing, which should have shamed her, but she didn't mind if she looked weak. Just this once. "If you're right, you and I have no future."

His mouth thinned. "Maybe we're already too late. How can they not see what's between us?"

She shook her head, letting her hair fall over her face. "If we don't know how we feel, how can they? They're just kids. We're the adults."

"Not anymore," Matt said. "I don't think I'm always an adult with you. I want what I can't have, and I don't know how to stop."

His voice, thicker with each word, pulled her to him. She swayed toward him, but as he leaned down to her, as his lips seemed to swell just a breath away from hers, the nursery door opened, and Caroline sprang guiltily away from him.

"Mom," Shelly wailed, "is Uncle Ford teasing me again? You don't really plan to fly with Matt?"

Caroline tried to speak, but her voice wouldn't come. She pressed her hand to her throat and forced herself to make words. "Only if he promises we won't crash."

CHAPTER TEN

WHILE MATT READIED the Cessna, Caroline returned business calls. Matt focused on the job at hand, rather than on the woman who'd avoided him with all her might since the day they'd painted the nursery. After he finished his checklist, he waited for her to end negotiations with a wallpaper manufacturer.

"Are you sure you want to do this?" he asked her.

"I don't have a choice. Uncle Ford told Aunt Imogen and Cate, and they thought it was a great idea. Like I'd know how well you pilot."

"The Navy trusts me," he said, slightly affronted.

"Yeah, I tried that argument. They said the Navy didn't love Uncle Ford the way we do."

"Get in the plane, Caroline." He helped her in. She wobbled at the door, and he caught her thigh, thinking she was about to fall. "You're trembling."

"I hate to fly. I never told anyone at home, because I didn't want them to think I'm a coward."

"You don't mind if I know?" He stroked her leg, trying to impart his confidence. As always when he touched her, he wanted more.

She caught his hand. "Don't, Matt." She rubbed

her leg, as if she could erase his touch. Hell of a thing to do to a man.

As soon as they took off, Matt headed out to sea again. The weather seemed calm today, and the sky was clear. Over water, they smoothed out. Matt turned north, but suddenly, there was a popping sound, and the plane tilted toward Caroline's side.

She grabbed the window and Matt's leg, her face ghostly pale. At her other side, the window was open. Adjusting the plane's position, Matt leaned across her panicked body, but he couldn't quite reach.

"Shut the window, Caroline, and tell me before you change anything on the aircraft."

"Did I do that? I needed some air."

"You're going to be fine. I won't let you get hurt."

She speared him with a chiding look that plucked out bits of his heart.

"I'm not that scared, Matt. You don't have to baby me."

"Sorry. In that case, you have to think about what you're doing up here."

"I'm sorry. I didn't know I should ask before I opened the window."

"No problem, but I wouldn't want to face Ford or Imogen or Cate if I let something happen to you."

She nodded without speaking again. This version of Caroline, too frightened to pretend she wasn't, intrigued him. Not that she'd asked for comfort.

"Do you want to go back?" he asked.

"Are we going to crash?"

"No. Trust me, Caroline."

"I did. I'm not sure why, but I did."

"You mean about the job?"

"It shouldn't matter to me. I don't want to care."

"If you keep gripping that seat so hard, you're going to pull it up."

She let go immediately, and Matt felt guilty.

"I'm sorry," he said again. "I was teasing, but listen, Caroline, I'm trying to get back as often as possible. Isn't that enough?"

"It has to be. I just don't understand why you have the choice. I couldn't leave Shelly, or any of my family."

"I don't have a family like yours. Jake and I got used to a long-distance relationship after my divorce."

"He seems to understand about the job."

Had she said it to comfort him? He checked his instruments before he looked her way again. She met his gaze, straight and level. For the first time in a long time, when he thought about Jake, he believed he'd done his best.

"Thanks, Caroline."

"For what?"

"Pointing out my son is an adult. He does understand, because he and Shelly have no choice right now, either."

"Are you saying they don't love each other? Just when they've convinced me?"

"I'm suggesting they would have waited until they knew they could support their child."

"They're just hoping to, with our help?"

Matt nodded. "But do you think he felt I let him down because I have to move?"

"No." She looked straight down, at the yoke moving in front of her. "I was the only one who fell apart. I still can't explain it," she said. She looked up, and her brilliant blue eyes caught him by surprise. He didn't bother to hide the fact she took his breath away. "I just don't want you to go," she admitted.

"But if I stayed, you wouldn't want me, either."

"Shelly and I are easing toward each other," she said. "I wouldn't do anything to upset her."

He didn't blame her. He couldn't when he finally understood what drove her. Family. Maybe she couldn't care more for a stranger than for her family. It was an answer he'd rather ignore. He wanted to come first with the woman he loved. He'd be about tenth with Caroline.

He shook his head, to clear it of any more wild thoughts, like "We could be together."

"Do you want to fly?" he asked her.

She widened her eyes. "Are you kidding?"

"I'm right here. I'll take over any time you want me to."

"You are a dangerous guy. You tempt me."

He smiled. "You're not afraid to take the controls, just to fly as a passenger?"

Color stole over her skin. "I have control problems. Honestly, I'm hardly ever sure I know what to do next, so I feel better if I can look as if I'm in control.''

"Sensible," he said, her honesty working its usual magic with him. "You just have to keep it level. Watch my hands. Forward on the yoke to go down, back to go up. I'll take care of the throttle—I mean the pedals.'' He pointed at the drawing of the airplane in the flight director. "As long as you keep this straight and the wings level, we're fine.''

"You'll take over if I get in trouble.''

"I don't want to die, Caroline.''

"That's right.'' Now, pleasure seemed to tint her skin pink. "I'll put my hands on the yoke thing, but don't let go until I tell you.''

"You're in charge.''

"Finally," she said with amusement. "If only the rest of my family gave me my due with so little fuss.''

He had to concentrate on loosening his hands as his pulse sped up. She'd just acknowledged him as a family member. She had no idea how he longed to be part of a family like the Talbots.

She curved her fingers around the yoke.

Matt touched her sleeve. "Let me take us up and down so you can feel how it responds.''

"Great idea.''

Matt demonstrated, and Caroline nodded her understanding.

"All right.'' She glanced at his hands. "I think I'm ready.''

"Yeah?" He assessed her level of bravado. She seemed appropriately serious. "Now, Caroline. It's all yours."

Matt kept his hands at the ready, in case he had to take over, but the moment he let go, the plane's nose dipped, and Caroline gently eased it back level.

"Perfect." Possibly, he'd overdone the praise, but a woman who was so frightened and yet had the courage to try to fly, impressed him.

"We're all right?"

He glanced at the flight director. "Steady as a rock. How do you feel?"

"Like a god."

Her rich voice aroused him, head to toe, instantly. Matt licked his lips and imagined tasting hers. "Does this mean Ford gets flying lessons?"

"I doubt it. What if his heart couldn't take this beating?"

"You're a stout protector."

Caroline looked puzzled, but before she could ask the question on her mind, a loud bang reverberated from the Cessna's motor. Caroline made no sound, but terror painted her face as she watched the propeller begin to slow.

"Let go." Matt pulled the yoke back to climb while they still could.

She'd been afraid to fly, wary of pilots, and now he had to get his mind off her before he killed them both.

He calmed his voice. "I've got it, Caroline. Nothing bad's going to happen.'' He turned the key. Nothing at all happened. He turned it again, though he expected what he got this time. No response.

''What'd I do?''

''Nothing. We blew a cylinder. It happens.'' He adjusted their angle of attack, his heart pounding like their lost cylinder. He seriously didn't want to hurt Caroline Talbot Manning.

''What are you doing, Matt? Can I help?''

''Just try to relax.'' He didn't want her tense when they hit the sand, and he was determined to fly them back to the beach. ''I'm setting glide rate, so we get as much forward distance as the aircraft can give us as it falls.'' He turned back toward Leith, careful to maintain his airspeed. Without the engine's roar it was strangely quiet. Only the soft rush of the wind hugged the plane's body. ''Caroline, I have to tell you we're going down.''

Finally, she whimpered. ''Shelly.'' Her longing shattered him, but he was determined to show her she didn't have to be afraid. He'd save them.

''You'll see Shelly. Let me finish. We're dropping about five hundred feet per minute. I'm going to declare an emergency and tell Leith tower what we're doing.''

''Which is?''

''Landing on the beach.''

''On the beach?''

''We can't vote. We have five or six minutes, and I can't be sure what we'd run into in a field. We can't see power lines on a road. On the beach, the gear will dig in. We may tip forward, but I intend to land so we jerk to a stop. I want you to bend over, the way you would on a commercial flight.'' It wouldn't help, but it would give her something to do. ''When we land, if you have feeling in all your fingers and toes, I'm dragging you out of here.''

''I'll manage if you get us to the beach.'' She peered out the window. ''Try to head as far north of Cate's house as you can. Just beyond her, the dunes start.''

Matt knew this terrain, but he nodded as he hit the mic switch. ''Leith Tower, this is Cessna 522Kilo declaring an emergency. We've lost our engine. Two souls on board.'' He glanced at the other soul tucked in her seat. She had yet to say she'd known better than to risk a flight with him. He prayed with all his might that he'd keep them from tipping over. ''Approximately two miles north of Leith Point, preparing to ditch the aircraft on the beach before the dunes.''

''22kilo, Leith tower, roger. Will notify police and fire. Will your engines restart?''

Impatiently, he hit the mic switch again. Of course he'd tried to restart the engines. He was idiotically flying the mother of his son's pregnant bride. This just proved they couldn't get involved with each other. They might both die together if he couldn't get his mind back where it belonged—in this cockpit. ''Tower, 22kilo, negative.''

''22kilo, Leith Tower, roger,'' the controller said.

"We've notified emergency services. Advise intents."

Caroline twisted to look up at Matt. "What does he mean 'intents'?"

"Get back down. He means if we change our plan, we should let him know."

"That two souls thing alarmed me."

She was teasing him. Her spirit wrung Matt's heart and tempted him again to give in to his own fear. "We'll land with a great story for Shelly and Jake."

"You've been in worse than this." Her tone asked for reassurance, but he had to admit to himself this time was different for one huge reason. He had a passenger who mattered to him. Desperately.

"We're over the beach now." Now or never. He wanted to keep flying out to sea. They were fine, drifting down toward earth, but trying to reach safety could kill them. He concentrated on the controls. "The slower we're going when we land, the better the gear will stick, so we're going to land at stall speed. You'll hear a horn, and it's going to wail. It's supposed to."

The houses grew larger. The wind tried to tumble them in the sky. Matt's own heart throbbed an alarm in his temples, in his stomach. "Dump the headphones, Caroline." He should have told her to get rid of those things before.

She pushed them behind her legs, and Matt adjusted the yoke. This end of the beach was private.

Hardly anyone was near the sand below, but it wasn't empty. He identified Jake's truck. Matt swore silently.

Then he put Jake and Shelly out of his mind. He had to.

Sand rose up at him. Waves on the left side of the plane seemed to leap in their direction. The stall horn sounded once and silenced and then blared in a long, urgent cry, and Matt held his breath.

He would not kill Caroline. He would save her and give her back to her daughter, and he'd never risk her life again.

Their gear kissed the sand and then dug in. The plane stopped as if some monster buried deep in the beach had grabbed them and tried to pull them under.

Matt was so intent on his passenger, he lost track of his own safety, and his head bounced off the yoke. Caroline uttered concern, but she stayed where Matt had told her to stay, and they didn't tip over.

At last came silence. Loud, unbearable silence. And Caroline straightened.

"You've cut your forehead again."

The light of life in her eyes meant everything to Matt. He ignored her comment about his head. "Are you hurt?"

"No. I'd like to hug the ground, but my knees are shaking. Can you help me out of here?"

Actual tears burned in his eyes. "I'll get you. Stay there."

He forced his door open and dropped onto the sand. He stopped and held on to the side of the plane because his legs were shaking at least as much as Caroline's probably were. Finally, he pushed himself upright and struggled around the plane.

After he yanked her door open he eased her out. Wrapping his arm around her shoulder, he struggled to help her across the sand. Her legs were as unsteady as his, and they tripped over each other until he judged they were a safe distance from the plane.

When he would have let her go, she held on. "I knew I shouldn't fly with you," she said.

"I hoped you weren't going to mention that."

"I'm reminding myself." He didn't care what she did as long as she wrapped her body around his. "Your job is dangerous, and so is your fun. We both have even more responsibilities than when Shelly and Jake were children. We can't ruin their lives when we're supposed to be helping them."

"Caroline, we're safe." He stroked damp tendrils of her hair away from her cheekbones and pressed his lips to the corner of her mouth.

With a sharp cry, she caught his face and kissed him back, branding him with passion no other woman knew how to wield. He locked his arms around her waist and gave himself up to the secrets she kept in her kisses, letting go only when Caroline broke away from him.

Bewildering Matt, she was already tidying her clothes when he could barely think straight. "That was the last time," she said.

"Like hell."

"I meant the last time you'd kiss me, not the last time I'd fly."

"I know what you meant, and you aren't ever getting in another airplane without me. You may be bad luck." He must be out of his weak mind. She seemed to second that suggestion as she stared at him with a hint of anxious suspicion hazing her anger.

"Bad luck?"

"I just don't want you flying with anyone else. I don't want you taking chances."

She dared to laugh at him, turning her back as Jake's voice shouted for Matt. "Oh, God," she said.

Shelly and Jake were running down the sidewalk. He'd forgotten them while he and Caroline mauled each other in the sand.

He glanced down the street toward Caroline's house. They must have been inside.

"Stop running, Shel," Caroline yelled. "Did they see?" she demanded, no doubt meaning the kiss. It was much more threatening than a mere crash landing.

"I doubt it. They'd have run down here a lot quicker."

Shelly suddenly did stop, but only to clutch at her stomach. Jake turned back to her.

"Is she in labor?" Caroline asked.

"She'll be fine. She's young."

"And pregnant."

Arm in arm, she and Jake came across the sand. Jake held back, his face pale, as Shelly skidded to a halt at her mother's side. She shoved Matt out of her way. "What did you do to my mom?"

"This isn't Matt's fault," Caroline said stoutly.

He knew why she was protecting him. She didn't want their respective children to choose sides.

"Are you hurt, Mom?" Shelly ran her hands over her mother's arms, but Caroline stopped her.

"My head nearly exploded when you started running over here."

"I'm fine. Maybe back in the dark ages when you had me pregnant women were supposed to act like invalids, but I'm fine. Sit down. Wait for the paramedics to examine you."

Matt nearly laughed at Caroline's affronted expression, but Jake broke in, his voice abnormally deep.

"Let them examine both of you, Dad." He hovered at Matt's side, on the verge of touching him, but not quite daring.

Why? Even at a time like this, he obviously cared, but he held back from normal human contact.

"We're all right," Matt said, and wrapped his son in the tightest bear hug his fear-weakened arms could manage. "We're all right," he repeated, but the last word came out in a puff of breath as Jake hugged him back, without the consideration of watery limbs.

"I'm glad I didn't know it was you. We'd just driven up when we saw the plane..." Jake said softly. "We went inside Caroline's house to call 911. Shelly realized it was you when she saw her mom's hair."

"The engine went out. Normally, I wouldn't even have worried, but with Caroline on board...."

"There were two souls," she cut in. "I'm kind of glad we made it."

"You were amazing," he said, not realizing he shouldn't. "She flew," he told Jake and Shelly. "And she's terrified to fly."

"You are?" Shelly asked.

Caroline made a sarcastic face of phony thanks at Matt. "I always tried to be brave for you, but the truth is I don't like flying."

"She took the controls anyway." Matt envied her will to fight her own weaknesses. He wished he could overcome his fear of losing his son. He never made a sudden move that might frighten Jake back into the cover of the woods, like the wild animal he sometimes seemed. In fact, he wouldn't have held Caroline if she hadn't reached for him first.

Being so alert to rejection made him feel less a man. Sirens had him looking up to see police cars and trucks bearing down on them.

The officers and paramedics spilled out of their vehicles. Caroline eyed them as if they were the enemy.

"Shel," she said, "go see Cate and Aunt Imogen. They won't want to hear about this on the news or the grapevine. And tell them to let Uncle Ford know we're perfectly all right."

Family first, Caroline's usual method of operation. Suddenly, he believed that "last time" threat she'd hurled at him. She'd avoid any more chances with him.

SHELLY TUCKED her hand around Aunt Imogen's waist and eased her into a chair at her kitchen table. "I'm sure Mom's fine."

She wished she'd insisted her mother and Matt come here when the police finished with them. She'd never noticed her aunt was getting older—well, not this much older, but Aunt Imogen had that gray-of-face look you only read about in books.

"She was walking around." Aunt Imogen locked a hand around Shelly's wrist. "You saw her walking?"

"They both looked as if she'd just torn a strip off Matt, too." Shelly felt for her father-in-law. "I'm not sure he's ever been this far on her bad side."

"He'll be fine. Where's Jake? You shouldn't have come here by yourself in your condition."

"Why do you all treat me as if I'm carrying plague? I told you Jake went to get Uncle Ford. Mom didn't want some busybody making the accident more dramatic."

"I shouldn't have let her go. Does she think I don't know how much she hates flying? Isn't it bad enough your uncle wants to risk his neck in those little planes?"

Shelly sneaked a quick glance out the kitchen window. Thank God Jake was coming back with Uncle

Ford. She patted her aunt's hand. "I doubt she'll go again."

"You got that right. Not if I have anything to say about it, and I'm thinking plenty right now."

Shelly stared at her. All her life, Aunt Imogen had been the family's strength. Her mom and Aunt Cate had gone to Aunt Imogen for reinforcements when they faltered. She'd gone when she needed help handling her mom's overprotective ways.

She stared at the table. The one time she'd avoided her family, she'd ended up pregnant at nineteen. And now—she glanced through the window at Jake—now she might just have made herself a burden on the man she loved.

Why hadn't she realized her bills with her family would come due? Soon, she'd be responsible for her child, but she'd also have to pitch in and give Aunt Imogen strength as she grew older. She'd have to listen to Uncle Ford's stories, not just for the fun of them, but to figure out what he was after when he told them. She'd seen her mom and Aunt Cate performing that trick when she was still young, but she'd gone blithely about her own life.

The porch screen squeaked open, and Shelly ran to Jake's side. She was too young for this much responsibility. Didn't anyone know? Was she fooling everyone in her family? Except herself?

Uncle Ford immediately stomped to Aunt Imogen. "You're taking this too hard, woman. They had a little accident, but I've flown with Matt. He knows what he's doing. He landed them safely, and they're both fine.''

She lifted a bewildered gaze to Shelly and Jake. ''And what would these two have done if he hadn't been able to land the plane? Do you know how young they are?''

''We've taken care of our girls all these years, Imogen, and we'd take care of Shelly and Jake, too. That's what we do, because we're family.''

Jake swallowed hard. His throat made a funny noise that almost made Shelly laugh.

''I have to go,'' he said. ''My study group...''

Shelly didn't believe her ears. ''You're meeting them after all this?''

''It's my responsibility, Shel. We'll be at Karen Beaufort's apartment if you need me.''

She shook her head. ''Your responsibility is here, with us.''

''I'll check back by on my way home.'' He offered Uncle Ford an unsteady hand. ''I hope you're okay, sir.''

Aunt Imogen nodded at him. ''Have a good study,'' she said.

He walked out, letting the porch door slam, and Shelly tried to decide which of the planters on the windowsill at her back she should throw at him.

''Forget it,'' Aunt Imogen said. ''He's afraid. He didn't bargain for this much responsibility.''

''Neither did I. Neither did you guys when my

mom and Aunt Cate came to live here, but you didn't throw them out.''

"He's twenty years old." Uncle Ford drew back a chair with the tip of his cane. "He's about to become a father. Let him concentrate on that for now, and later, we'll figure out how to assure him we won't move into your spare room and drool at him for the next twenty years.''

CHAPTER ELEVEN

SHELLY CLOSED her apartment door and braced herself against it, running her hands over the mound of baby that danced inside her body.

Jake would be late again tonight. His study group was meeting at the library this time, but one of the other members had to do a shift at the college bookstore until nine o'clock. Jake had said he wanted to take advantage of the hours between class and the meeting to get in some extra study time.

It would have been fine, but tonight the empty apartment reminded her of the five weeks that had passed since they'd seen her mom and Matt crash land on the beach. She'd never gone this long without seeing her mom, but something had happened to Matt and Jake and her mother that day.

Matt and Jake made excuses to see each other. Her mother had suddenly produced a buying trip she couldn't put off another day. She was off on an antiques tour of the South.

Shelly pushed away from the door and wandered down the hall to the baby's room. She should make something to eat and study for her own calculus exam, but when she was this tired, she didn't want food, and she needed to wash and iron the curtains her mom had ordered for the nursery.

A key in the apartment door made her turn. She went back into the hall as Jake rammed the door into her book bag.

"Shel?"

"Back here." Awfully glad to see him, she hurried down the hall.

He moved her bag so he could come inside. "Are you okay?"

"I thought you were going to study."

"I was, but I thought we could eat dinner. You look funny. Did something happen?"

She looped her hair behind her ears. "Maybe I missed you."

He kissed her swiftly. "What were you doing in the baby's room?"

"I'm going to wash the curtains."

"Weren't you waiting for your mom to help you hang them?"

"She didn't come by before she left, and I don't expect her to show up when she comes home." She couldn't keep the accusation out of her voice. "I think she's trying to put distance between us."

Turning them both, he pulled her toward the kitchen. "You miss your mom."

"I'm glad you want to be involved, Jake, and I'd never want you to feel left out, but I want to know why Mom's pulling back. And then all my friends suddenly seem to think pregnancy's catchy. I don't have anyone to talk to.''

"I haven't been home much either." Jake flexed his shoulders. "Do you think Caroline's still mad at my dad over the plane crash?"

"That's not it. I think she's got a beef with me." She stroked her belly. "We only have two more months. Could she be dreading the baby?"

"I don't think so." He hugged her. "I really don't think so. Even if she is, I'm not." He rested his chin on her head. "Maybe she and I have something in common. I'm afraid I can't be the husband you need, or a good enough father for the baby. When Dad and Caroline crashed I saw how your family takes care of each other, and I got scared I couldn't measure up."

"Why didn't you tell me?" Relief lightened the heavy load on her shoulders. "I thought you were sorry we got married. I was afraid my family had finally scared you off. I'll have to take care of them one day the way they've taken care of me."

Jake tightened his arms. "I'm glad we'll be able to give something back," he said.

"How are things with your dad?" she asked.

"Good. He forces a hug on me every time I see him, and he's always showing up out of the blue." A chuckle from low in his chest rumbled against her cheek. "I kind of like it. Funny, isn't it? I'm a grown man, but the fact my dad wants to hug me makes me feel as if he really loves me again."

A wave of protectiveness swept through her. "He always loved you."

"Yeah, but we didn't connect. I think he was waiting for me to let him back in, and I was waiting for him to let me down. He doesn't though. Let me down."

Shelly sighed, envying him. "I miss my mom. At least she could tell me why she's not coming around."

"Maybe she hates the apartment." He glanced around the small kitchen, at the table that seemed to take up most of the room. "I'm sorry I can't give you more."

Everyone in her family had offered to help them, but neither of them wanted help. "I love our place, Jake. You make me mad when you act as if it's not good enough." She broke away from him and opened the refrigerator door. Pulling a foil-covered bowl to the edge of the top shelf, she peeled the corner back. "How do you feel about chicken soup?"

"Terrified. We had that two weeks ago." He planted his hands on her shoulders. "You take a shower and relax. I'll make some tuna salad."

Their staple. If tuna went extinct, they'd starve inside a month. "I don't want you to make me dinner."

"Your mom would hate the way you try to be a housewife for me. We're in this marriage together, and my dad taught me to make tuna salad when I had to stand on a chair to help him."

"Okay, I give up." She waited in the kitchen doorway. "Maybe I'll try to call my mom." She wanted his opinion on the idea.

"Will she tell you if something's wrong?"

"Have you seen her hide anything from me?"

"If she thought she was protecting you."

"You think I should wait for her to come back."

"My birthday is next week. Let's talk to her then."

Maybe she wanted to be a June Cleaver kind of housewife occasionally, but she didn't need her husband to fix her problems with her mom. "I'll talk to her by myself." They were having a picnic on the beach at her Aunt Cate's. "You just keep your dad out of the picture."

"Maybe he's the problem," Jake said. "He's always hanging around when she's with us."

Shelly's mouth dropped open. He was right. As far back as the wedding, wherever her mom went, Jake's dad popped up right behind her. And then there had been the strange tension between them after the crash. She'd put it down to shock, but what was going on?

"We asked them to shop for the baby stuff together," she said sharply. Please, God, don't let my mom have an affair with Jake's dad.

Jake looked as if she'd hit him over the head. "What do you think I said, Shel?" he asked.

"I don't know." Just in case he really didn't get it—and he was wrong—she decided not to spell out the disgusting possibility. Shelly felt hollow inside. Her mom and Jake's dad?

"What, Shelly?"

"Nothing. If you don't mind making the tuna, I'm going to take that shower."

Did everything in her life have to turn into a family affair? Even her marriage?

AUNT IMOGEN DROPPED her bomb the night of Jake's birthday picnic. Inside the tent they'd set up outside Cate's house, Caroline held Melinda, and Cate cradled Mary. Shelly sprawled on her back, rubbing her distended belly, sparing the occasional groan as her baby apparently performed Olympic dives.

Aunt Imogen flipped back the tent flap and entered, bearing homemade peach ice cream. "A bowl for each of you ladies. Ford said if you were too lazy to come out of here and ask for it yourselves, you should go without, but frankly, I don't want to deal with getting it home to the freezer. He makes enough for an army."

She distributed the bounty and then took a spot beside Caroline on the blanket.

"He'll call you lazy, too, Aunt Imogen," Shelly warned her.

"I don't care. I wanted to talk to you all about Whitney."

"I've been waiting for this." Cate's satisfaction made Caroline feel slightly guilty. She'd never shared her conversation with Aunt Imogen in the attic.

"Have I been unconscious? What's going on with you and Admiral Randolph?" Shelly flicked an annoyed gaze at Caroline. "Seems like my whole family is up to something behind my back."

Alarm bells began to clang in Caroline's head. She avoided her aunt and sister as they eyed her with increased interest.

"Wait your turn," Aunt Imogen finally said. "I just wanted to tell you I think Whitney's going to ask me to marry him, and I intend to say yes."

"No!" Cate's happy exclamation, which meant, "I can't believe it" when obviously, she could, roused Mary, who grumbled at her mom. Leaning toward Aunt Imogen, Cate massaged her daughter's back. "Come give me a hug. I can't get up."

Aunt Imogen made the rounds before she sat down again. "How about you, Caroline? What do you think?"

"I'm still fine with it. I kind of thought you'd call me while I was gone to tell me he had asked." She was glad she'd returned from her cowardly shopping trip in time. Avoiding Matt and keeping Shelly from finding out how she felt about him, had seemed important enough to manufacture the series of small trips that had kept her busy for weeks. Now she felt foolish. She'd missed her daughter, longed for Matt's steady presence, and she might have missed the most important announcement Aunt Imogen would ever make.

"We're taking it slowly," her aunt said. "I wanted to prepare you all. I know you depend on me, and you still can."

"But will you live here?" Shelly asked.

"Mostly. Whitney does a good bit of traveling, but we'll make our home in my house."

"I say it's about time," Cate announced.

Aunt Imogen laughed, and her pleasure warmed Caroline. "That's exactly what your sister said," Aunt Imogen told Cate.

"When was this?"

"In my attic, when we were looking for baby things. I told her first, because I wasn't sure she'd take it well."

Cate nodded, annoying her twin. "Change isn't always Caroline's best friend."

"Why would you care, Mom?"

"I'm glad." Caroline looked from face to beloved face. "Whitney's a lucky man, and I'm glad someone will be taking care of you for a change, Aunt Imogen."

"This matriarch work has been trying," Aunt Imogen teased, "but I wouldn't have traded it. I think he came back to Leith just in time."

"You knew him before, didn't you?" Shelly asked.

"He was married to one of my best friends."

"Did you love him then?"

"Shelly," Caroline said, "how can you—"

"I want to know how easy it is for a woman to love a man who's…inappropriate for her."

Those warning bells practically deafened Caroline.

"I didn't have an affair with him, Shelly." Aunt Imogen sounded hurt, but Shelly ploughed on.

"Like you, Mom. What if you fell in love with someone like—say—Matt? Would you have sense enough to leave him alone?"

Caroline tucked Melinda's light blanket around her tiny body. The baby wriggled, no doubt in response to Caroline's tension. "What do you really want to know, Shel?"

"Maybe we should talk alone." Shelly sat up. Aunt Imogen and Cate, both staring at her as if they didn't know her, suddenly sprang to their feet.

"Give me Melinda, Caroline." Aunt Imogen scooped the baby out of her arms. "We'll keep everyone else out of here until you finish talking."

"Which had better be in a hurry." Cate looked at Caroline suspiciously. "You've been keeping all kinds of secrets."

They left the tent and silence fell with the flap. Caroline mulled over her options. She'd tried to give her daughter freedom. She hadn't known she'd have to fight for her own.

"You shouldn't have asked that in front of them," she said. "Tonight was Aunt Imogen's night."

"I didn't want to ask, but I have to know if you can be as responsible as Aunt Imogen."

Caroline took a deep breath. "When you were a child, I based my whole life on what was best for you, but we're both adults now. You have no right to question me—"

"It affects my family. What's up with you and Matt?"

"What are you talking about?" she asked, unable to hide the guilt that dripped from her voice.

Shelly leapt on it. "There *is* something between you. I don't believe it. Jake noticed that Matt's always around you, or you're always around him, but I still didn't think you could be desperate enough to go out with my father-in-law."

"Desperate?" Caroline couldn't help thinking of the mess Shelly had made of her own life before judging her mother's. "In what way?"

"To keep a toehold in my life." It was an accusation. "Are you sleeping with Matt? I didn't believe it. I was trying to trick you."

"You should have asked me straight out. I would have told you the truth."

"Did you?"

"Sleep with him, or tell you the truth?" Caroline scrambled to her feet. "I haven't done anything to be ashamed of."

"How do I know if anything could possibly shame you?"

Caroline blinked at the stranger who'd somehow inhabited her daughter's body. "You're out of line. That part of my life no longer has anything to do with you."

"If you're dating my father-in-law, I have plenty to say."

"I've tried to back off and give you and Jake privacy." Partly because she was afraid this would happen, but also, because she'd wanted Shelly to feel comfortable in her marriage. Without her mommy.

Her daughter grabbed the tent flap and struggled to her feet, but she would have fallen if Caroline hadn't helped her. "You've been so busy with Matt, you didn't have time to put curtains on my baby's window."

"You're wrong. I am attracted to Matt, and I care about him. But I think that's because he's such a good father. I never intended to let you find out he even matters to me. I won't act on it, Shel, but I can't help how I feel. Any more than you could with Jake."

"Fine. Throw the baby in my face."

"I'm trying not to, but this is none of your business, and you know Matt's leaving for Maryland right after Halloween."

"Not a moment too soon, I'm thinking. I'm not blind, and I've watched you two all day. You wouldn't have worked so hard at staying apart unless you were dying to be together."

Shelly flounced out of the tent as proudly as her distended body allowed. "Oh, sorry, Matt." Distance and the tent muffled her voice.

"What's the matter?" he asked.

"Ask my mom. You'd rather talk to her anyway."

Matt ducked inside the tent. "What's wrong with her?"

"She knows we're…" Caroline shrugged. "We're whatever we are."

"Come with me. We'll worry about Shelly later."

"Where do you want to go?" She studied him closely. He looked anxious. "What's more important than Shelly?"

"Ford. He wandered off down the beach, and I can't find him. I wanted to tell him you were going to let him fly."

"Am I?" She followed him out of the tent, only slightly alarmed. "He's probably down by the dunes."

"That's the direction he went, but, like I say, I can't find him. Are you coming? I could ask the others, but I didn't want to alarm anyone if he was all right."

"Look at me. I'm on your heels. At the risk of sending my daughter into early labor."

Outside, the night was warmer than she'd expected. Whitney, Alan, Aunt Imogen and Cate stood at the edge of the water. Pointing at the bright, moonlit sky, Whitney was angling his hand, no doubt describing a flight.

Pilots.

"Uncle Ford won't thank you for chasing him down like this," Caroline said as she strode at Matt's side toward the dunes.

"A Talbot who doesn't welcome friendly concern?" He kept moving, but reached for her arm when she couldn't match his pace. "You astound me."

With a weak grin, she hoped Shelly had taken private refuge with Jake. She pictured her extremely pregnant daughter maneuvering in the uneven sand. Even by the light of a full moon, it wouldn't be safe.

They evaded the others in the firelight easily. Soon, they left the clumps of tall grass behind. Vegetation was thinner along the dunes. Caroline spied a pile of something dark on the sand. A lump, like a pile of clothes. That's what they called bodies in mysteries.

And she'd made fun of Matt for worrying.

"Uncle Ford?" she shrieked and started running. "Matt, did you check the water?"

"I looked, but I can't see past the foam on the shore." He headed toward the road. "I'll get flashlights. Keep yelling."

She had to gasp for air. It was like a horrible dream. She couldn't drink in enough air to yell, but she had to. "Uncle Ford!"

She skidded to a halt at the pile of clothes. They were his clothes. Her momentary relief fled as cool waves licked at her feet.

She bent and hooked her uncle's brand-new Hawaiian print shirt off his shoes. Then she turned to the ocean and simply screamed.

No answer from the water. Her heart filled every part of her body and pounded to get out.

"Uncle Ford?" She scanned the darkness, kicking off her own shoes as she fought panic. "Uncle Ford," she yelled for all she was worth.

The waves got louder and colder. They stole the last of her breath as she waded in, falling in her haste. Toward the breakers, she saw a flicker of light and dark. Could that be her uncle bouncing out of the water in his T-shirt?

"Uncle Ford, you'd better answer me!"

Why would he go farther than those chilly first steps? The dark and light object seemed to rise out of the water again.

"I'm coming." If it was him, and if he floated past the breakers they'd both turn up in Greenland in a few months. "Relax," she yelled. If he saved what strength he might have left, he could help her swim back to shore.

Swearing at the progressively colder water, Caroline angled toward her uncle and swam. She could hardly hold her breath in the icy water. At a faint sound, she strained to see him. His arm lifted languidly. He must be exhausted. Terrified, she remeasured her distance from him.

"Stay up," she bellowed.

"Hurry."

At last, his tortured breathing reached her over the choppy surface.

"Cate?" he said. "Or Caroline?"

"Caroline." Was he delirious? He turned on his back as she reached him.

"I can't tell you apart with your hair wet. And it's dark out here."

"Let me feel your heartbeat," she said, as if she could do anything to help him.

"No way. Just start for shore, while I can still swim."

Without the sand to reflect the light, the moon offered little illumination. Caroline twisted her hand in
the neckline of Uncle Ford's T-shirt. Her fingers
brushed against his back. His unnaturally cold skin
horrified her.

"Tell me the ocean sucked you out of your shoes
and shirt, Uncle Ford." She began to kick back toward shore.

"Isn't it refreshing?"

"Freezing." And more so if she backstroked.
"This is October—what were you thinking?" She
turned back over. "I'm going to put my arm around
you and try to sidestroke."

"Just for a second, and then I'll be able to swim
by myself again."

"Fine. Relax." A strong undertow tugged at them,
and the shore slipped farther away. "Where's Matt?"
Had no one else heard her yelling from shore?

"Is Matt out here, too?" Uncle Ford asked, tensing
his body to peer around him.

"Lie back again, Uncle Ford. He asked me to help
him look for you, but if you're going to be as reckless
as he is, I'm afraid you can't spend time with him
anymore."

"I'm sorry, Caroline." A laugh at the end of his
apology ruined its effect.

"Stop laughing at me and kick your feet. You'll
stay warmer."

A head burst out of the water at her shoulder, and

Caroline screamed long and hard, even after she recognized Matt's hard-edged profile.

"Caroline," he said, calmly, "I asked you to wait while I got the flashlights."

"I found him," she said. "Get out of my way."

Uncle Ford flipped over. "Matt, old buddy, I can always count on you."

Indignant, Caroline urged him onto his back again. "You're counting on me right now. Did you tell the others we needed help, Matt?"

"I heard you screaming and started back without the flashlights or anyone else to help us. Give me Ford."

"I'm not a piece of furniture," her uncle reminded them.

Caroline considered screaming again. "Why don't you both shut up and swim? Uncle Ford's cold, and I can't feel my toes."

"Give him to me. I'm stronger than both of you."

She had to admit he was right. She couldn't risk Uncle Ford's life to prove a point. Only the sound of the waves and their harsh breathing accompanied them to shore. They struggled onto the sand, and all three collapsed on their backs.

"Why are you acting so crazy?" Caroline demanded.

"I'm a Talbot," Uncle Ford said, a jester to the end. "I have a reputation to uphold."

"Not funny. Why do you insist on terrorizing us?"

"Give him a break, Caroline."

"You're to blame for all this, Matt. If you hadn't taken him up in that plane the first time—"

"She's right," Uncle Ford said. "I'm alive, and I'm having a hell of a time. I'm sorry about tonight, but I wanted a last swim for the summer."

"Did you have a first swim?" Caroline demanded, launching herself onto one elbow as the cold wind wafted over her. Uncle Ford had been out here longer than she and Matt. "Where are your clothes now? It's freezing."

"I don't know, I left them on the sand. And stop babying me. A first swim isn't the point. I was celebrating, but maybe tonight has taught me moderation."

"Let's hope," Matt said, still a bit breathless.

"Uncle Ford, you've got to be more responsible."

"You're responsible enough for the whole clan. I don't see any reason to give up on life yet."

"Ford, lay off her if you can't thank her for saving your life. Caroline, run to my car and get anything warm out of it. We'll look for his stuff."

"Cate had extra blankets in the tent."

Resisting the night air's cold touch, Caroline ran for their picnic site. Inside the tent, Aunt Imogen and Whitney sat together, and Shelly sprawled against Jake's lap. Cate and Alan looked up at Caroline's sudden appearance.

"What happened to you?"

"I need the extra blankets. Uncle Ford and Matt are wet."

Cate handed them over, and only she stayed behind. Alan grabbed all the blankets except one, and ran past her toward the dunes.

"Stay here, Shelly. Don't run."

"Imogen and I will walk with you, Shelly." Whitney offered.

Caroline glanced back at her daughter as her own feet seemed to sink into the sand. By the time she and Jake reached Matt and Uncle Ford, Alan had wrapped them both in the largish baby blankets Cate favored.

Uncle Ford wasn't grateful for the fluffy yellow square whose ends he clutched in front of his chest. "I'm going home," he said, "before someone sees me like this."

"You're not sexist, too? Yellow is a universal color." Caroline pressed her hands to his cheeks, needing to do something for him. "You're awfully cold. Maybe we should take you to the emergency room."

"Not a chance. I'll call the EMTs if I have a problem, but why don't you let me decide if I need to?"

"I'll drive you home, Uncle Ford," Alan said. "Will you tell Cate?"

"I'll tell her." Jake tugged at Caroline's sleeve. "You should change into dry clothes, too." Then he loped off down the beach as if his concern for her had embarrassed him.

Matt held out his hand to Caroline. "Come here." He wrapped his arm and a blanket around her.

"Keep that, Matt," she said, not wanting him to treat her as if she were fragile. Now that Uncle Ford was safe, her legs were wobbly and her delayed reaction made her feel vulnerable. "Your front is exposed."

"Then share with me. Put your arm around my waist."

Terribly aware of Alan and Uncle Ford, both pretending not to notice her and Matt, she followed orders. It seemed wiser than arguing. They staggered, making about the same progress as they had the day they'd crashed.

"Why don't you take Matt to your house?" Alan suggested. "It's closest." He and Uncle Ford split off toward the cars parked in front of his own home.

Matt sighed as Jake reached Shelly, Imogen and Whitney ahead of them. "Are you up for more questioning?" he asked.

"Maybe we should go to my house. I don't want Shelly to see us like this."

"I don't want to see anyone else right now." His tender tone almost sent her back into the water. "You scared me half to death, Caroline."

"Welcome to the club."

"What do you mean?"

"I'm afraid every time I know you're flying. More so, because we haven't had many good times. We'll never know what we could have been."

He hugged her and she melted against him, not caring that Shel might see them.

"You should let Shelly know you're all right."

"Jake will tell her. I don't want her looking us over for some telltale hint of passion."

Matt's laugh made her shiver, but his body heat had already begun to warm her. "She wouldn't think anything as crazy as that."

"She accused me of sleeping with you so I could keep butting into her life."

"She's pregnant. Pregnant women tend to imagine the worst."

She looked him over. "You're such a Neanderthal. I'm not surprised I want you so much. You're par for the course for me."

He yanked her closer, his touch somehow gentle, despite his possessive grip. "That's all good, right?"

She nodded, her gaze still intent on the family she didn't want to see for one of the first times in her life. Matt stepped away from her, and cupped his hand around his mouth. "Whitney, I'm taking Caroline home to change her clothes. See you out at the base tomorrow."

"Right," the other man bellowed back, as if he were addressing the troops from the quarterdeck.

"Aunt Imogen, Shelly, I'm fine," Caroline called. "Good night."

The older couple waved. Shelly stood completely still. Caroline worried, but she still welcomed Matt back under the blanket. She limped across the street, exhausted and too tired to avoid the pebbles in the road.

"You're barefoot," Matt said.

"I took off my shoes before I went in the water. We must have come out at a different spot."

"Do you want to go back?"

And risk running into a member of her family again tonight? "I don't care if they float to the North Pole. For a little while I thought Uncle Ford and I were headed there."

"Why'd you do it, Caroline?"

"What?" The sharp edge on his question cut her. "Why did I try to save my uncle from drowning?"

"Instead of calling for help."

"I was yelling at him, so he wouldn't give up before I reached him."

He pulled her close again, crowding her with the bulk of his body. "Promise you won't ever scare me like that again."

"You've crashed two planes since I've known you. I have a long way to go before we can compare records."

"But I'm trained to fly out of dangerous situations. I react to the problems. You jumped in and started swimming out to sea."

"Uncle Ford needed help."

"And you could both have died."

She shuddered, because he was right. "What else could I do? You'd have done the same thing. You did do the same thing."

"And if I hadn't, you'd still be struggling to get him to shore. That undertow was so strong I thought it was going to drag you past the breakers before I could get to you."

"I thought the same thing when I was trying to reach Uncle Ford." She accepted the way he crowded her under the blanket, but not his reproach "We're all safe, so let's drop the subject."

She tugged away from him and ran up the sidewalk to her front door. Matt had parked in front of her house, and now he stopped to take something out of his back seat.

Caroline opened the door and went inside. Matt came after her, not waiting for an invitation. She should tell him to leave, but she wanted him with her tonight. She'd deal with her heart—and Shelly—later. Caroline glanced at the green material in Matt's hands.

His flight suit.

"Oh no," she said.

CHAPTER TWELVE

MATT FOLLOWED Caroline's stricken gaze to his flight suit and nearly laughed out loud. He didn't understand her fixation, but he wasn't above pandering to it.

Watching her swim for her uncle, he'd known Caroline was the greater part of her family's charm. He was falling in love with her. Maybe loving Caroline would be the wisest decision he'd ever make. Maybe with her, he could give commitment a chance.

He held up the flight suit, hoping to waft a few pheromones her way. "Do you mind if I change?" he asked.

"Not if it forces you to take a break from insisting I should have let Uncle Ford drift out to sea."

He didn't go on about the terror that had kicked him in the gut as he'd watched her dive into the waves. She used Shelly and Jake as a shield to keep him away, but he wasn't naive. She felt the same attraction that troubled him. A woman didn't kiss like Caroline if she was uninvolved.

"Listen to me, Caroline. You Talbots have given me and Jake the first family I've known since I left my parents' farm. The only thing worse than watching you drown would have been watching you and Ford die."

Caroline shut the door, her gaze disturbed. "You talk to me as if we're any man and woman."

"Why can't we be?"

"Because you're the father of the groom and I'm the mother of the bride, and if we look at each other the way you're looking at me, we create complications that could destroy our children's marriage."

"They'll learn to accept us the way we learned to accept them. I wanted to kiss you breathless when we climbed out of that surf. My hands itch to touch every inch of you—to make sure you're not hurt. I don't talk this way to every woman I meet. Jake and Shelly will have to understand."

Her blue eyes wide, Caroline backed into the wall.

"You're wet." He tugged her gently toward him, but didn't hold on. "You'll damage the paint."

"Are you playing a game with me?"

"I'm holding myself on a tight leash—because you don't want me to touch you, and I think I should listen to what you want."

She swallowed, still pressing both palms into the wall she was ruining, as if he were a one-man firing squad.

He gave up. "I'll change in the downstairs bathroom."

"What are we going to do, Matt?"

Her question stopped him in midstride. When he turned, Caroline had finally taken a step toward him.

The fear in her gaze made him angry—with the infamous Ryan and his successor, Patrick, with her renowned, wild-living family, with her, for thinking a couple of mistakes made her off-limits for the rest of her life. "We could tell Shelly she's right about us."

"She's not."

"But don't you want to find out if she might be? Something happens to me every time I think about you, Caroline, and I can't stop thinking about you."

"It's physical attraction, and it doesn't last."

"I've felt lust, and it was different." He'd never been the partner to beg for commitment. "Tonight I wanted the right to insist you call the police instead of diving in to save your uncle."

She laughed with arrogance that matched his. "We could be together fifty years, and I'd never give you that right."

He accepted her challenge. "You're afraid you might want me to have rights."

"I am, and I can't change."

"You're afraid of hurting Shelly and Jake. But you know, we're adults. We can go back to being friends if we break each other's hearts."

It seemed like a smarmy speech, and it cost him when she laughed again, but he'd meant what he'd said even if he couldn't convince her.

Caroline didn't need him to solve her problems, but he longed to ride to her rescue. He'd break his neck trying to prove she should take a chance on him. The problem was, she wanted nothing from him, and he didn't know what to offer.

He slid his arm around her waist. She watched him, tense, clearly ready to leap out of his reach. He leaned down to kiss her. She could have pushed him away, and she held herself stiffly in his arms for so long he was about to pull back. Then with a sigh, she slid her hand across his throat, teasing his upper lip with her thumb.

"What if you're one more mistake I'm not supposed to make, Matt Kearan?"

She chipped away at his ego, but a chance of happiness with her was worth a few bruises. "What if I'm the one chance you're supposed to take?"

She smiled, a swift flicker of amusement and daring. He kissed the bow of her upper lip, but she twisted her mouth beneath his, offering him welcome and need.

Immense hunger overwhelmed him, and he took all the passion she could give. Her soft moan in his mouth fed his desire. She'd run screaming if she knew how primitive his need for her was. He wanted to make her see she needed him and no one else.

He kissed her mouth and her eyes and the delicious thrust of her cheekbones. He slid his hands down her shoulders and tried to undo the top button on her wet blouse.

When he couldn't open it, she stepped back from him.

"Matt," she said. Her gaze a promise, she unbuttoned the shirt, revealing a sheer, white silk bra that molded her taut breasts.

"Wait." He curved his fingers around the swell of her flesh, and her nipples peaked even harder. "Where is your shower?"

"Upstairs."

He took her hand, bracing himself in case she changed her mind. Dancing around him, she turned into her room, and he followed, but he crossed ahead of her to switch on the bathroom light. Still holding her hand—almost afraid to let her go, he slid the glass shower door open and turned on the water.

Second thoughts clouded her gaze when he turned back to her.

"I can leave." He would if she asked him to, but he prayed she'd let him stay with her.

"No." She dropped her shirt on the tile floor at her feet. In a soaking, gold madras skirt that clung to her hips and the bra that all but bared her breasts, her beauty took him by surprise. He turned her toward the mirror.

"Look at you." He wanted to look at her. For the rest of his life, for long days and longer nights. Leaning down, he caught a strap between his teeth and pulled it over her shoulder. More laughter colored the breath she eased between her lips.

"I'm seducing you," he protested, feeling a little foolish as he rubbed his mouth. "That thing tastes salty."

"I washed it in ocean water tonight." Her teasing

tone, low and thick, rode his nerve endings like a slow electric current.

He ran his hands up from her waist, seeking the jut of her rib cage, the powerfully sweet curve of her breasts. As he slid his palms over her nipples he grew hungry to taste the salt from there. Her eyes darkened as she concentrated on her own reflection, as if she'd never seen the sensuality that shook him. He unfastened the back catch of her bra and dropped the scrap of silk.

Sighing as if the weight of her own flesh aroused her, she reached behind her back to pull him closer. He buried his face in her damp hair, falling in love with the scent of sea and Caroline.

Wrapping his arms around her, he teased the underside of her breasts with his forearm, gently brushing her soft skin. With his mouth, he followed the line of her throat, groaning as her pulse fluttered against his lips.

He stepped back and yanked his own shirt over his head. Caroline turned to him, covering her breasts. He held her hands where they were and licked the long line of her ring finger. At the end of her nail, he pressed his lips to her skin. She whispered his name again, and he parted her fingers with his, baring her wine-dark nipple to his tongue.

Deliciously salty. She seemed to swell in his mouth as she slid her hands to the back of his head and rubbed herself against his lips. He suckled until the salt was gone, and all he tasted was Caroline. Even better.

He mouthed the underside of her breast, possessively memorizing the curve, her fullness. He wanted her badly. He wanted to help her believe she could belong to him.

Hooking his fingers in her skirt he tugged it and her panties down her long legs. Caroline shifted restlessly, and he held his breath, half expecting her to stop him with second thoughts.

She shifted away from him, but she only stepped inside the shower and held the door for him. He shucked off his wet khakis and his underwear. He felt foolish in his socks, but Caroline wasn't laughing as he peeled them off.

"Come in, Matt, before the water gets cold."

She waited for him beneath the spray. Caroline wound her arms around his neck and buried her face in his chest. He lifted his own face to the warm water and then tilted his head out of the way so he could wet Caroline's hair, too.

"Are you shy?" he asked, as she still refused to look at him.

"Afraid again. I shouldn't have watched you undress."

Despite her lowered voice, he heard her as if the small glass shower were their own world where she would reach for him in her own time.

He took soap from the dish at his elbow and sniffed the fresh musky scent that reminded him of her. He ran the bar across her shoulders. Tonight she would smell this fragrance on him, too.

He soaped his hands and then set the bar back in the dish and ran the lather over Caroline. Her skin glowed beneath his palms. The suds covered her breasts better than her bra had, but he wanted to see her. He moved so that the water rinsed the soap off her, and she smiled at him, letting him play.

He washed the rest of her body, learning her most secret curves, the pulse points that made her gasp, the kind of touch that prompted her to arch against him.

In his head, the same warning sounded again and again. She might let him love her tonight, but in the morning, she could decide he was too unsafe for her.

How could he persuade her he was just risky enough? He was capable of matching her passion for passion, commitment for commitment, if she'd give him a chance to stay in her life.

Suddenly, she reached behind her back for the soap, and she slid the bar across his chest. Her fingers scraped his skin, awakening him to the power she hid from the rest of the world. She pushed the soap across his hip, brushing his hardness.

"Caroline," he said urgently.

"You can dish out the teasing, but you can't take it."

"This side of you always startles me." And he wondered why she hid such passion.

Her forehead puckered. "I'm not sure anyone ever knew me like this."

"Good." An image of Caroline with anyone else filled him with frightening jealousy.

She smiled against his chest, but suddenly, her tongue traced a hot path across his skin. She tasted him with the same craving he'd felt for her. His heart raced, trying to burst out of his chest. He caught her mouth against him, kissing the top of her head as she roused him to explosive need.

He turned her against the shower wall and gently parted her legs. She groaned as he teased her eager flesh, but when he brought himself against her, she stopped him.

"Wait," she gasped.

He thought she was saying no, and he backed away from her.

"I forgot—" She broke off, a blush staining her skin. "And I don't have anything...."

"Oh." He hadn't exactly come prepared either. "I'm sorry. I didn't think—"

She eyed him, her gaze dissatisfied. "It's been so long, I haven't—well, I don't know what to do next, but we can't finish this."

He nodded, trying to be a man, rather than an over-eager boy.

"Except," she said, looking alarmed and ashamed, "I could look in Shelly's bathroom."

He felt empathy. He didn't want to think of their children just now. "Did they ever stay here?"

"No, but she might have stored something in her bathroom."

"Go see."

Caroline grabbed a towel as she left the shower. Matt backed into the warm water again, but after he rinsed one last time, he stepped onto the rug and toweled himself dry.

Caroline came back, negotiating the tile floor on slippery feet. She held up a foil square. "Are you still in the mood?"

He assumed the question was rhetorical. "Are you?"

"I'm trying not to think of Shel."

"I believe I can take your mind off her." He took her hand and pulled her back into her room, pausing only to shut her door and turn the lock. "Just in case the Talbots come check on you."

He led her to the chintz-covered bed, but when she turned to pull the comforter back, he tugged her towel free and rubbed it over her long back. She turned, surprised, and he eased her onto the crisp sheet.

She lifted her face, baring her throat to his mouth. He felt powerful as he realized she liked him to kiss her there. He scraped her soft skin with his teeth, and Caroline rewarded him by looping her legs around his waist.

Kissing a luscious path to her breast, he ran his hand possessively up her strong thigh. He wanted to know her, needed to recognize the muscles that quivered against his palms. He took her nipple in his mouth again, tasting her skin with hungry familiarity.

After a few heady moments, she urged him to her other breast.

He groaned, glorying in the private dance she wasn't afraid to lead, but it had been a long time for him as well, and he reached for the packet she'd dropped beside her. Sheathing himself, he turned back to Caroline, and she guided him with her hands on his hips.

Their voices mingled as he entered her gently, taking only what she offered, waiting for her to show him when she was ready for more. Her body loved his with exquisite generosity. He thrust a little harder, unable to hold back.

He looked into her eyes, and she closed her lids, but not before he saw the storm of her need for him. He opened her mouth with his.

She met the first thrust of his tongue, arching her hips, and he lost his rhythm in a surge of unexpected delight. Caroline's hands, still on his hips, measured a pace that pleased them both until she suddenly lifted her back off the bed and seemed to hang in the air, wrapping her arms around him.

Her first quiver undid the last residue of his control. He met her cry with a hoarse moan that rose out of the depths of pleasure she gave him. They clung, rocking until their breathing slowed and they relaxed against each other.

"That wasn't so bad, was it?" he asked when he could speak again.

Her laughter filled the room and his head and his

heart. He rolled onto his back and pulled her against his chest. After he tucked the sheets around them both, she made herself comfortable in the crook of his shoulder. He fell asleep to the sound of her breathing.

CAROLINE WOKE to the joy of Matt making love to her again. It was slow and languorous, a gift of feelings she neither doubted nor trusted. Afterward, they showered again and she offered him breakfast. Her body tingling from his touch, sated with loving, she was glad when he turned down food.

"I have packing to do," he said. "I fly three nights this week, and then I have a going-away party on Friday."

"And you leave on Saturday?" Saying the words as if they didn't hurt, she amazed herself.

He straightened from tying his sneakers, his gaze watchful. "I'll be back, Caroline. It's unfortunate we waited until now to find out how we felt, but it's not the end of the world."

What was he saying? "We can't go on with this," she said, even more amazed that she had to tell him. "I can't give you up."

"You don't have me to give up. Last night was—last night. This morning, you go back to packing, and actually—" She read the clock on her nightstand. "I have to measure for cupboards in Mrs. Russell's day-care center."

"You were just using me for last night?" he asked,

almost laughing because he obviously knew the concept was out of her ken. "Forget it. That's not you, and it's certainly not me. I'll see you before I leave."

"I don't think you should. Shelly's already suspicious, and I don't want her to know about last night. I'll make up an excuse for not going to see you off."

"Caroline, if I come back tonight, you'll welcome me to your bed."

She glared at him, and he held up his hand.

"I'm not being a chauvinist. I'm stating a fact. We're starving for each other, and last night won't fill us up."

"We're forbidden. That's the problem, and I don't see a solution. My daughter thinks I want you because being with you somehow makes me closer to her. I won't feed that fire."

He dropped his foot to the rug. "You have to learn to stop forcing me out of your life, or I'll take you seriously."

"I am serious."

He stood, and he looked so irritated, she thought he was going to walk away. But, as he crossed the room, his hard mouth softened. He cradled her nape and bent to kiss her senseless. Her helpless response shamed her. She had no control where he was concerned.

Her impulses had always landed her in trouble. She rubbed her mouth, as if she could ever get rid of his taste.

He laughed. "You won't be able to say no any

more than I will. You're a generous lover, Caroline. You make me feel as if I'd crawled out of a desert, and I can't turn back.''

''Generous,'' she fumed, longing to see herself in his eyes. ''We make each other feel wanted. You and Jake have the family you've always tried to give him, and I won't risk his and Shelly's happiness with an inappropriate relationship.''

She'd learned a long time ago where such Talbot tendencies could leave you—on the outside, looking in, feeling like the bad example her daughter should try to avoid. ''My family is everything to me, Matt.''

''Good luck trying to put me out of your mind.'' His thumb massaged the back of her neck. ''The beating on your door tonight will be me.''

CHAPTER THIRTEEN

CAROLINE FOILED Matt's promised siege by taking another buying trip through the estate sales of Northern Georgia. She mapped out a week's worth of sales advertised in the Atlanta paper and followed the trail on back roads that led through cold, barren trees. Frost greeted her each morning, but not one particle of ice felt colder than the block of craven fear that held her prisoner.

On Saturday, when she knew Matt was flying to Maryland, in Icarus' private plane, she found herself watching the time. Saturday night, as she checked into a bed-and-breakfast in Helen, Georgia, she thought for one irresponsible moment about getting back in her car and driving farther north.

Naturally, she didn't. She spent a restless Sunday at the bed-and-breakfast and drove home Monday. Back at her cottage, she listened to the messages on her machine. Matt had called often, but as the week came to an end, his messages became more abrupt. Finally, as he'd waited for his plane to take off on Saturday, he'd called her and given her his new phone number.

"And, Caroline," he'd said, "come to your senses before it's too late for us."

On Tuesday, she was supervising the installation of Mrs. Russell's new cupboards when Shelly came into the classroom. Six weeks from her due date, she looked placid, pregnant and overheated.

"Mom," she said, "can we talk?"

Caroline gestured to the dust and the workmen sweating over the cabinets. "I can't leave yet. Bo," she said to the foreman, "you're not supposed to have to force those in. Did I measure something wrong?"

"No, but it's like building a puzzle. Don't you worry, we'll make them fit."

"In one piece," she said, and he nodded, turning back to his work.

"Go on with your daughter. By the time you get back, we'll be on our way."

"That's what I'm afraid of. I don't want to start over with new cabinets that come out of my own pocket."

"Mom, let them do their work. This won't take long." Shelly led her to the open window. "The dust is choking me."

Caroline smiled at the waddle in Shel's walk. The baby had dropped. It wouldn't be long now.

Caroline knew she'd made the right decision about Matt. She wouldn't spoil the last days of Shelly's pregnancy, even to spend a few precious hours with him. She certainly wouldn't complicate the first months of Shelly's marriage with a relationship that had already come between them.

"Mom, what's bothering you?"

Caroline stared at her, immobilized. She wasn't a very good liar. "I'm not sure what you mean."

"I tried to talk to you while you were away last week, but you kept cutting me off."

Because she'd wanted to talk about Matt, about his party and the dinner they'd planned with the rest of the family to see him off. "I was busy. I told you I had several pieces in mind when I went up there."

"Well, let me apologize for what I said on the beach. When you stayed away instead of saying goodbye to Matt, I realized what I'd done."

"You didn't do anything." Caroline controlled a sigh of relief. She'd been afraid Shelly might have realized she hadn't wanted to say goodbye to Matt.

"You were obviously afraid I'd think the worst about every word you two spoke to each other. I had no right to make you so selfconscious. I could tell he was hurt you didn't come."

He should have hidden his feelings better. "I didn't schedule all those sales on purpose. You must be exaggerating." She hugged Shelly. Her daughter would be a mother herself, soon. Very soon, from the look of her. "Let's drop it, and you tell me how you're feeling."

"I couldn't be better, as long as I finish finals before the baby shows up. Dr. Davis says it'll be a race." Shelly shook her head, refusing to let Caroline distract her. "But I need to tell you I know you wouldn't have an affair with Jake's dad. You're responsible, and you don't have flings. You're not that kind of woman, and Matt isn't the kind of man who'd jerk your feelings around."

A fling. Jerking her feelings around. Caroline's heart ached. Even Shelly didn't believe she and Matt could love each other for a lifetime.

"I know how much family matters to you, Mom."

"Family is everything." Even to her own ears, Caroline's mantra was beginning to sound mechanical.

SHE STOPPED answering her phone, and, after a couple of weeks, Matt appeared to grow tired of talking to her machine. She wasn't surprised when he gave up on her.

This year Aunt Imogen was doing Thanksgiving at her house. Matt had planned to come back, but on the rainy night before Thanksgiving, Shelly called to say he'd decided to stay in Pax River because he couldn't take the Friday off.

His new plan didn't surprise Caroline either. She'd expected his work to come between him and family. Still, she wandered her empty house, restless and resentful as she realized how she'd counted on seeing him across Aunt Imogen's dinner table tomorrow.

Disgusted with her own weakness, Caroline forced herself to settle in a chair with a book and a mug of cocoa. Three hours after Shelly's call, she took off her glasses and set her book aside, not having read a single page. She turned off the television and switched off the living room light. Stretching the kinks from her back, she was heading for the hall when her door shook beneath pounding that sounded like an enraged drum solo.

Shelly! The baby wasn't due for another two weeks, but babies often came on their own time. Caroline yanked the door open, fully expecting to see Jake.

Matt, his hair soaked, his face as unreadable as the cloud-riddled night sky, took her breath away. Raindrops bounced off the shoulders of his brown leather jacket, but she was so glad to see him, she couldn't find her voice to ask him out of the rain.

An unusual bolt of November lightning slashed the sky behind him, and she forgot all the reasons she should send him away. She launched herself into his arms, famished for the press of his mouth to hers. His kiss healed her pain at having gone without him for the past several weeks. In his equally desperate embrace, she had plenty to be thankful for.

"Let me come inside and make love to you," he said against her ear.

Shivering, she pulled back. "I want you to." She wasn't sure she had a choice. If she did, she was choosing Matt. She brought him out of the cold rain, into her home.

"Wait," he said, as she turned toward the stairs. "Last time we didn't talk. Let's talk."

She'd rather not. Words always got them in trouble. "Shelly said you were staying in Maryland."

"I didn't want anyone to expect me, in case you sent me away."

A gust of wind sheeted rain at the door, and she remembered how wet he was. "Do you have dry clothes?"

"My flight suit," he said with an unexpected hint of humor.

She shook her head. He hadn't needed its magic last time. "I'll get you a towel."

When she came back downstairs, gripping a couple of towels as if they were talismans that could save her from herself, he hadn't moved. A small puddle had formed around his feet where he stood in the glow of an old ship's lamp.

"I thought you were Jake." She held out the first towel from a cautious distance.

He rubbed his head and emerged. "Why—something wrong with Jake?"

"No," she said slowly. With his hair standing on end, he looked more handsome than ever. He made her home feel full again. Another burst of wind rattled the door, and Caroline turned her back on him to close it more securely. She shouldn't have thrown herself at him. She shouldn't have admitted she wanted him in her bed. She couldn't stand losing him all over again.

"You hammered so hard, I thought it must be Jake—that Shelly was in labor."

"Already?"

"She'd only be about two weeks early."

"I'll be glad to see her." He shrugged out of his jacket and then reached for the second towel. "Will I still be here tomorrow, Caroline?"

His scrutiny robbed her of breath. "Staying is your choice," she said.

"Am I staying with you?"

Yes hovered on her lips. She needed this man at her side. She needed his strength and the sense of being cherished he gave her, but apart from Shelly, she didn't trust the longevity of Matt's feelings.

He'd proven her wrong about Jake and Shelly's maturity, and she hoped he'd been right about their marriage. Neither of those things meant he was the one for her, and she cared too much about Matt to risk anything less.

She was safer here in Leith, with her family around her. They were her shelter. They gave her love that never hurt.

"You can't stay here with me."

He lowered the towel at his side, and the terry cloth dropped from his fingers. He didn't seem to know he'd opened his hand.

"You lost a husband once," he said. "It wasn't your fault. You loved a footloose pilot who didn't want the family you need, and you chose Shelly over him. I'm not those men, Caroline."

His black gaze bludgeoned her with disappointment that made her wish she'd been a better woman for him. A braver woman. "How am I supposed to believe in you? Because of those men you mentioned, I don't know how to trust my own judgment. I can't endure the pain of losing you any more than I already have, and Shelly can't see you as someone I should love."

"Shelly doesn't matter in this discussion," he said.

"Shelly always matters to me. Shelly matters first. I won't hurt her, especially after I helped her into a marriage I could ruin if I make her father-in-law a bone of contention. If she and I argue about you, she and Jake will, too."

"I want to be with you. I want commitment from you. I want a life that revolves around us. I'll deal with the fallout."

She opened the door again. "I don't believe you've ever experienced true fallout. You should go."

As he opened his mouth to answer, the phone trilled. Caroline waited for him to go. He stared her down, unmoving, and she slammed the door and went to the phone. Jake's voice at the other end didn't startle her. She'd expected this moment since the day she'd seen Shelly at the children's center.

"We're on our way, Caroline," Jake said. In the background, Shelly's voice murmured. "Shelly wants to know when you'll be there."

She turned toward Matt, but he must have realized who she was talking to, because he'd stalked across the room on silent feet, and now, he was staring at her with terror in his eyes.

"I'll come now," she said. "What about your dad?"

"I've been trying to reach him on his pager, but he doesn't answer. I wish he'd been able to come."

"Jake," she said, deciding she had to tell him. His unfailing love for Shelly had taught Caroline to love him. "Please be careful how you answer this, but he's here with me. Do you want to talk to him?"

"Better not right now, but I'm really glad."

"I'll bring him to the hospital."

"Thanks. Caroline?"

"Yeah?"

"Don't worry—about anything. We'll work it all out."

"I love you, Jake."

"Yeah, I guessed you did. Hurry, okay?"

"On our way." She hung up and turned to Matt. "He's glad you're here, but he didn't want Shelly to know you were with me. Do you have any dry clothes?"

"I'm fine—only wet on the outside. Let's go."

She hurried to the hall closet and grabbed her jacket. "I miss your Jag."

"It's a lot faster than your car," he agreed. "I'll drive."

She let him, and they flew. As soon as he parked, they shot out of the car and headed for the hospital entrance.

"What are you going to say about my being with you?" he asked.

"Nothing." She jumped the median that separated the entrance from the parking lot. "That you wanted to surprise Jake." Taking his hand, she stopped him. "Shelly will be all right, won't she?"

"Women have babies every day. You had her."

"I'm petrified."

He kissed her hard. "I'm with you."

This late at night, the lobby was almost empty, and they stood alone, waiting for the elevator. When the doors opened they hurried inside. Caroline brushed away unexpected tears and jumped when Matt flattened his palm against the small of her back. She twined their fingers together.

"I think I'm mostly happy," she said.

"Me, too, but it's a brand-new experience."

At the maternity ward, the doors opened on echoes of raucous noise. Caroline laughed. "That's us," she said.

Apparently, one of the nurses didn't share her amusement. Marching around the corner of her desk, she lit out for a room down the hall, her soft-soled heels all but digging into the floor.

"We'll follow her." Matt kept Caroline's hand in his. She let him hold on to her. Support flowed between them, a mighty river that threatened to run away with her.

She couldn't give in, wouldn't risk making another father unavailable for Shelly. At the door of the waiting room, the nurse's voice met them.

"I'll have to ask some of you to leave if you can't

keep the noise level down,'' she said. ''We have pa-
tients sleeping on this— Mr. Talbot, how are you?''

''In a fury,'' Ford's voice boomed. ''I left my
house so suddenly I forgot my hearing aid. You
wouldn't have a spare on your person, Emma?''

''Why, I don't know.'' The blond woman adjusted
her coiffure. ''If you keep it down in here, I might
just let you take a look-see later. I'll check on your
niece for you.''

''That man is a marvel,'' Matt said.

''You'd think so. Like seeking chauvinist like, I
guess.''

Matt laughed and they joined her family.

''Matt,'' Ford thundered, and then he made his
slow way across the waiting room. In pajama pants
and a crisp oxford shirt, he looked as if he'd dressed
in the dark. He threw himself on Matt much the way
Caroline suspected she had. ''When did you get here?
Shelly called me earlier to say you weren't coming
for Thanksgiving. I'm glad to see you—want to fill
you in on my flight lessons. I soloed last week.''

''And lived to tell,'' Matt teased, his bond with the
older man clear to Caroline across the room.

''How's the job going?''

''Fine,'' Matt said. ''Great, but I miss everyone
down here.''

''I want to discuss what my instructor's been teaching me. See if you think we're going in the right
direction.''

Caroline enjoyed her uncle making man-talk. He'd

adopted Matt as he had no other male in their family. Dan and Alan put up with it admirably. She'd be brokenhearted if someone came in and shoved her aside in Aunt Imogen's heart.

"I want to hear everything," Matt said, turning to hug Aunt Imogen. "As soon as we hear from Jake. Has he been with Shelly all this time?"

Aunt Imogen nodded. "They got here about the same time we did," she said. "We'll hear soon." Her gaze flickered over his shoulder, over Caroline's as well. "Whitney," she said, and everyone shouted welcome to the newcomer.

"I thought I should be here," he said. "Jake called me—didn't know you were coming, Matt."

Surprising Caroline, Cate appeared at her shoulder as Matt hugged his old friend. "Hey, sis." Cate wrapped her arm around Caroline's waist. "Come join the party—at least until they throw us out."

"Where are the twins?" Caroline asked.

"My neighbor's watching them. She's probably sound asleep on the sofa in their room, but at least she's there."

"I'm glad you're here."

Cate tightened her arm. "Me, too. Scary, huh?"

"About the same as when you had Mary and Melinda." Caroline kissed her own twin's cheek. "I don't think I've seen you without them in a year."

"Have I been so busy with them I've neglected you?" Cate pulled her to a chair, and they formed their own world apart from the others.

"I'm not myself, and I don't know what to do about it, but I'm glad you're here tonight."

"I noticed you came with Matt." Cate made her observation sound like a question.

"He wanted to surprise Jake tomorrow."

"And you," Cate said. "He wanted to surprise you, too?"

"Why me?" Caroline glared at her watch, trying to put her sister off track. "How long has it been? Did you see Shelly?"

"For a second." Cate looked wise, but she went along with the subject change. "She was in mid-contraction, so she wasn't exactly chatty, but you'd have been proud of Jake for the way he talked her through it. I think those kids are going to be okay."

Caroline's heart nearly dropped to the floor. "Oh my God, Cate, they are just kids."

"They have all of us. We've never let each other down."

Caroline looked across the room, at Matt, tall and strong, his body a secret she knew intimately. As if he felt her gaze, he turned, and his smile was for her alone, a communication between lovers.

"Caroline," Cate said, "what have you done?"

This time Caroline gave in, surprised her twin hadn't guessed before now. "The worst possible thing. A Talbot thing."

"Do you love him?"

Cate's question made Caroline look away from Matt. "I'm not allowed to love him. In a way, he's

Shelly's father now. How can I risk taking him away from her?''

''What do you mean?''

Caroline looked into her sister's gaze, taking comfort from her mirror image, from the secrets they'd kept and traded throughout their lives. The power of their loving past lay in the grip of her hand on Caroline's.

''If I let myself care for Matt, and it doesn't work out, it's worse than a divorce. Shelly would have to choose between her mother and her husband's father. What kind of life would I be making for her?''

''What if it does work? How can you not take the chance?''

''Because she's the reason I've made every choice I have since the day she was born. I can't put someone else between us.''

''You wouldn't be in this relationship alone. Matt wants Jake and Shelly to succeed as much as you do.''

''If it didn't work, I couldn't be his friend. I'm not grown-up enough.''

''Give him a chance. Remember what you said to me at the kids' graduation when I admitted I didn't trust Alan to love me the way I needed.''

Caroline turned away from Cate. ''It's not like you and Alan last year. I have no past with Matt, no son. I'm not carrying his children.''

''But you could if you'd let him love you. Listen to me.'' She made Caroline look into her eyes. ''Love will come after you. You can try to hide, but it finds you. Why fight it?''

Cate hadn't lived through all those years with Shelly, wondering what she'd done wrong that meant her daughter had to go without a father. Cate hadn't spent her adult life believing it was safer not to love if loving always resulted in loss.

''I'm not you,'' Caroline said. ''I have my own life and my own past, and I don't know how to be as generous as you.''

''You're being stingy with yourself.''

Caroline looked at her sharply, but the waiting room door bounced into the wall, and Jake came into the room.

''Dad.'' He searched their faces blindly.

''Son.'' Matt took him by the shoulder. ''What's wrong?''

''The baby's coming too quickly. They want to do a C-section.''

Caroline sprang to her feet. Before she knew she was moving, she was at Jake's side. ''Shelly,'' she said.

Shock blanked his expression. ''She's afraid. The doctor swears she'll be all right. I wanted to come tell you, but I have to go scrub. I should be back in about an hour.''

Turning, he pushed Matt out of his way so he could run back to his wife.

Cate nodded at Caroline. ''She'll be fine. We were born by C-section.''

"Jake was a C-section." Twenty-year-old guilt colored Matt's brittle speech. "I was flying back from a temporary assignment, and by the time I showed up, he was home, and Lisa was back in fighting condition."

Caroline wanted to wrap herself around him, to offer him protection from his own misgivings. He ran his hand down her arm, catching her hand. She let him link their fingers and pull her to his side.

"I'm here now," he said, to himself? To her? "I don't want to be that man anymore."

She let him take her to a chair. The rest of the family crowded around, their voices subdued, their love flowing freely. Caroline made crazy promises to herself. She'd never do anything, never think another thought that might impinge on Shelly's happiness if only she and the baby were all right. When Jake finally returned to the waiting room, Caroline stood, pulling her hand from Matt's.

Jake didn't have to speak. The light that bathed his face shouted good news. The whole extended family swamped him, congratulating, hugging, crying, touching him because he was a connection to their Shelly.

At last, he struggled free. "I have to go back. Shelly's fine, and I get to watch our son's first bath. Well, they're supposed to wipe him off, but I remember whole years when that was the only kind of bath I took—huh, Dad?"

Matt agreed, laughing. Jake stumbled as Dan

pumped him one last time on the back, and then he
flew out of the door.

"What did they name him?" Uncle Ford asked.

"Who cares?" Matt muttered, dropping onto the
magazine table.

TOWARD MORNING, Dr. Davis told Caroline Shelly
wanted to see her. Shel's weary smile tugged at Caroline's heart.

"You saw him, Mom?"

"He's gorgeous." He was—all eight pounds of
him, a squalling, healthy, dark-haired infant boy.
"What are you going to call him?"

"Jake's already calling him Matty, so I think we've
named him after Matt."

"He'll love that."

"Do you love him, Mom?"

"Shelly." She pulled away, reluctant to start that
all over again. "I don't want to argue about Matt
here."

"Wait." Shelly reached for her. And since she was
still Caroline's daughter, Caroline went back to her.

"I was wrong. I have no right to tell you who you
can care for. I should be glad, the way you were glad
for Aunt Imogen, that you've fallen in love with such
a good man."

"Should be," Caroline repeated, hearing only that
Shelly was willing to move on, not that she understood.

"I'm trying. The moment I first held Matty, a lot of my life with you became clearer."

That hurt. Had she been such a dictatorial mother? So hard to understand? "Did you need so much to be cleared up?"

"Sometimes." She hid a yawn behind her extremely young hand. "Mom, will you send Jake in? I'd like him to bring Matty back for a visit before I fall asleep."

"I'll get him right now." She left. Shelly'd probably meant to comfort her, but she'd just given Caroline more reason to question herself.

Jake waited in the hall. He wrapped one lanky arm around Caroline's shoulder. "I'll love her all my life. Her and Matty."

"Did you tell your dad?"

He grinned. "I thought his face was going to split. He likes my boy's name." Jake sobered. "I think he likes you too, Caroline."

"Thanks for talking to Shelly."

"I hope it works out."

She nodded. Unfortunately, all the good wishes in the world couldn't guarantee a happy ending, and she needed a guarantee. She focused on Shelly and the baby instead of Matt, and she found herself dancing down the hall until she flitted into the waiting room and found only Matt waiting.

"I should have noticed how quiet it was," she said. "Where's everyone else?"

"At Aunt Imogen's. We're having breakfast, and

then we thought we'd have Thanksgiving next weekend when Shelly and the baby can come.''

"Will you be there?''

"That depends on you.''

"You won't come back if I don't give in. Sounds like a threat.''

"I'm not saying I'll never come back, but I have a hard time pretending I don't want to be with you again. You walk into a room and I feel as if I've come home.''

She knew what he meant, but she wasn't willing to point out that they couldn't trust their feelings. Today was for family, not for arguing.

Breakfast was a rowdy meal. Alan helped Aunt Imogen cook, and Cate and he forced Mary and Melinda on anyone who had a spare arm or a lap. After breakfast Whitney and Imogen insisted on doing the dishes together to the melodies of their favorite Christmas carols. Finally, they emerged, with a tray of fluted glasses.

"What's that?'' Dan asked. "Looks like champagne.''

"We'd like you all to join us in a toast,'' Whitney said. He passed among them with the tray, and then he went back to Imogen with the last two glasses. He handed one to her and raised the other. "To Imogen Talbot, love of my life, who has finally consented to become my wife.''

Caroline immediately searched for Cate among the crowd. The sisters shared a tearful smile as they crossed the room to each other and then went to their aunt. Her tight embrace made Caroline believe in possibilities.

"You're choking me, girls." Aunt Imogen broke away and Caroline hugged Whitney, laughing as he blushed. Cate even planted a kiss on his cheek.

"Drink up, everyone." Aunt Imogen lifted her own glass so that light sparkled in the bubbles. "Christmas is coming, and I want to open our family celebration right this moment. Drink with me to love that took a while to bear fruit, to a season of fruitfulness and hope."

Caroline stopped with the glass at her lips. Did she want to wait to make the same toast in her seventies? She lifted her glass and wished her aunt well.

From behind, Matt wrapped his arm around her waist. "They're lucky to find each other after all this time."

"You say that to remind me I need you."

"You do." He nodded toward Aunt Imogen. She and Whitney moved between their relatives in a sweet waltz. "Just as she needed him."

"She's had longer to think about it."

"Come here." He strolled toward the front door, stopping beneath a sprig of mistletoe. Caroline gazed at it, knowing he was going to kiss her, wanting him to, but hoping she'd have the will to stop him.

He tilted her chin with one finger, and she went into his arms. He didn't speak. If he had, she might have been able to resist, but he opened her mouth with his and she gave up the fight.

Kissing him was like breathing in life. She clung, relearning his body, comforting herself with the potency of his longing for her.

He lifted his head, and she looked at him in a haze of desire and burgeoning frustration with the crowd at their backs.

"Is family enough now, Caroline?"

She blinked, wanting to destroy him and devour him all at the same time. If deciding how to live the rest of her life was that easy, she'd never have let him go to Maryland without her. Bracing her hands on his chest, she pushed out of his arms.

He nodded, a small smile on his mouth, but she got the feeling he wasn't amused. He took a cell phone out of his pocket. "Stay inside. I'll call a cab." Without looking at her again, he opened the door and left.

CHAPTER FOURTEEN

IT WAS A HARD Christmas season. Matt grew more distant, but no less important to Caroline. All around her, people seemed to travel in pairs, in packs of pairs.

Two newly married couples came to her the week before Christmas to ask for help with their new houses. Good for her company. Bad for her sinking morale.

Her family provided little help. Cate told her flat out she was selfishly hurting Matt because she'd turned chicken. Every time Jake looked at her, Caroline sensed he was accusing her of keeping his father away. Shelly said nothing, but her silence contained a hint of relief that Caroline hadn't acted on her feelings for the father of the groom.

Aunt Imogen was the worst. Now that she'd decided to take the plunge, she leapt on every opportunity to remind Caroline how many relationships lasted. She sent golden anniversary announcement clippings from the paper and dire e-mail warnings. Her last, most hysterical and most effective caution had read, "Fear is simply a crutch for a woman who believes passionate love can't be true."

Only Uncle Ford seemed to understand. He took

Caroline out for dinner one cold night to repay her for helping him frame aerial pictures of Cate's and Aunt Imogen's houses. Which probably meant one of them had done the same service for a picture of her house.

"Why do you like flying so much?" she asked him over their coffee and Christmas songs in The Captain's Lady, a diner on the beach.

"Freedom," he said with no extra thought. "I only regret I didn't start twenty years ago. I wanted to, but I was always afraid."

"Of what?"

"Well, there's crashing," he teased, and his affectionate gaze healed her. "There was the chance I might not be good at it. That's what scares you most, isn't it, Caroline?"

She snapped to attention. "I might not be good at what?"

"Marriage. You've fallen in love with Matt, and he wants you, but you think you might have bad marriage vibes, or maybe you think you're not a woman a man can love forever."

"Uncle Ford," she protested, her wounds opening all over again.

"You're wrong." He reached across the table, and she placed her hand in his. "You love Matt, and I knew he loved you before he realized it, but you want him to sign some sort of contract."

"Has he talked to you?" she asked, hardly able to breathe.

"He didn't have to."

She sighed, as disappointed as she was relieved. "I've never asked for a contract. You all think I'm a nut."

"Not a nut, but you and I share a profound fear of commitment. I'll admit you at least have reasons, but, Caroline, I found my love in an airplane. For now it's enough, but I'm hoping to graduate to human companionship. Is safety the only gift you want this Christmas season?"

"No." She tightened her fingers around his. "If you could change being alone all these years, would you?"

"Yes." Releasing her hand, he sat back in his chair. "If I could embrace commitment instead of running from it, I'd have been married at least five times."

Caroline laughed. "Five times? That's what I'm afraid of."

He shook his head. "I said it wrong, another problem I have. I'd have married the first of five women I regret not marrying, and I'd still be happy with her today."

"But how do you know? How can anyone know?"

He tapped his chin. "Maybe you're not allowed to know until the end of your life. And then if you're still with Matt, you'll know he was the right one."

"And if he's long since left me?"

"You may be glad you tried to honor the longing and devotion I see when he looks at you and you look at him.'' Uncle Ford fished an envelope from his lapel pocket and dropped it on the table.

''What's that?''

''A ticket to BWI in Maryland. One way,'' he said with a smirk. ''I don't believe you'll need the return. And I included a car rental. I bought it back when Matty was born, but I waited until the day I scheduled your flight to give you a chance to come to your senses. Four days before Christmas you might be out of luck in getting tickets of your own.''

''I'm spending Christmas with my family,'' she said, nudging the envelope in his direction.

''Tempting though, isn't it?'' He pushed it right back at her. ''Get on that plane tonight, and you might be able to talk Matt into flying you back here in time for Christmas dinner. I'm sure he'd love to remind you what a good pilot he is.''

''You just want Matt back here because he's your buddy.''

''I miss him,'' he agreed. ''But I don't cry for him at night. How about you?''

She stared at the ticket. She cried all right. She yearned for the mere sound of his voice. Memories of his touch scalded her with frustration. Most of all, she longed to stop believing in her own worst fears. Why were they easier to believe in than Matt?

''Family isn't enough, Caroline.''

She stared at Uncle Ford, startled that he'd found the perfect words to push her onto the plane. As she realized she could spend this night with Matt, her heart broke into a marathon run.

"I still don't believe in happily ever after," she said.

"Why don't you mix a little happiness with your fear? Say he leaves you—what have you lost?"

Every day of the past month she'd told herself she couldn't bear saying goodbye to Matt again. So she couldn't risk offering herself to him. She'd been wrong.

If she had to say goodbye, she'd know what true love felt like—even if it turned out to be temporary.

She didn't want to be seventy-nine years old, looking back on empty regret. She wanted her regret to be chock full of memories only Matt could give her.

"MATT, DO YOU KNOW what time it is?" Henry Camp bared his watch face at Matt from across his desk. "Four days before Christmas, it's nine-forty-seven at night. I should be home wrapping gifts and mulling wine with my wife. Instead, I'm sitting at my desk, listening to the one man who can do your job telling me he wants to quit. After less than two months?"

"I love the job, but I need some changes, Henry." He'd told himself to give up on Caroline, but he couldn't. He'd given up on Lisa. For years, he'd reconciled himself to being a long-distance father to Jake, and only now had those walls finally fallen. He refused to settle for less with one more person he loved. Caroline might be right about the damage they could do to their family if they failed each other, but he didn't intend to fail. "Jake's baby is a month old, and I've seen him once. I want to be home more often."

"Home," Henry said, disgusted.

"In Leith. Give me a week, Henry, a week out of every month. It could be good for the company, too. I'm a pilot—I know what kinds of facilities we'll need. I know the people in Leith. I'm a good liaison."

Henry straightened. "We didn't consider that when we hired you." He frowned. "But what about operations here? You have schedules to meet."

"I can train Douglas. We flew together on the Enterprise. He's a good man. Besides, I can get back up here with a couple of hours' notice."

"All this to see a baby."

"Not just a baby. Jake's baby." Matt rubbed his forehead. "And there's someone else."

"A woman?" Henry mocked him.

"I hope so." A week a month might not be good enough for Caroline, but he had to try. "Think about it, Henry. If you don't think the company could benefit, we'll talk again."

"You'll quit you mean?"

Matt hesitated. His usual MO didn't include threatening good friends who'd done him a huge favor, but this was more in the nature of a warning, so Henry could find someone to take his place.

"I might have to." He stood and resituated the

chair in front of Henry's desk. "I've given twenty years of my life to flying, but now I need my family." All of it, Talbots and Palmers and new Randolphs included.

"I think I can spin it for the company's benefit," Henry said. "In fact, I think it makes sense to give you an opportunity to check on this facility as we put it together, but I'll have to let you know."

"I appreciate your help." Matt didn't bother to hide his relief. "You can reach me at Jake's apartment. I have a seat on a morning flight tomorrow."

"All right." Henry picked up his phone and began to dial. "I'd better let them know I'm finally on my way home. Next time you want to ruin my Christmas, see me right after lunch."

As he drove through snow toward the little house he'd found in the Maryland woods, Matt tried to plan his campaign to win Caroline. What more could he say to her? He loved her. He wanted her for his wife, and he'd never let anything between them hurt their children.

Why couldn't that be enough?

There were only two lights on his street, and a car was parked beneath one of them. Matt drove up slowly. Kids sometimes parked down this lonely road, and certainly, this car's windows were fogged.

What were they doing with a flashlight? It swung around the car's interior as he turned into his driveway. He stopped. Could be someone's car had stalled, and the driver needed help.

The other door opened as he got out of the Jag.

A tall woman climbed out of the car, her long legs unfolding for an eternity. She stood, yanking her short skirt down her thighs, and Matt froze. He knew those thighs.

The streetlamp spun copper light in Caroline's hair. She wrapped her short black coat around her waist. How the hell could she look so doubtful when the only thing holding him back was the fact his feet seemed to be staked to the ground?

"How long have you been here?" he asked.

She turned and tossed something back into the car. "My flashlight," she explained with a nervous smile. She shut her car door and came across the street. "I bought it at the service station out by the interstate when you weren't home by dark. You work late hours."

"Don't you have my office number?" He breathed in her scent, the intangible texture of her that had stayed on his skin after they'd made love.

"I was too nervous to call." She nodded toward the car. "I worked on my business plan. I'm hoping I'll have to make changes."

He liked the anxious strain in her voice. It made him feel less like an idiot for hoping he figured in her new plan. "What kinds of changes?"

She shivered. "Can we go inside?"

He stood out of the way for her to precede him up his sidewalk. He hadn't shoveled in a few days, but he liked watching her hips sway as she negotiated the frozen snow.

"Caroline, are the kids all right?"

She turned so sharply she nearly fell. He took her arm to steady her.

"Matty's growing like kudzu. I should have told you they were fine right away," she said. "They don't even know I'm here."

He opened his door, and she went inside. He switched on a light that illuminated the room his landlady called the "parlor." Her grandmother's rag rug covered the pine floor in front of the fireplace. Matt shrugged out of his coat and dropped it on a long, newspaper-covered sofa. He reached for Caroline's coat, but she shook her head.

"I'm cold. I'll keep it for a few minutes."

"Why are you here?"

She rocked on spiky heels that made her calves flex and his mouth water. Her gaze confused, she turned away from him, as if she were reluctant to let him see her face.

"I—" She spun to face him and squared slender shoulders he could easily span with both hands. "I came to ask you for another chance. Being with you scares me out of my mind, but I'm more frightened of trying to live without you. I love you, Matt Kearan, and I'd like you to be part of my life."

Hope burst in his chest. He let her declaration repeat in his mind. Every word of it. He didn't want to mistake her meaning.

"I'd like you to marry me," he said. "Without you, my life is only a series of events."

She laughed, but she sounded as if she were also crying. "You're not worried we'll hurt each other?"

He went to her, sliding his hands beneath her jacket. She wore some soft sweater beneath it. Warmed by her body heat, the silky yarn made his head spin.

"We'll definitely hurt each other," he said, restlessly relearning the curve of her waist, the jut of her breasts. "But then we'll make it all better."

She wrapped her arms around his neck. "Why are you so willing to forgive me? I wondered if you might want a pound of flesh."

"I love you." He couldn't think of a reason to be angry. "I believe you were as confused as you seemed, and I only wanted you to want me."

"A man who doesn't hold grudges," she said. "What am I going to do with you?"

"Oh, I intend to concentrate on more than a pound of your flesh, but I believe we'll both enjoy it." He pulled her arms from around his neck and then gently pushed her jacket from her shoulders. "Pink cashmere." He molded the material against her back. "Remind me to buy more of these sweaters."

"Where were you tonight?" She struggled with the knot on his tie as he began to walk her backward toward his bedroom.

"Persuading Henry Camp to give me a week each month in Leith."

She tiptoed to kiss him, her mouth sweet and yielding. "I don't know Henry Camp, but I think I love him a little, too."

"What changed your mind, Caroline?"

"Sadly, I'm not sure I've changed, but I think I can learn to." She slid his tie from beneath his collar and tossed it over her shoulder. "You're worth the risk."

"Did you miss me?" His arrogance returned, surprising even him.

"I ache for you. Uncle Ford talked to me about the difference between regretting the loss of a man I loved well and regret at having never tried to love him. If I'm going to lose you, I want to love you like crazy first."

"That Ford. He's my best friend, but you won't lose me."

She grinned, her wide mouth curving in an invitation he intended to accept with all his heart. "I want to look back on my life and see you with me."

"You're always bravest in a crunch. Did you know that?"

"I can't let a dare go untaken, thank goodness." She hooked her fingers in the hem of that delicious sweater. "I really love you, Matt. I have almost since the start."

"I'm the kind of man you need. A stayer." He kissed the corner of her mouth, where her smiles began. "And you're the woman for me, a woman wearing a pink sweater that fascinates me."

He curved his hands around her hips, but then she peeled her sweater over her head before he could stop her. "Caroline, I was deciding how to get that off you with my teeth."

She slid her hands across her belly, as if she were hungry. A storm had begun to churn in her eyes, passion-driven, whipping to life only for him.

"There's still my skirt," she said.

Chuckling, he led her into his bedroom. Life in a locker on a ship had never trained him to be tidy, and Caroline stumbled as she surveyed the other storm in this house. His clothing, more newspapers on the bed he hadn't made.

"You're not the queen of pristine anymore," he said. "You're in love, and love is messy."

"My love is a tornado, and this room looks exactly the way you make me feel. What am I getting myself into?" she asked.

He knelt behind her and caught her zipper tab between his teeth. "Looks like paradise to me," he said. He slid his hands beneath her skirt. Her short gasp as he molded her thighs made his senses sing.

She caught his arms to hold herself up. "After we make love, can I read the newsprint off my favorite places?"

"What are your favorite places?" He dropped her skirt, and she knelt to face him, her eyes sleepy and yet, full of heat.

"Let me show you," she said.

As her warm mouth drank from his body, he knew he was about to lose track.

EPILOGUE

MATT FLEW THEM BACK to Leith on Christmas Eve. Caroline exuberantly professed herself to be impressed with his skills, until he finally told her to go in the back and finish her plan for hiring an assistant who could run the business while she was in Maryland with him.

Secretly, she hoped Cate would join her in the business. Alan seemed to be doing well enough these days that he might be able to spare her, and with her office at home, Cate could bring someone in to look after the twins.

After they landed, they were walking toward the office when Uncle Ford came out to greet them. He hurried across the tarmac on his cane.

"Matt, old buddy." He clapped his buddy on the shoulder, and Matt turned to give him a real hug as Caroline beamed at the two men she loved most in the world. "What are you doing here?"

"Surprising you all," Caroline said wryly as he finally found time to hug her, too.

"I was surprised when I heard Matt's voice talking to the tower."

"What are you doing out here so late? You can't fly at night yet," Matt said.

"No, but my friends are out here."

"What's up with your horses these days?" Caroline asked.

"Mostly, Dan looks after them," he admitted with a sheepish look. "What are you doing here tonight? Dinner's over."

Caroline turned the thin gold band on her finger and waited for Matt to answer. With male pride that made her want to cry, he lifted her hand.

"My wife wanted to spend our first night of marriage under her own roof," he said.

Uncle Ford stared at the ring. Its glow in the near dark distracted Caroline, too.

"Young woman, when you surrender, you knock down all the walls." Uncle Ford grabbed her for another embrace before he congratulated Matt with a series of thundering slaps on his back. "Don't let me hold you up. Of course, Imogen's going to give you hell for not letting her do a wedding for you."

Caroline slipped her arm around her husband's waist. "We had a lovely wedding." No one in attendance except the two who mattered. Tomorrow she'd be ready to share Matt with her family again.

In the morning, they drove through the tinsel-lined streets of Leith. Caroline, sated and exultant, ran her hand up Matt's arm.

"I wish we could have slept in a little longer," she said.

He dropped a possessive hand on her thigh. She'd worn his favorite black skirt again, with the new green cashmere sweater he'd given her that morning. He slid his fingers beneath her hem.

"We could pull over," he said.

"Shelly will find us hard enough to take without our getting arrested for making love on the side of a street." She studied the lights that crossed above their heads. "I already miss the snow. It made Christmas more Christmassy."

"I hope you won't get tired of it by spring."

"I hope I manage to convince you I could get tired of snow, but I won't run away from you again." She leaned over to kiss away his unconscious grimace.

Grinning, he brushed her cheek with the back of his hand. "Marrying me was persuasive."

At Aunt Imogen's, they dragged the two plastic bags that contained their gifts out of the trunk before anyone noticed they'd arrived. As they staggered up the sidewalk, the door opened and Cate came onto the holly-draped porch, Melinda in the crook of her elbow.

"I'm stunned," she said, looking it. "I was rocking Mel to sleep when Uncle Ford told me to look out the window. What are you two doing here? Shelly and I had a bet you wouldn't show up until spring."

"And miss Matty's first Christmas?" Matt said. "I don't think so."

"He's inside with his mommy and dad."

The door burst open again, and Jake flew at his

own father. "I knew you'd get here." He nearly knocked Matt down.

Laughing with pure joy, Matt held his burdens at his sides. "I'm glad to see you, son."

"Let me take one of those." Jake took a bag.

"Mom, you're home." Carrying Matty on her shoulder, Shelly pushed through the door. "I'm glad you came for Christmas." She came down the steps, but she stopped in front of Matt. "And I'm glad you're together. I know you love my mother."

"We'll take good care of each other," he said.

Nodding, Shelly turned to Caroline. "Are you happy, Mom?"

Caroline felt herself blushing. She slid a sideways glance at her husband. "Ecstatic." She leaned over Shelly's arm to peer at Matty, who slept peacefully despite the commotion. "He's grown in the past four days."

"You're telling me." Shelly leaned toward her Aunt Cate to kiss Melinda's cheek. "I can't quite believe he'll ever be this big girl's size."

"Let's get them out of the cold," Matt suggested.

They walked into the house where Aunt Imogen met them in the living room doorway. "I thought I heard voices out here. Caroline, Matt, you look different somehow."

Alan appeared with his other daughter in his arms. "Hey. Glad you made it back. Cate, I think Mary's hungry. Should I warm a bottle for Melinda at the same time? Give me a hug, Caroline."

As Caroline responded to his last command, Aunt Imogen caught her left wrist.

"What's this on your hand?"

"We were going to explain," Matt said hastily as Whitney Randolph rose from fiddling with the lights on the bow-sprinkled Christmas tree. The rest of the family trooped into the room to stare at Caroline's wedding ring.

"This is quite a coincidence. I'm surprised you young people don't know how to really keep a secret." Aunt Imogen fished something out of her pocket and slid another gold band onto her own finger as Whitney looped a possessive arm around her shoulder.

Shock silenced the Talbots, a once-in-a-lifetime moment Caroline didn't expect to experience again.

"Aunt Imogen," she said, "this is why you refused to talk about your wedding."

"It was Whitney's and my Christmas present to each other. We saw the base chaplain yesterday. And you?"

"Also yesterday," Matt said. "Justice of the Peace at Annapolis."

"Mom, you're married?" Shelly asked.

"What do you think of that, Shel?" Aunt Imogen lent Shelly a supportive arm while Jake took the baby from her. "First, your mom has to share Cate's birthday, and now my anniversary."

"I never thought you'd marry Matt."

"I have more reason to consider myself lucky

enough to be your father," Matt said. "And I love your mother more than my own life."

"Before next Christmas, I'm going to have to find myself a woman-friend," Uncle Ford said. "I'm feeling left out."

"Shall we wassail?" Whitney suggested. "Shelly looks as if she could use a cup."

"No." Shelly shook her head with decision. "I just want my mom to be happy." She turned to Caroline. "Maybe I'm vain, but I really thought what you felt for Matt had more to do with my leaving home."

Caroline shook her head, blushing as she thought of the ways she and Matt had shown each other the depths of their love over the past four days.

"You were wrong," she said. "I'm blissfully in love with my husband." She smiled at him, enjoying an intimate bond she'd never known with anyone else. "Who knew?"

He caught her, his embrace loving. "I think you may owe me for that, wife."

She lifted her eyebrows. "If these eavesdroppers can find something else to occupy their interest, I believe we can talk terms."

"Where's that wassail, Whitney?" Uncle Ford cut into their public display. "Let's drink to the Talbots. Oh, and all the rest of you, too. Get that formula going, Alan, and then we can drink to family."

HARLEQUIN *Super*ROMANCE®

Old friends, best friends...
Girlfriends
Your friends are an important part
of your life. You confide in them,
laugh with them, cry with them....

Girlfriends

Three new novels by Judith Bowen

Zoey Phillips. Charlotte Moore. Lydia Lane.
They've been best friends for ten years, ever
since the summer they all worked together at a
lodge. At their last reunion, they all accepted a
challenge: *look up your first love.* Find out what
happened to him, how he turned out....

Join Zoey, Charlotte and Lydia as they
rediscover old loves and find new ones.

Read all the *Girlfriends* books! Watch for
Zoey Phillips in November, *Charlotte Moore* in
December and *Lydia Lane* in January.

HARLEQUIN®
Makes any time special ®

Visit us at www.eHarlequin.com

HSRG

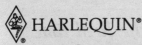

Hugh Blake, soon to become stepfather to the Maitland clan, has produced three high-performing offspring of his own. But at the rate they're going, they're never going to make him a grandpa!

There's *Suzanne*, a work-obsessed CEO whose Christmas spirit could use a little topping up....

And *Thomas*, a lawyer whose ability to hold on to the woman he loves is evaporating by the minute....

And *Diane*, a teacher so dedicated to her teenage students she hasn't noticed she's put her own life on hold.

But there's a Christmas wake-up call in store for the Blake siblings. Love *and* Christmas miracles are in store for all three!

Maitland Maternity Christmas

A collection from three of Harlequin's favorite authors

Muriel Jensen
Judy Christenberry
&Tina Leonard

Look for it in November 2001.